The Duke Goes Down

He flinched. "I beg your pardon?"

"I said 'ha.'"

"Yes, I heard you." He shook his head as though trying to make sense of what was happening. "What does that mean?"

"Oh, did that sound not capture my complete disbelief on the matter of your kissing expertise?"

His eyes narrowed.

She continued, "You must confess, there is no way I can ascertain the truth of this. I can do nothing to dissuade others from believing this particular allegation—ack!"

In one smooth move, he reached out, closed his hands around her arms and tumbled her against his person. His mouth claimed her lips before she could form a more coherent exclamation.

He was kissing her.

By Sophie Jordan

SOPHIE JORDAN

The Duke Goes Down

THE DUKE HUNT

AVONBOOKS

An Imprint of HarperCollinsPublishers

THE DUKE GOES DOWN. Copyright © 2021 by Sharie Kohler. All rights reserved. Printed in the United States of America. No part of this book may be used or reproduced in any manner whatsoever without written permission except in the case of brief quotations embodied in critical articles and reviews. For information, address HarperCollins Publishers, 195 Broadway, New York, NY 10007.

First Avon Books mass market printing: August 2021

Print Edition ISBN: 978-0-06-303563-8
Digital Edition ISBN: 978-0-06-303564-5

Cover design by Nadine Badalaty
Cover illustration by Chris Cocozza
Cover images © Getty Images
Author photo by Country Park Portraits

Avon, Avon & logo, and Avon Books & logo are registered trademarks of HarperCollins Publishers in the United States of America and other countries.

HarperCollins is a registered trademark of HarperCollins Publishers in the United States of America and other countries.

FIRST EDITION

21 22 23 24 25   QGM   10 9 8 7 6 5 4 3 2 1

You made it through 2020 and you're still going.
This book is for you.

Chapter One ❧

A garden party, 1838

*T*he day was bright. The weather perfect. The guests attired in brilliant colors that seemed to celebrate the occasion, as though the heavens wished to shine down on the birthday of the privileged and lauded heir to the Duke of Penning.

But it might as well have been a funeral to Imogen Bates.

There was no pleasure to be had for her. She smoothed a trembling hand over her ruffled skirt. It was a new frock. Mama had insisted on the extravagance since it was to be such a special occasion. Mama's words. *Such a special occasion.* Papa went as far as to proclaim it an honor.

Other far more apt descriptors leapt to Imogen's mind. None of them flattering. She would have preferred to stay at home among her books or visit one of her friends in the village—all girls who were never invited up to the duke's grand house on the hill. Lucky them.

Oh, why couldn't I be one of them now instead of stuck here?

Imogen wore a matching blue and pink bow in her hair that was ridiculous. A great monstrosity at the back of her head that threatened her very balance. Mama was trapped under the delusion that Imogen, at ten and five, was still three years old. She would not yet permit Imogen to wear her hair up off her neck as most of the girls in attendance this afternoon did. Other than a few thin plaits coiled atop her head, her hair hung loose down her back.

Mama called her lovely. Papa said she looked like a princess.

Imogen knew the truth. She looked more like an enraged peacock in full fan.

There were dozens of people in attendance. All close friends of the duke's family. Bluebloods. Titled. Wealthy. Gentlemen with jeweled signet rings and ladies in tea dresses that far outshone any gown her mother had ever donned—or, for that matter, any gown Imogen would *ever* don. They were modest people rubbing elbows with the crème de la crème of the *ton*.

At least Imogen and her family were not invited to the evening festivities. She would be spared that wretchedness. She did not have to sit down to dinner with any of these people and make conversation with whomever sat beside her. She did not have to feel inadequate in her modest and juvenile attire. She did not have to suffer dancing among them—or even worse. *Not* dancing. Either scenario would be a veritable punishment.

The garden party predominantly consisted of young people. Naturally. As it was a weeklong house party to celebrate the birthday of his lordship, the heir apparent, the guest list was abundant with his friends.

Imogen started across the lawn toward Mama who was chatting with several of the heavily powder-faced dames. Her mother spotted her coming. Of course. She had not taken her gaze off Imogen for very long since they had arrived and Mama thrust her away like the proverbial bird from its nest, forcing her to socialize with those of her own age.

Imogen wasn't normally shy or reticent, but the young people here all touted old and renowned titles after their names. The young gentlemen went to Eton with Penning and the young ladies all took their curtsies at Almack's. Imogen was achingly aware that she was not one of them.

As she advanced, Mama gave a hard and swift shake of her head in a clear warning that Imogen should not join her with the matrons.

Imogen stopped, frowning. She was aware that Mama wanted her fraternizing with the young lordling and his friends, no matter how vast the gap between them.

No matter that Imogen would rather rub shoulders with a pack of rabid hyenas. Hyenas would at least acknowledge her.

Sighing deeply, she turned back and obediently ambled through the garden where a game of croquet was being played out.

She stood to the side watching, trying not to feel obtrusive as a group of young ladies and gentlemen played a lively game, whacking their mallets and laughing merrily. Unfortunately the longer she stood there, watching, being ignored, the more awkward she felt.

After several minutes of that misery, she decided to move along. Clearly not back toward her mother and the old dames where she was not welcome. She felt like a dinghy, cast adrift, lost at sea.

It really was a dreadful day.

She looked around helplessly before settling on the quietly beckoning pond as a potential refuge. She strolled toward its calm waters, stopping when she noticed a group of young men congregating at the edge, initially obscured behind the large oak with bowing branches. They skipped stones, laughing and chatting congenially.

At the center of them stood Penning's unmistakable form. He cut a dashing figure with his dark hair and sharply hewn profile. She recognized only one other person in the group. Amos Blankenship. Like the young duke-to-be, he was easy to identify, but for different reasons.

Amos Blankenship was blinding in his lime-green-and-gold jacket. Amos's father possessed untold railway shares and his son reveled in his family's wealth, oft tearing through the village in a flashy new phaeton. They might not possess title, but money like theirs paved the way for them and bought them position. The Blankenship family took pride in leading village society. Mrs. Blankenship was the epicenter of all social activity . . . and the town's biggest gossip.

Imogen studied the group of young gentlemen undetected. The young Lord Penning was no longer boyish. All his softness was gone, replaced by hard edges—a fitting observation on this, the celebration of his eighteenth birthday. He was a man now. She looked down self-consciously at herself, fisting a handful of ruffles in disgust. Whilst she was an overdressed little girl.

He reminded her of one of the chiseled Greek gods at the British Museum she'd visited not very long ago. Except he was attired in clothes, of course. Just last summer she and her cousin Winifred had giggled and gawked at the naked statues longer than they ought to have done. Their mothers would not have approved, which only made them revel in their silliness. There was something to be said of being away from their mothers' gimlet stares that brought out the ridiculous in them.

Deciding she could not stare at the young men forever and remain undetected, Imogen turned in a small circle, renewing her search for a place where she might take refuge. Her choices were limited. She could not return to the house where the older gentlemen assembled over their drinks and cigars. No one wanted to include her in croquet. Mama would not welcome her with the other matrons, and she dared not approach the urbane lads near the pond.

Her gaze arrested on the conservatory in the near distance. She lifted her skirts and walked briskly toward the building.

She sent a quick glance over her shoulder. Satisfied no one was observing her, she unlatched the door and slipped inside. Instantly the loamy smell of plants and vegetation assailed her. She inhaled deeply and started down a row, colorful flora on each side of her. She felt pleased with her resourcefulness. If she only had a book, she could spend out the remainder of the afternoon quite contentedly here.

She stopped before a pair of potted lemon trees, relishing the scent of citrus on the air. She reached out to stroke a well-nourished leaf. She was debating whether or not plucking one of the fruits would constitute stealing when she heard the creak of the conservatory door.

She whirled around, seeing *them* before they spotted her. Penning and his friends. Apparently they'd departed the pond and decided to invade her sanctuary. *Monsters.* Could she find no peace today?

With a muffled whimper, she dropped down before they could spot her and scurried under a table. It was undignified, but then so was she in this dress.

Imogen squeezed herself into the smallest ball possible, wishing she had the power of invisibility.

The voices grew louder, more raucous.

She slunk lower and buried her hot face in her knees. What had she done? She should have revealed herself once they entered the building and then pardoned herself from the conservatory. As simple as that.

Now she was trapped. Crouched beneath a table, cowering without a shred of dignity, praying the young gentlemen soon took their leave so that she might emerge.

Alas the muffled thud and shuffle of their footsteps came closer.

She hugged herself tighter.

There was the scratch of a match being struck.

Ah. So that's what they were about. Evidently they did not wish to join their papas indoors for cigars, but would indulge among themselves.

"Is your father still keeping that opera singer?" one of them asked.

Imogen had a fairly good notion what he meant by "keeping." She might be a vicar's daughter, but she was not wholly ignorant on such matters. She read. She read a great deal. She devoured books her parents would not approve should they know of their content. And then there was Winifred in her life.

Imogen spent a few weeks with her London cousin every year. Winifred was very worldly and knew a great many things. Things Imogen's parents would not deem proper—or Winnie's parents for that matter—but Winnie knew of them nonetheless, and she imparted such knowledge to Imogen.

The reply came: "No, he's moved on to an actress."

"Indeed? I might pay the opera singer a call then. I'm a man about Town now. I've got an interest in setting up an attachment for myself. Something regular to see to my needs."

"You've just finished your schooling and you want to take on the responsibility of a mistress?" another voice inquired with a snort.

"She's not a wife," came the quick rejoinder.

"A mistress knows how and when to use her mouth . . . and it's not to harangue a man."

This earned several chuckles and remarks of agreements. She thought she recognized Amos Blankenship's braying laugh.

Imogen's face burned.

Penning had yet to comment—she knew his voice well enough—and she was inescapably curious to his thoughts on the matter. Did he, too, plan to take a mistress? Perhaps he already had one now that he was a man of ten and eight. For some reason the notion of this made her cheeks sting. He was a young man of the world now. If he did not have a mistress yet, he likely soon would.

The notion should not offend her. Truly, it should not affect her one way or another.

She shifted her weight and the motion nudged a small stack of planting pots stored beneath the table to her right. She cringed at the slight clanking and hugged herself tighter, holding her breath, waiting for what felt like imminent discovery.

What would they do if they found her? The mortification was almost too much to contemplate. She was hiding under a table like a mischievous toddler.

But then she was dressed like a toddler, so perhaps they would not be overly surprised.

They were still talking and she released her

tight little breath. Thankfully they were too caught up with each other and their cigars to take notice of her.

". . . after dinner," one of the gentlemen was saying. "She has promised me a walk in the gardens."

"Now that is a lovely mouth *I* would not mind being used on me."

More chuckles.

More of Amos's bray.

"You best be careful." Penning's familiar voice rang out and she could not help easing her arms around her knees and leaning forward, eager to finally hear him speak. What would he contribute to this wholly inappropriate conversation?

Of course he would be as scandalous as the rest of them. She should expect no less. She recalled him well enough, even if he had spent the bulk of these last years away at school. He'd been an incorrigible boy. She doubted he had changed that much. Mama always said a leopard never changed its spots.

Imogen rather enjoyed this moment of invisibility. No one, especially gentlemen such as these fine toffs, ever spoke their true minds in her presence. She winced. These toffs never even spoke to her at all. She was beneath their consideration.

How different the world would be if people

spoke their true thoughts. Chaotic perhaps, but there would be no confusion.

You would know who the monsters were.

Penning continued, "You shall be betrothed by the end of this house party if you do not exercise some caution."

"Well, married to Lord Delby's daughter would not be such a terrible fate? I can think of far more miserable futures than that," a voice contributed. "The lass is comely. Her papa is well positioned and with deep pockets. It would be a brilliant match for any of us."

"Well, if you don't mind marrying straight out of Eton, then I'm happy for you," Penning said in that all-knowing way of his that had not changed since he was a lad of ten. He always had that air to him. It irked her then and it irked her now. Arrogance must go part and parcel with his noble birthright.

"You expect to do better, Penning?"

"He *is* Penning," another lad chimed in with an incredulous laugh. "He will have his choice of heiresses. Beauty, charm, rank . . . he can take his pick."

"Aye, I'll have my pick," he agreed mildly. *Arrogant prig.* He spoke as though he were shopping for ribbons at the village market and nothing more significant than that. "But nothing would lure me into marriage for another decade at least."

Invisibility, indeed, proved useful. She was correct on that score. He had not changed from that lad who treated her to hard silences, resentful of their parents forcing them to spend time together and vexed when things did not go according to his wishes.

"You mean the vicar's daughter is not your fate then?" a voice trembling with mirth asked.

Imogen stiffened where she crouched. They spoke of *her*?

Masculine laughter broke out.

Hot mortification washed over her, but she strained for Penning's response just the same, curious to hear if he would heighten her humiliation or alleviate it.

If he would be a decent human or not.

"Amusing," he said, "but no." Despite his words there was no amusement in his voice. Only hard denial. Stinging rejection that should not sting because she should not care.

She took a bracing breath.

Of course, he would not agree that their fates were entwined. That would be absurd. A vicar's daughter and a future duke should not even be mentioned in the same sentence, and yet here, among this group of lads, it had somehow happened.

It had happened and she did not like it one little bit.

"Come now, Penning. Once you get beyond all the ruffles and bows, she's a fetching lass."

"I do not see it," he countered.

The heat crept higher in her face.

"Indeed," another voice seconded. "I would not mind exploring beneath all those ruffles and bows."

The burn of humiliation now reached the tips of her ears.

"You lads are debauched. She's a child," Penning blustered. "And a sanctimonious one at that."

She should feel grateful in his defense, except she did not appreciate being called a child. *Or* sanctimonious.

"She's woman enough for me. And I would not be required to put a bag over her head during procreation like the chit my father wishes me to wed."

"No, but you would need to put a bag over her personality," Penning rejoined.

Laughter.

She flinched, feeling their laughter as keenly as the cut of a knife.

She did not know what offended her more: Penning with his clear abhorrence of her or his blue-blooded friends with their lewd comments. It was difficult to decide.

"Come now, Penning. She's a fair lass and there

likely isn't much feminine enticement to be had in this little backwater. No brothels here, to be sure."

"Unfortunately," Amos inserted.

The voice continued as though Amos had not spoken. "All your visits home for holiday and she's right down the road. Mightily convenient. You've never been tempted?"

Tempted? Outrage simmered through her. As though she were free for the picking. For *his* picking.

She had never rubbed on well with Penning. He never appreciated being stuck with her on those afternoons Papa visited the duke. He'd made his displeasure abundantly clear, treating all her attempts at conversation with scorn. And now she knew why.

You would need to put a bag over her personality.

His next words only further confirmed his enduring dislike of her. "She might not be hideous to behold, but other things matter."

Might not be hideous to behold? Such a ringing endorsement. That was as much credit as he could grant her? *Wretch.*

"And what would those other things be, Penning? What is more important than a wife who is fair of face and not a chore to bed?"

"I can think of little else that matters more than possessing a lovely wife," another voice seconded.

Possessing? Is that what these lads thought? That a wife was a possession? Papa did not think like that. Is that what Penning thought? She wanted to believe gentlemen did not think this way, but she knew the reality. Men controlled the world and women had to fight and claw their way for a foothold in it. She'd accompanied Papa on many a house call to visit a downtrodden wife, crushed beneath the boot of a domineering husband.

Their neighbor to the east was one such example. Mrs. Henry had five children and a brutal husband who was never satisfied with any of her wifely efforts. She was frequently "falling down." Mama often tended to her after these mishaps—beneath the critical eye of her husband, of course. As though he feared his wife might tell Mama the true cause of her *accidents.*

Imogen held her breath, waiting for Penning's response, her shoulders tightening to the point of discomfort.

Penning chuckled lightly. "One's disposition must be considered. A wife will not stay young forever. Looks fade and then you're left staring across the dining table at someone you can hopefully abide."

"And you cannot abide Miss Bates?"

"Let us just say she has the disposition of a rotten lemon."

Imogen pulled back as though struck.

Everyone laughed. Even Amos, and she had only ever been solicitous to him.

Not just a lemon . . . but a *rotten* one.

"No one is telling you to marry the chit, Penning. Dalliance does not require that level of commitment."

As though dalliance with me is a given? As though I would simply fall into his lap with wild abandon?

"There are any number of females I would rather kiss than a sanctimonious vicar's daughter who finds it diverting to discuss the weather and the latest infestation of wheat mites."

She dropped her hands onto her quaking knees and inhaled a pained breath.

She never knew what to talk about in his exalted presence—and wheat mites *could* ruin a crop. Clearly he could not be bothered with topics so beneath him.

Still holding onto her knees, she rocked slightly. It was one thing to suspect he didn't like her and another thing to hear him say it out loud—another thing to hear him talk about her with all his friends. To hear him laugh and ridicule her to them.

She blinked her suddenly burning eyes. *Rotten lemon.*

The young toffs continued talking and laughing, but she could scarcely hear the rest of their words over the buzzing in her ears.

They moved on to other subjects, but she remained crouched where she was, battling anger and nausea, breathing in the aroma of cigars and wondering how long she had to suffer in silence.

She didn't know how long she waited. It felt like hours, but it could have been minutes. Eventually their voices turned to low rumbles as they moved toward the door of the conservatory. They were leaving at last. Hinges creaked and then silence fell and she assumed they had departed. After a moment, she emerged from beneath the table and rose up into the smoky air.

They were indeed gone.

She turned and grasped the edge of the table as though drawing strength from her ruthless grip. She inhaled and beneath the lingering scent of cigars she caught a whiff of loamy fauna. Imogen looked down at her hands and noticed the small matchbook near her left pinky finger. One of them must have left it.

The door to the conservatory creaked open and she whirled around.

There at the end of the aisle, between stretching foliage, the door drifting shut behind him, loomed Penning.

He'd returned.

He'd returned and now he stared down the length of the walkway where she stood. He regarded her and there was no point in running or hiding. It was too late. She was discovered.

"I forgot my matchbook," he declared.

"Oh." Turning, she plucked it up from the table and faced him again, glad for the stretch of space between them. Hopefully he could not detect the way her hands trembled.

"Were you in here this entire time?" he asked mildly, a tinge of disapproval in his voice.

Disapproval? She would have none of that from him. *She* had done nothing wrong. At least not in comparison to him. "I was."

"You might have announced yourself."

"I did not wish to intrude."

"But you wished to eavesdrop?"

"Not particularly. It was not my intention."

"But you *did* eavesdrop," he said more than asked.

"On your vile conversation?" She lifted her chin. "Yes. I heard it."

He sighed as though afflicted. That was some irony. *He* was the afflicted one? After all the terrible things he had said about her in front of his friends? In front of young Amos Blankenship, no less. No doubt the duke's words would make the rounds in the village. Everyone would look at her and think: *rotten lemon*.

"I suppose I should apologize then." Clearly

any apology he issued would not be sincere. He doubtlessly felt compelled as their fathers were friends.

"You should not do or say anything you do not mean. You never have to do that with me. It's no longer necessary." Palming the small packet of matches, she forced herself to stroll forward down the aisle toward the door—toward *him*—with great composure. She was proud of herself for that. Attired in the most ridiculous frock, still bruised raw from his words, she moved closer to him with a semblance of equanimity.

Upon reaching him, she stopped and held out her hand. "Here you go."

He looked down and turned his hand over. Taking great care that they should not touch, she dropped the matches into his open palm.

"Thank you," he murmured, all the while peering carefully at her face, as though he was searching for evidence that she was not as calm as she appeared—that she was not unaffected. He would be right if he perceived that, but God willing he would not. She did not want him to know how hurt she felt.

He knew the ribald nature of his conversation with his friends. He knew she should be scandalized and offended—and she was. She was actually fine with him knowing those things. As long as he knew she was not crushed. She would not have him know he possessed the power to hurt her.

"Pardon me." She nodded to the door he was blocking, indicating she wanted to pass.

"Of course." He stepped aside, still looking as though he wanted to say something. God spare her whatever lies and platitudes he would offer forth to soothe her. She did not want his sham of an apology. She would not believe him, at any rate, and he could not expect her to—not on the heels of everything she had overheard.

She was well clear of him and out the door when she suddenly stopped and looked back at him.

Bathed in sunlight, he stood in the threshold, one shoulder wedged in the doorjamb, an eyebrow lifted questioningly. And it occurred to her then. He was not sorry. Indeed, not one little bit. There was no regret in that supercilious arched eyebrow of his.

She moistened her lips, outrage bubbling up inside her. "I would just like to say . . ."

"Yes?" he prompted.

"I would have you know . . ." He continued to stare at her in patient expectation, and she blurted, "Wheat mites can be very serious and decimate an entire crop. An entire shire can suffer the ravages of wheat mites."

That said, she turned and left him.

Perhaps she should have said something else. There were a great *many* things she could have said that were more stinging, but that was the one thing that had popped out from her mouth.

She had heard Penning speak unrestrainedly. Now she knew his true mind. There was no confusion. No obscurity. This particular monster no longer hid in the dark.

She'd glimpsed the real Penning, and she would never forget him or his words . . . even as she managed to avoid him in the days and years to come.

At future gatherings, she kept her distance. Greeted him as required, but said little else. An outsider looking in would think naught of it. One might remark that the vicar's daughter was merely reserved in nature around her betters.

Only young Penning would be able to read more into her reticence. *If* it even occurred to him to do so. If he cared. Perhaps he recalled that long-ago lawn party and the girl in the garish pink dress who stared at him with wounded eyes. Perhaps not.

In the years that followed, young Penning attended her mother's funeral alongside his family. Imogen was aware of him there, a tall, silvery-eyed figure on the periphery, an unwanted presence amid her grief.

Two years later, on the death of his father,

Imogen returned the courtesy and did the same, standing among mourners and offering stilted condolences.

Following the demise of the old duke, there was little occasion for them to interact further.

Five years passed with minimal sightings.

She heard of his exploits, of course. The young illustrious Duke of Penning spent most of his time in London, expanding his reputation as a feted nobleman about Town whilst Imogen's life turned to that of caretaker.

She settled into spinsterhood and loyally tended to her father and the vicarage and the people of Shropshire, telling herself it was all she ever wanted. This duty was her calling.

It was enough.

Her life was one of purpose. She harbored no regrets even if, on occasion, the whisper of *rotten lemon* chased through her mind like a slithering snake. Especially every time she came face-to-face with Amos Blankenship in the village. That snake slithered yet.

Her single consolation was the proverb Mama had frequently chirped: *As you sow, so shall you reap.*

The Duke of Penning would have his turn.

She did not know when or how, but when it came for him, she would not pity him.

Chapter Two ❦

Ten years later, 1848

The once glorious and venerable Duke of Penning sat as bold as he pleased in the first pew of Imogen's church.

Except he was a grand duke no more.

The young nobleman had gotten his comeuppance.

The mighty had fallen from his perch and landed upon earth to mingle alongside the rest of them—even if he still happened to sit in the pew reserved for the Duke of Penning and his family.

Duke no more.

A tight little smile of satisfaction curved Imogen's lips—until it occurred to her that she was sitting in church and harboring some decidedly less than charitable thoughts over one man's misfortune. Not very virtuous behavior. She tried to stamp down her glee. It was not well done of her.

Her fingers tightened around the edges of her prayer book, digging into the leather, and she sent a guilty glance where the erstwhile duke sat beside his mother, looking unreservedly bored as her father pontificated from the pulpit—and any guilt she may have harbored for her less than charitable thoughts toward the man vanished.

Impudent man. Once the *real* duke arrived, he would then sit among the denizens of Shropshire like the mortal he was. Her smile deepened. She longed for that day. The final reckoning come to fruition. Mama had been right. *As you sow, so shall you reap.*

Her gaze drifted back to the front of the church. Papa stood on the other side of the altar, one hand gripping the pulpit for support. He scarcely looked up from the parchment as he haltingly read, squinting through his spectacles. She silently encouraged him. *Come now, Papa. You can do it.*

He was no longer the rousing orator he once had been. He had not been that in some time. Not since his last fit of apoplexy, but as long as Papa was still here with her, and he could stand up in front of his congregation and read the sermon she had written for him, then all was not lost. He still enjoyed society, and society enjoyed him. It was enough.

Imogen shifted restlessly in her pew. Penning—no, that was not correct. He had ceased to be the Duke of Penning for nigh on a year. One would think that fact would have fully absorbed into her head by now.

Mr. Butler attempted to hide his yawn behind his hand. Rude man.

Why was he even here today? He rarely ever put in an appearance at the vicarage—or Shropshire, for that matter. It was typically left to his mother to grace the hallowed confines of their country church.

To be fair, he was still glorious. Dark locks and silvery gray eyes. He was a dark angel. Imogen well knew that angels came in all shapes, however. Ever since she was a child and found herself launched into a pond on the Penning estate, choking on pond scum, the little lordling's laughter ringing in her ears, she knew what manner of angel he happened to be.

The boy had been a devil then, and the man was no better now. A smile again threatened to overtake her lips. He would soon learn that the world no longer bowed down to him.

Papa finished and the congregation lifted as one to their feet.

Imogen collected Papa's cane she was charged with keeping for him, and stepped out from her pew. Moving forward, she patiently held out her gloved hand for Papa to accept as he stepped down from the dais. He took his cane, gripping it with one hand and latched onto her arm with his other, leaning a significant amount of his weight on her. Fortunately she was sturdy. Helping Papa to and fro over the last couple years had developed muscles where none had previously existed.

They started down the center aisle together as the choir sang its departing hymn. Her gaze landed on Mr. Butler for a heartbeat. He wore an impatient expression, as though he could not wait to be free of this church. Imogen sniffed in disdain and snapped her gaze forward.

She and Papa took their positions just outside the double doors. Pasting a smile on her face, she nodded and smiled and greeted the denizens of Shropshire. Papa managed this part of his duties quite well. He still loved the social aspect of his role. That had not changed. He had always been a marvelous listener. He smiled and nodded and appeared wholly invested in conversations flowing around him—even if he was not quite the loquacious speaker he once was. Even if it took him a long time to arrive at his words. That did not mean he failed to appreciate the community around him.

Imogen likewise nodded and smiled and said all the right and usual things as congregants exited the church.

Thank you for coming. Have a lovely day. How is your dear grandmam? We would love to join you for tea this week. Oh, my what a splendid bonnet! My compliments on your freshly painted fence. It is the highlight of Shropshire.

The banalities ended as the last family passed through the doors and moved on. Imogen and her father turned to face the bustling churchyard.

As with every Sunday, members of the congregation lingered and mingled. There was nothing unusual with such a sight. The duke—blast it! Mr. Butler—in their midst, however? That was unusual, and highly suspect as far as Imogen was concerned.

In the last year since his disinheritance, he had not accompanied his mother to church. It was a curious thing. What brought about this development now? Why was he here? Should he not be in London leeching off his friends now that he found himself without rank and funds? At least she assumed he was without funds. She was not privy to the nature of his finances. Or perhaps now that the truth of his birth had been revealed those friends wanted nothing to do with him.

She tugged down on the brim of her bonnet so that she might survey him more inconspicuously.

He stood beneath the shady drape of a tree, adjusting his hat, looking resplendent in his blue frock coat and brocade waistcoat, his cravat impeccable beneath his chin. He still dressed in the height of fashion. At least he was fashionable by

Shropshire standards. Evidently it would take more time for his state of penury to become perceptible to the outside world.

"Come, daughter." Papa patted her gloved hand and together they stepped down the front stone walk of the church.

Mrs. Blankenship and her daughters immediately waylaid Papa. Imogen stepped to the side, largely forgotten as they started chattering excitedly about their impending house party. Their guests were very important and well-heeled people from London. The entire shire was invited to the country ball they would be hosting on the third night of their house party.

Imogen smiled as though interested in the banter, but she had no interest in balls. At nearly six and twenty, balls were no longer high on her list. Indeed, they had not been for some time.

Lifting her face, she let the rare sunlight skim over her skin with no fear of any resulting freckles. Her nose was already spotted with them. She'd been born that way. Freckled and cheeky, her mother had oft asserted.

Lowering her face, she allowed her gaze to roam over the inhabitants of her beloved Shropshire—or at least those who had shown up to hear her sermon today. It filled her with secret delight when people complimented Papa. No one could know they were her words—that would not go over well at all—but *she* knew and that was enough to make Imogen feel warm inside.

She squinted against the bright morning glare.

Mr. Butler no longer stood alone. He had moved and was now chatting with the very elegant baroness. She frowned slightly. Strange indeed. Imogen had never seen them in conversation before.

The widow was not in the first blush of youth—or even the second blush of youth. Of course she was no ancient dragon either. She had to be close to a decade older than Mr. Butler, but she was still an exceptionally handsome woman with vividly dark hair and translucent skin.

Her daughter stood near her, shifting awkwardly from slippered foot to slippered foot as her mother conversed with the former duke. The baroness touched the girl's arm, and brought her in closer, determined, it seemed, that she participate in the conversation. Mr. Butler angled his head and listened with a rapt expression as the blushing girl murmured something.

Oh, dear. Imogen narrowed her gaze on the trio. She dearly hoped Butler had no designs on the baroness's daughter—and that the baroness would not actually humor his designs if he did.

The young girl would soon be traveling to London for her first season. Once she turned ten and eight, she would officially be on the market. She would doubtlessly find more suitable choices there than an illegitimate scoundrel, who clearly only had interest in her dowry.

A year ago he had been living the life of a spoiled nobleman, paying no mind to the baroness or her daughter or anyone else in the village of Shropshire. He cared naught for anyone or anything save his own pleasures.

Obviously, he'd had a change of heart. The baroness was no longer beneath his notice. In fact, her daughter would now be quite the catch for the likes of him and well he knew it.

She felt her lips purse in disapproval. Imogen could not stand by silently as he ruined the poor girl's life. She knew all about young girls with their shimmering hopes who fell prey to silver-tongued devils. She knew too well.

Mercy Kittinger sidled close to Imogen's side.

"Your duke is looking as dapper as ever this morning," she murmured for her ears alone.

"He is not *my* duke. Or a duke, for that matter," she corrected her friend while trying not to sound too gleeful.

Mercy stared at Mr. Butler in a considering fashion. "'Tis a shame to see though."

"What's that?"

"Young Annis staring after the duke calf-eyed. You must not approve." Mercy looked at her knowingly. Her long-time friend was well versed in Imogen's dislike of the former duke. She did not fully understand it, of course, but she knew of it. Imogen had never shared the particulars of that day in the conservatory. Some shames were best kept private.

"She's young and impressionable." Imogen shrugged. "Mr. Butler is handsome and still possesses an air of consequence. It will take time for others to see that he is no longer eligible." Papa chortled at something Mrs. Blankenship said. It reassured Imogen to see him happily occupied. "Will you be attending the Blankenships' upcoming ball?" she asked her friend.

Mercy sighed. "I suppose I must. Grace will not forgive me if I keep her from it. She says I keep her isolated enough at the farm." Mercy's anxious gaze tracked to her sister, where she stood laughing with a gaggle of other young girls.

The Kittinger farm was sprawling and took up a considerable amount of land to the east of Shropshire. The Kittinger house itself was almost an hour's ride by carriage. They did not often make trips to the village. Sunday was usually the only day Imogen could visit with her friend, unless she made a special trip to call on her, and lately she preferred to stay close to home in case Papa had need of her.

Imogen turned her attention back to Mr. Butler

as he bestowed a brilliant smile on the baroness and her daughter. "I am certain that wretched man will be in attendance, wooing all the unattached young ladies who have two ha'pennies to rub together."

"I think he's looking for a bit more than two ha'pennies," Mercy offered. "He's searching for an heiress, and Shropshire does boast a few of those."

Imogen made a sound of disgust. "Can you imagine it?" *Now* he would join their ranks. *Now* those heiresses were good enough for him. She sighed. "Dukes are the worst."

"Except he is no longer a duke . . . as you are fond of reminding."

"Indeed. Indeed, he is *not*." She nodded once in accord.

Mrs. Blankenship's twin daughters edged away from Papa's and their mother's side to stop before Imogen and Mercy.

"Good day, Miss Bates, Miss Kittinger," they greeted in near unison. Turning then, they tracked Mr. Butler through the crowd. The girls sighed dramatically. "Penning is so handsome, is he not?"

"And no longer Penning," Imogen offered with false cheer, but they did not seem to hear her.

"He has accepted Mama's invitation to our ball," Emily, the more effusive of the Blankenship sisters, trilled, very nearly dancing in place. "It is so thrilling."

Imogen canted her head. "Is it?"

Emily continued as though Imogen had not spoken. "He's never attended *any* of our fetes before, although we have been invited on occasion up to Penning Hall."

"There has been nothing held at the hall following the late Duke of Penning's passing. Not so much as a tea since then," Imogen reminded, unwilling to let the point slide. She wished everyone would recall how little Mr. Butler had to do with anything or anyone in Shropshire. Unlike his father, he cared not one whit for their community. His present interest was only spawned by his need.

Emily fluttered her hand in dismissal, still staring dreamily after Mr. Butler.

It really was too much. What would it take for others to realize he was no grand catch anymore?

"And there is his other . . . affliction," Imogen heard herself declaring.

Emily glanced at Imogen sharply, proving she was not completely oblivious of her remarks. "What affliction?"

"Yes, what affliction?" Mercy seconded, her expression rightly wary. She knew me only too well.

"I should not speak of it . . ." Imogen hedged, her mind working feverishly, wondering if she dared say what was even teasing at her mind.

Now both the Blankenship sisters were looking at her expectantly, waiting.

Imogen cleared her throat and glanced around as though to make certain there were no eavesdroppers . . . although she knew once she uttered the words, they would be the tattle of Shropshire. The girls, like their mother and brother, could not keep a secret, but that would be the point of what she was about to do.

"Well . . . the man is stark bald. He wears a wig," she rushed to whisper. "It's quite unfortunate. Oh, they've done their best to conceal it with a very realistic-looking wig. The best money can buy, but he's been bald ever since he was a lad."

The girls gasped, swinging their gazes to rest on the former duke. "No! His hair seems so very real."

"Doesn't it?" Mercy murmured. Imogen shot her a quelling look.

"Indeed. It is very convincing." Imogen nodded with feigned grimness. "However, if you were to give it a hearty tug it would pop clean off his head." She made a popping sound with her tongue against her cheek and the girls' eyes widened even further.

The sisters exchanged looks and with a quick farewell, they beat a hasty line for their mother, doubtlessly to fill her ears.

"What have you done?" Mercy asked with a chuckle and rueful shake of her head.

"I'm simply protecting the unsuspecting females of Shropshire from a grasping and disingenuous man."

"By starting a rumor? And when this reaches his ears, which you know it will, and he finds out you are the source . . . what then?" Mercy arched an eyebrow.

Imogen felt a flicker of misgiving . . . until she once again caught sight of the man in question, escorting the baroness and her daughter to their waiting carriage.

Young sweet Annis had settled her hand on his arm and blinked up at him worshipfully. Imogen blinked, suddenly seeing herself as she had once been, so much like Annis, young and hungry for the love and attention of a handsome young man. Susceptible.

No. It would not be. The girl must be saved.

No fabrication was too wild—or wrong—if it saved a vulnerable girl from making a mistake she would regret all her life.

"I've done no harm, and I'm not afraid of him." Imogen crossed her arms. "Mr. Butler has no power over me."

Mercy made a skeptical noise in her throat. "I hope you're right."

Chapter Three ❧

*T*he day following Perry's uncharacteristic attendance at church, he was hiding in the wine cellar, three sheets to the wind, when Thurman found him.

"Your Grace," Thurman intoned with all the disappointment only an ancient butler could wield. "Dinner is served."

Perry understood his disappointment. He was disappointed, too. His booted foot slid out in front of him. He kicked at nothing in particular.

He lifted the paper his mother had given him earlier in the day and waved it wildly in the air. "It's official, Thurman. The banns are posted. Lady Circe is betrothed to that sod, the Earl of Westborough. Can you believe it? She will marry that oaf? When we were at Eton he liked to jump off the roof of the conservatory and see if he could land in the rhododendron hedges. More oft than not he missed, and landed on his head. He's a stellar grade arsehole."

Just another disappointment. Another one of the many things he had thought to have for himself but did not. Propped against the wall between racks of wine, Perry turned an eye to the myriad bottles, contemplating which vintage to crack into next. If ever there was a time to get foxed, this was it.

"Forgive me, but it must be said. Do you really think it advisable to wed someone named after the goddess Circe? She was a necromancer known to seduce men and change them into swine."

Perry peered up at the steely-eyed retainer from where he sat on the ground. The man had served his parents faithfully since his predecessor had retired in Perry's infancy. He stuck by them, moving into the dower house with Perry's mother rather than remain at Penning Hall to await the new duke. Loyalty like that could not be bought.

"She was beautiful and could carry an intelligent conversation," Perry countered.

Thurman's lips twisted as though he tasted something tart. "And also vain and short-tempered. Word has it she treats her staff abominably."

Perry sent Thurman a sharp look. "You never mentioned that before."

"A vain and short-tempered noblewoman bears mentioning?"

"She was not *any* noblewoman. I was considering marrying her," he reminded reproachfully. He was damned close to asking for her hand when the bottom had fallen out from his world.

"It was not my place to interfere."

"But now you don't mind telling me of my near miss?" He snorted.

"I thought you might be glad of it now. Count yourself fortunate."

Fortunate? He supposed he was. He could not imagine being married to Lady Circe now that he had fallen so low. What if they had wed before the truth of his illegitimacy came to light? She would despise him. At least he did not have to endure that, waking beside a woman who loathed him for the circumstances of his birth. At least now whomever he married would know what she was getting—*a bastard born son of a duke without a penny to his name.*

Perhaps he should set aside the entire notion of marriage, pack a bag and leave. Head for some distant land where he might start anew and make his fortune. Men and women were doing it every day. Sailing across the pond. Canada. New Zealand. South America.

With a muttered curse, Perry lifted the bottle of wine he had been nursing and took a deep swig. A final swig, it would seem. He gave it a small shake, and looked through the mouth to eye the hollow interior. With a regretful sigh, he tossed the empty vessel to the ground at his feet. "A fine year. Pity 'tis gone."

"Your mother awaits, Your Grace," Thurman reminded.

Perry spread his arms wide. "As you can see, I'm not fit to sit at my mother's table." He then wagged a finger at the stern-faced butler. "And Thurman, you know better. I'm not 'Your Grace' anymore."

"Old habits are not so easy to alter."

They certainly were not. He was still learning that himself. It was difficult to break the customs of a lifetime.

"Call me Perry."

His mother's butler shuddered. "I would never demean myself to call you that revolting moniker."

Perry chuckled. "Very well. You may call me by my truly *revolting* name then."

Peregrine.

It was the type of ostentatious name that belonged to a duke. Not a bastard like him—the bastard he'd turned out to be. But he would let Thurman have his way.

Thurman waved toward the door. "Your mother . . ."

Perry looked down at himself. His clothes were hopelessly wrinkled, and wine stained his cravat. "In my present state, she would not wish me at her table." His mother was fastidious and exacting in nature. A duchess through and through. She would not approve.

"Perhaps." Thurman sniffed and started to leave, but then he stopped. "If I might be so bold as to inquire, how was your time in Shropshire yesterday?"

"You mean did I manage to corner the baroness and her daughter in the churchyard?"

Thurman inclined his head slightly in acknowledgment. There was not a fraction of shame in the motion. The old gentleman had taken Perry's descent hard, perhaps only second to the unhappiness Perry's mother suffered, and he wholeheartedly supported Perry finding an heiress.

In fact, Thurman and Mama had spent a great deal of time strategizing over that very matter, insisting that Perry attend church and all local happenings where the few heiresses of Shropshire congregated.

"Fret not. I did engage with the baroness and her daughter after church. Well, mostly the baroness. The girl hardly speaks." Truth be told, her widow mother was more intriguing than the callow daughter. "I escorted them to their carriage."

"They were amenable?"

"As always," he said, feeling wearier than he should.

He had begun courting with the intent to wed well over a year ago when he was still the duke. Naturally he had not courted anyone in Shropshire then. He'd thrown himself into the season and the London marriage mart like a good nobleman. The time had come and he had resigned himself to taking that next step toward the proper state of matrimony. Now, however, the act of courting felt so very desperate and soul-crushing.

"Very good. The baroness's daughter is by far the most eligible female Shropshire can boast."

It did not bear mentioning that while she might be the most eligible female in the shire, Perry would never have bestowed any amount of attention on her before. Harsh perhaps. And yet true. It was simply the way things had been in the before times.

The before times. When he was a duke and life had been decidedly uncomplicated. When he had everything he ever wanted. Before a pair of dour-faced gentlemen, agents of the crown, had arrived in his drawing room alongside the morose-faced Penning family solicitor. It had been the most lowering moment in his life.

Initially, given their expressions, he had thought they were before him to deliver the news of a death . . . and he supposed, in effect, that was precisely what they were about on that ill-fated day. Only the loss they were there to proclaim was his own.

He'd sat stunned, hands limp at his sides, speechless as a slab of marble as they'd imparted the news of his illegitimacy. It was all a blur. He vaguely recalled the pop and crackle of the fire in the great hearth. The scent of leather from the armchair he sat ensconced within filling his nose.

As dark and somber as crows, the gentlemen had circled him within the shrinking space of his drawing room, citing their proof. They presented him with several signed documents and witness statements.

Perry remembered looking at those papers, trying to process the words, the parchment brittle in his shaking hands. He'd felt like a lad in school again, attempting to decipher a particularly difficult Latin text. Latin had not been his best subject.

In the rubble of his shock, he recalled feeling a sense of gnawing guilt. Perhaps that was because of the grim lines of the faces watching him, the tight set of their mouths. Judgment was writ all over their expressions. Condemnation. As though he were somehow culpable. As though he had set out to defraud the true Penning duke of his rightful life.

It had not been his doing. None of it. He had

led a life of blissful ignorance, unaware of the truth waiting to materialize.

Truth always had a way of doing that, of revealing itself and illuminating the darkest, hidden corners. It could not stay buried forever.

The wrongdoing had belonged to his parents alone, but his father was dead now and unable to answer for his deception. That left only his mother.

When all had come to light, she had behaved as though she were the victim of a hoax. A cruel hoax perpetrated against *her*.

"It was your father's idea," she had wept when Perry demanded an explanation from her.

Fortunately she'd been in Town for the season and Perry had not needed to travel far to arrive at her house in Mayfair to confront her. She was just rousing herself at noon and taking her breakfast in her private rooms, comfortably attired in her dressing robe with her hair hidden inside a turban—as she had done ever since he could remember. As children, he and his sister knew not to bother his mother until late in the afternoon.

"He said the title belonged to his son, no matter if you were born before we were wed. He was off on the Continent when I learned I was increasing." She sniffed and dabbed at her nose with a lacy handkerchief. "He wanted a grand tour before he settled down."

"What for?" Perry had snorted, pacing a hard line in her chamber. "It seems he was having quite a bit of fun sowing his oats right here in England. Why did he need to go abroad for his diversions?"

"Peregrine." His mother lifted her tear-stained face from her handkerchief to glare at him reproachfully. "Don't you dare cast judgment on me. It's not as though you have led a saintly existence. Have you?"

His mother was the daughter of a marquis. She came from an old and venerable family. She had always known she would marry the Duke of Penning and one day become the Duchess of Penning. That had been taught to her alongside her letters and embroidery. He supposed this certainty might have accounted for her willingness to prematurely consummate her union. She must have felt her future was assured.

Perry did not know what his mother or father could have been thinking. Clearly they weren't using good judgment. He could only guess that they had been afflicted with youthful short-sightedness and functioning from the waist down . . . but he would rather not contemplate his mother and late father together in so intimate a fashion. It was all too much. He was already battling nausea over finding himself in this grim situation.

"*I* never lied to the world," he had told his mother in the face of her censure and accusation. "I never stole a life that wasn't mine."

I just lived that stolen life.

The color had burned hot in her cheeks. "Once I sent word to your father, he returned as soon as he could . . . as soon as he was located." A grimace crossed her face. "It just took some time for word to reach him." She paused and tilted her head. "I believe he was found in the Netherlands." She shrugged as though that were of no account now. "Alas he did not get here in time. You were born as he was en route home."

"A great inconvenience, that," Perry said with all the bitterness one might feel in such circumstances. Not that he imagined many people ever found themselves so similarly devastated. His situation was wholly unique.

"We married as soon as he returned."

"Little good that does me now."

"We shall contest this!" His mother struck a fist on the surface of the table, her eyes bright with the impulse to fight.

He'd grimaced, recalling the grim visages of the crown's agents in his drawing room, armed with documentation that verified the true date of his birth was before his parents' wedding, an event that took place at a small church in Yorkshire. That alone served as a flag.

Why had his mother not been wed in grand style in St. Paul's Cathedral in front of hundreds of members of the *ton* as her sister had done? As her mother had done? As all the previous Dukes of Penning had done?

A small wedding at a remote shire in Yorkshire was certainly not in keeping with tradition or with his mother's enduring need for spectacle and admiration.

His parents had been married in near seclusion and without pomp because she had been hiding her newborn son from the world.

"You want to contest it?" He shook his head. "Why? Are they mistaken? Was I born *after* your marriage? Am I legitimate? Am I *not* a bastard? That is the only point that matters here."

She glared at him in mute frustration, her lips pressing together mutinously. "It is not right."

"And yet it is indisputable."

They would not take on the laws of primogeniture and win. Surely she knew that. Certainly she was not so arrogant to believe she was an exception to long-standing tradition and the rules that governed their land?

She stabbed a finger toward him. "You are not the only one affected here, Peregrine."

He blinked at her sudden attack on him.

"Oh, the shame." She pressed her hands to her flaming cheeks. "Thank Providence your sister is already married to Geston and can weather this."

"Indeed," he'd said wryly. "Thank Providence for Thirza's good fortune."

At least one of his parents' offspring would be untouched by the day's revelations. But then Thirza was the legitimate one. She had nothing to fear other than the barest tangential shame. Her marriage to the Earl of Geston would spare her the worst of the damage. Thirza's mother-in-law was a great friend of the queen, after all.

His mother had looked at him with sudden dawning horror. "What of me? You don't think I shall lose my title and widow's jointure, do you?"

In that moment, he could have been justly scathing toward his mother who had so little thought for him and *his* ruin, but he did not possess the inclination.

It took energy to be angry and hostile, and he found he lacked the will. It had already been an emotionally fraught day.

Instead, he had marched across the room and sank down across from his mother. He reached between them and took her hand, giving it a comforting squeeze. "You will be fine."

And he was correct.

She was fine.

Even though it was well within the crown's

right to strip her of her title as the Duchess of Penning for her involvement in the fraud, no one wanted to drag things out in so dramatic and punitive a fashion. It would be a public embarrassment for all. So Mama had weathered the backlash.

She fortunately retained her widow's jointure, and most of her friends stood by her. They weren't so spiteful as to hold against her an indiscretion from almost thirty years ago—not when she ultimately married the man in question. Besides . . . if they renounced her then they would not be privy to all the despair in her life—or rather, in Perry's life. They wanted a front-row view for that spectacle. Shunning Mama would prevent them from that pleasure.

As predicted, his sister was saved and untouched by the disgrace. She was actually even more popular than ever—still the darling of the *ton*. Everyone wanted to be close to her to hear all the juicy bits of her brother's downfall.

Whereas his mother and Thirza were spared, there was nothing to be done for Perry.

Perry wholly and fully felt the sting of his life going up in smoke all around him. The smoke was *still* all around him. Most days he struggled through the haze.

Thurman was still talking as Perry dragged his attention back to him.

His mother's butler was shrugging. "If the baroness's daughter does not come to fruition, then we shall move on to the Blankenship lasses."

Ah, the giggling Blankenship chits.

The sisters might possess significant dowries, but they lacked rank, which had been a priority once. He winced at his complete about-face. It made him feel an arse—but that was nothing new. He'd generally felt like an arse these days. Ever since the wretched truth of his illegitimacy had come out.

It did not occur to Mama or Thurman that these heiresses might want more for themselves now that he had . . . well, nothing.

The Blankenship sisters had been kind enough to his face, as were most people, but who knew what they really thought and what they said behind closed doors.

No one in Shropshire had rebuffed him directly. Perhaps it was because his mother still occupied the dower house and was an important personage in the community. Or perhaps the residents of Shropshire were genuinely kind and accepting in true Christian spirit.

Except her.

Ironically, the vicar's daughter treated him to her usual disdain. She was nothing like the kind and accepting residents of Shropshire or her benevolent father in that regard.

Miss Imogen Bates had always managed to look down her nose at him even though he stood a good half foot taller. She had not concealed her distaste for him—not since they were children and his mother had forced him to spend afternoons with the vicar's daughter whilst his father and the vicar engaged in long philosophical conversations. What lad wanted to spend the day with a girl? Especially a priggish one who never wanted to do the things he wanted to do.

"And if the Blankenship lasses do not come to scratch, then we shall move down the line."

Perry wasn't even certain what—or whom—was down the line, but he was certain he would be told. Ever since he'd moved in with his mother, she and Thurman had resumed old habits. They treated him like a green lad who needed instruction on every matter—from how to attire himself to which ladies he should court. It was unendurable and yet he'd put up with it ever since he'd been evicted from his properties.

"Of course." Perry gave a two-fingered salute. Unless he wanted to permanently spend his days residing with his mother in the dower house, he had best heed their advice and consider any young lady touting a dowry. That was the sad truth of matters.

Bloody hell.

Perry started eyeing the bottles to his right,

desperate for another drink to numb his mind from the bleakness of his life.

He had no wish to spend the rest of his life leeching off his mother. Rather, he amended, the rest of *her* life. Her widow's jointure would see *her* through the rest of her days, and she was granted the dower house until her passing. There was no provision for him, however.

He'd been raised a duke.

He'd been *told* he was the duke.

That had been the provision left to him. That was his legacy.

All lies.

The dukedom belonged to another and Perry was on his own, without property. Without funds. With only his wits and the strength of his two hands and the charity of his mother. He winced.

His gaze fell on the discarded paper again where the betrothal of Lady Circe to the Earl of Westborough was stamped in ink for the world to see. He squeezed his eyes tightly shut for one long blink as though the sight pained him. When he opened them again, the portentous words were still there. Irrefutable.

He swallowed against the bitter taste coating his mouth, longing to open one of the fresh bottles surrounding him, but he resisted the impulse. He'd imbibed enough for the night. He needn't drink himself to oblivion. That was the act of a desperate man. He was not that. All was not lost. He would persevere. He would find another heiress. His life would improve. Somehow. He would make certain of that.

"Did, er . . . nothing untoward happen yesterday when you were in the village?" Thurman queried.

Perry considered that for a moment. The question seemed rather arbitrary, which was not a word he would have applied to the rigid butler in any sense. If one word could be applied to Thurman, it was *deliberate*. "Why do you ask?"

"You did nothing to offend anyone whilst there?"

Perry contemplated that, playing the morning over in his mind. "No. Not to my knowledge." True, it was not in his habit to consider how others might perceive him, but certainly he would know if he had caused offense to others when he was out and about.

"Think on that a bit," Thurman prompted, clearly convinced Perry should recollect.

"What are you getting at, Thurman? Speak plainly, man."

"There have been . . . stories circulating."

"Stories?"

Thurman appeared discomfited. A definite first for the man. He might not be nobility, but he carried himself with more hauteur than a king. "They would best be described as . . . rumors, I fear."

"Rumors?" he echoed. "Since yesterday?" He snorted. "I attended church with my mother. No more than that. What could have happened that was so scandalous in such a short passage of time?"

"I would not say these rumors are scandalous precisely . . . merely unfortunate for the subject. And in this case, the subject is you."

"Me?" He pointed to himself with bewilderment. "Well, out with it, man."

"It is purported that you wear a wig and are stark bald beneath."

"Bald?" He reached for his hair and tugged fistfuls of his thick locks. "Does this look like a bloody wig to you?"

"All rubbish, certainly." Thurman nodded forcefully.

Perry released his hair. "What else? What else is being said about me?"

"Nothing too . . . damaging."

"Thurman," he warned. There was clearly more.

"Only that you possess twelve toes."

He shot up straight, his outrage a lightning bolt to his spine. "S-slander!" he sputtered.

The only thing Perry had going for him was his charm and appearance and now that was under attack, too. *Brilliant.*

Thurman lifted one shoulder in a shrug. "In ancient times, it was believed a sixth toe was a blessing reserved for kings."

"Except it does not apply to me because I have five toes on each foot." He waved angrily to his boots.

"And there are those who believe it to be a witch's curse," Thurman admitted, still continuing as though Perry did, in fact, possess extra toes.

"With my recent misfortune, I am certain there are more than a *few* people who believe me cursed."

He dropped his head back against the wall with a *thunk.* "What am I going to do?"

The question was posed more for himself, but Thurman answered. "You'll go to the Blankenship ball and waltz so closely with every heiress present so that they will have no doubt you're in possession of a full head of hair."

"What of this twelve toes nonsense?"

Thurman made a sound in his throat that reflected how little he thought of that rumor. "Nonsense indeed. And if it were true, who really cares about one's toes?"

"Ladies," Perry snapped. "Ladies care about

toes. Especially the ones who are superstitious when it comes to extra ones."

Thurman shrugged. "And I am assuming this bad kissing business is a rumor, too."

"Bad kissing?" he demanded.

Thurman blinked. "Did I not mention that is also being bandied about?"

Indignation swelled up in him, threatening to choke him. "No, my good man, you failed to mention that."

"Oh." Another shrug from Thurman. "I did not think it overly significant compared to the other rumors."

Not overly significant that he was a bad kisser?

Perry lowered his head into his open palm. That ranked as significant to him. To females, too, he knew, it ranked as *extremely* significant. "The ladies tend to care about that, Thurman."

Thurman offered up yet another unhelpful shrug and gestured toward the stairs leading from the cellar. "Dinner, if you remember, sir? Please do not keep your mother waiting. She abhors tardiness." With that, the butler turned and took his leave.

Bad kisser?

Perry's ego stung from that. Perhaps more than it should have, but that was one complaint that had never been lodged against him, and London was a place where gossip thrived. If such tittle-tattle had been spun about him among the *ton*, it would have reached his ears in record time. As, apparently, it had done here in Shropshire. Gossip was gossip everywhere. He grimaced at that cold truth.

This bad kisser rumor was perhaps the most damaging one of all. He had to clear his reputation on that matter. He needed to prove his kissing prowess and soon, so that the eligible ladies of Shropshire knew that particular rumor bore no substance. Of course, it meant finding a candidate who would not mind advertising the fact that she had kissed him. Not necessarily an easy task.

Again, the idea of uprooting himself and seeking his fortune on some far distant shore dangled before him and the notion was not without merit.

In either circumstance, staying here or leaving, he would have to prove himself. That much was undeniable.

Staying, he would have to see about tackling *all* of these rumors and doing his best to quell them. Finding the source seemed the most obvious solution. Find the culprit and stop him.

Or, most likely, stop *her*.

Chapter Four ❧

*T*he Blankenship ballroom was crowded with all of Shropshire.

As in years before, it was a delightful country ball. Extraordinary, really. It was the only of its kind, Imogen suspected, where yeomen and tradesmen and their families mingled alongside the shire's well-heeled gentry: dancing, drinking, eating until one was red in the face.

The finest silks merged with the poorest of wools. The Blankenships did not discriminate. Class distinction was not observed at these affairs. Once a year the tables groaned beneath enough food to feed two villages. Even with Mr. Henry and his insatiable appetite present.

The slovenly man owned a small pig farm just outside of town, and from the state of his muddy boots and soiled trousers, he had not likely freshened his clothing before he quit his pig stalls for the day and ventured forth tonight. Mr. Blankenship really was singular in his ability to overlook such a man tromping mud—and other substance Imogen dared not examine too closely—all over his floors.

She watched him with a faintly curling lip. As an agent of the shire's vicarage, she knew she was supposed to serve all the denizens of Shropshire with goodwill and love in her heart. However, she held no goodwill in her heart for this man.

He sat at a table, waited upon most diligently by his wife, a woman very much with child. Their eleventh child, in fact. Although that did not stop the man from snapping his greasy fingers for her to hurry and fetch him yet another plate of food.

Mrs. Henry had been with child every year since Imogen and her parents moved here. As soon as one baby arrived another was on the way. Mama had oft grumbled that some men in life were as feral as beasts of the field and could not be civilized.

Mama had helped in the delivery of several of Mrs. Henry's babes whilst Imogen helped with the children—a task that their own father felt too beneath him. Mr. Henry usually sat drinking his ale and stuffing whatever food Imogen and her mother had brought into his mouth, leaving scarcely enough for his own children no matter how generously they had packed the basket.

Aside from her burgeoning belly, Mrs. Henry was thin as a reed, her features haggard this evening. Her hair fell untidily from pins into her face. Or perhaps that was a deliberate attempt to disguise the bruise purpling her eye. Imogen noticed it though. Just as she had noticed all of Mrs. Henry's bruises and scrapes over the years. This one did not escape her detection either. Whenever Imogen inquired about them, the farmer's wife always had some excuse: a fall, a collision with a door, one of the little ones threw a spoon and struck her.

Imogen did not believe a single one of her excuses.

Unlike his wife, Mr. Henry possessed great ham-sized fists and was a bear of a man with a large belly that pushed against his too-snug vest and jacket. He tore into a turkey leg with his teeth as though it had wronged him and he wished to punish it. Just the sight of him made Imogen wish she were a man with the power to punish *him* so that he never lifted a finger to his hapless wife again.

Imogen tore her gaze from the detestable farmer and scanned the room. A cornucopia of lanterns cast everyone's faces in a merry yellow glow as the orchestra played a lively tune. Mercy's younger sister, Grace, called out a greeting as she whirled past in a spirited reel. Imogen waved after her.

Miss Lockhart, the housekeeper up at Penning Hall, was in on the fun, too. She whirled past in Mr. Blankenship's arms.

Papa applauded Mr. Blankenship for hosting these affairs, and had done so ever since they first moved here years ago. He praised him quite effusively from the pulpit for organizing occasions that unified the community. Some might say it was just good sense to sing the praises of a man as wealthy and influential as Mr. Blankenship, that it could only work to the benefit of the village and the good vicar. And yet Papa did not think like that. He was not after his own gain. His mind did not work for selfish purposes.

However, Imogen did not agree with her father. Contrary to what he said, the Blankenship ball did not unify *all* of Shropshire society—not that Imogen contradicted her dear Papa on that point.

Delightful occasion or not, the late Duke of Penning had never graced any of the Blankenship balls. He might have invited the Blankenships up to the grand manor house for an occasional fete, but that was different. The late duke could invite whomever he wanted into his space. He had the right to pick and choose. He was a duke. He could do anything he wanted—but what he clearly *never* wanted to do was mingle with the many varied denizens of Shropshire in the Blankenship ballroom.

And this certainly was not the kind of event the once most precious and valued Penning heir would ever attend. He certainly had not in the days *before* he inherited the dukedom and definitely not *after*, in his glory days as the Duke of Penning. Before the truth came out. Only now, apparently, did he deem it a good enough venue from him.

Now he attended. *Now* he was here.

She lifted her nose a notch as though his presence carried with it an unfortunate odor.

People watched him as he moved about the room. Yes, Imogen watched, too, but she was *not* gawking at him for the reasons they were.

Everyone in this village held him in awe. As though he were *still* the duke. Still a nobleman in their midst. It was most vexing.

The Duke of Penning was not in this room. Indeed not. Only Mr. Butler was in attendance.

Penniless *and* rankless, albeit handsome, Mr. Butler.

Imogen nodded once and told herself to stop searching him out. She'd done enough of that. It felt rather desperate. It made her feel like one of the ladies who couldn't keep their eyes off him. Usually it was because of his dashing good looks. He cut an impeccable figure in his smart and still fashionable attire.

But there was more to it tonight. There was a difference. There were more to the stares he was eliciting.

For a start, the long looks he garnered had nothing to do with his appearance. Not anymore. Not this night. The whispers behind fans and gloved hands were all about the latest *on dit*.

The rumors circulating about him.

She need not hear everyone's words to know what they were saying—more or less. They were speaking the words she herself had breathed to life. The *on dit* she had created.

"You've been busy," Mercy's sudden voice remarked.

Imogen jerked at the arrival of her friend beside her. Her hand flew to press over her startled heart. "Oh," she exhaled. "Mercy, dearest. How lovely you look this evening. Is that a new gown?" Imogen leaned forward to press a kiss to the young woman's cheek.

Mercy gestured to her gown—a garment Imogen had seen her friend wear many times before. "This tired thing?" In fact, Mercy had worn the same gown to the Blankenships' last two country balls, and Imogen well remembered it.

Mercy's farm was quite prosperous, but one would never know it from the humble manner in which she lived. Plump pockets did not prompt her to spend money on herself and buy new frocks. She saw to it that her sister was always outfitted accordingly, but not Mercy. She never indulged in fripperies for herself.

She also had her brother with whom to contend. She often bemoaned the fact that Bede was a bit of a spendthrift. Since finishing school, he spent very little of his time at his family home. He rarely visited—even on holidays. Imogen could not recall the last time she had seen him. He left the management of the farm to Mercy, devoting most of his time to his leisure pursuits in Town. Mercy was, in effect, the head of her family, shouldering all the responsibilities whilst her siblings led carefree existences. It was likely why Imogen was so drawn to her. Mercy understood all about obligation and duty to one's family.

"Yes," Imogen insisted. "Your dress is lovely."

"Tsk! Rubbish." Mercy swatted her with her fan. "Now you're just trying to distract me with your *lovely* lies." Mercy's dark eyes danced. "And speaking of *lies*."

Imogen ignored the pointed mention of lies, asking instead, "Why would I be attempting to distract you?"

"To keep from talking about all the natter floating about town. Would you know anything about that, Imogen? Hm?"

Imogen sighed and decided not to pretend ignorance of her friend's meaning. They were well beyond that. Mercy had been there, after all. She had stood witness to the first lie Imogen had uttered regarding Mr. Butler—when Imogen informed the Blankenship sisters that he was stark bald and wore a wig.

"Just a few more carefully placed words here and there." Imogen sniffed and took a sip from her glass of punch. "No more than that."

Mercy lifted an eyebrow and sipped from her own punch. "Apparently a few more carefully placed words served its purpose. It took not five minutes upon arrival before I heard the latest tattle about Mr. Butler. You're quite the yarn spinner. I never realized you possessed such an imagination."

"I can be creative when called upon."

"And you're called upon to be creative now?" One of Mercy's dark eyebrows arched sharply.

Imogen gave a mild shrug, and lifted her glass for another sip, returning her attention to the dance floor. Mercy followed her gaze. They watched the colorful dancers for several moments. Standing by and watching was a familiar habit.

Like Imogen, Mercy was not interested in attracting a dance partner. Imogen might once have had dreams of dancing the night away in the arms of a dashing gentleman, but it had been a long time since she harbored those kinds of aspirations. As two firmly on the shelf spinsters, it had been several years since either Imogen or Mercy were even asked to dance at one of these things. They were content to chat and watch and keep a vigilant eye on Mercy's sister who *did* have those aspirations.

Although tonight Imogen found herself distracted from their usual easy flow of conversation. Mercy's words of caution from the other day echoed in her mind. *When this reaches his ears, which you know it will, and he finds out you are the source . . . what then?*

Indeed. *What then?*

Imogen tried to envision that moment and what she would say. What would she *do*? Was there some way she might avoid the man? Could she feign ignorance? Deny all accusations? Or should she simply confess her actions and tell him why she had felt compelled to ruin his matrimonial prospects? She cringed at the notion of having such a conversation with him. Such a candid exchange would not be an easy thing.

Pushing the unwelcome prospect from her mind, she did her best to follow Mercy's conversation and contribute her own remarks. It was difficult. Maintaining a discussion while tracking Mr. Butler was a challenge.

She watched him edge the ballroom, heading toward Emily Blankenship with long strides and a steely-eyed purpose. Blast the man for still looking so very handsome. His change in circumstances had done nothing to alter his physical appeal. Unfortunately.

Emily's eyes widened at his approach. In a less than discreet move, the girl spun around and dove awkwardly down the corridor for the ladies' retiring room, reminding Imogen of a hen fleeing the fox.

Imogen lifted her cup to her lips to hide her smile.

Apparently Mercy did not miss the little interaction either. She tsked. "Well. Your words have certainly done the trick."

Imogen shoved the guilt away that threatened to beset her. She would not let such emotion torment her. She knew the manner of man Mr. Butler was, and she knew the hope that brimmed in these young girls' hearts. She would not permit him to crush any of them.

He was only looking to find an heiress and use her for his gain. He needed an heiress for what she could bring to him, for his own salvation— not for who she was. Not for reasons of affection or respect. And while Imogen knew that was often the way it was in marriages—they were rarely formed on the basis of love or fondness— she could not look at him without remembering that disagreeable lad by the pond . . . and later the young nobleman in the conservatory.

Why was it that the wretched memories were always the ones that stuck with you?

The warm memories, such as her mother's

laugh, her mother's face . . . those grew dim with time. The harder Imogen tried to pull those memories from where they were buried in the far recesses of her mind, the more elusive they became.

But not the wretched memories. Those were clearly imprinted. Never to be erased. It was not fair how it worked out like that.

"You realize you could be ruining him."

Imogen stiffened at Mercy's words.

"His fate should not rest on me or anyone. Nor should it rest on his marriage to someone else. His fate is in his own hands." Her parents had always told her that—happiness came from within a person.

"You think so?" Mercy queried thoughtfully.

She heard the doubt in her friend's voice, and even felt a little bit of it creeping in on herself, but she chose not to react to it.

Mercy could not understand. She had no personal experience with Butler. She had not been the one to suffer those afternoon teas at Penning Hall that her well-meaning parents insisted were obligatory given the Duke of Penning's total and unfettered influence over their lives.

That's what being the Duke of Penning was. Power. The position meant power and absolute authority over those born mere mortals.

That was why it had been so gratifying to

learn that the prized Penning heir was in fact no heir at all. He was mortal.

No winged seraph, but mortal. Vulnerable to wounds. Just. Like. Them.

Just like Imogen.

Even at a young age Imogen knew her family existed at the Duke of Penning's whims. His pleasure with her family dictated everything for them. How many frocks she and Mama possessed, how often they indulged in desserts, their summer trips to visit family in London and whether they took spring holiday in Brighton so that they could frolic in the sea waves.

From the start, Imogen had been aware that they were just as beholden as the lowest scullery maid to the Duke of Penning. Also from the start, resentment had simmered within her at the unfairness of it all.

During those obligatory visits, whilst the adults conversed, Imogen was stuck with the young lordling and his overly beribboned little sister. The two rotten children wanted nothing to do with Imogen, and clearly viewed keeping company with the vicar's daughter akin to torture.

They'd done nothing to conceal their aversion about keeping company with her.

They'd done nothing to make her feel comfortable.

In fact, they had made her quite miserable.

Chapter Five ❦

A shallow pond, 1831

𝓘mogen was eight years old when Papa was chosen as the new vicar.

She recalled arriving to Shropshire and her first visit to Penning Hall, a requisite upon Papa's appointment to the role. As it turned out, the old duke heartily enjoyed a theological discussion. She had no notion on that first day that it would become routine and the first of many miserable afternoons spent at the grand house.

Imogen sat in awe in the well-appointed drawing room with its sky-reaching ceiling and the myriad gilt-framed paintings—some landscapes, some portraits—covering every inch of wall space. She thought the place a palace.

Her legs swung in front of her, several inches above the carpet as she sat on the sofa in her best Sunday dress. Mama reached out and pressed a gloved hand over her knee in a clear attempt to settle her anxious movements.

The Duchess of Penning smiled, and it was a

blast of dazzling brilliance. "Would you like to play outside with the children?" She gestured with an elegant hand. "My son and daughter are outdoors with the governess. They would be most happy to have your company."

How naïve she was to have believed that. Imogen thrilled at the notion of other children. She was eager to make friends in her new home, and she imagined that this girl and boy, even if they did happen to live in a palace, would be her bosom friends.

She eagerly followed one of the maids out of the drawing room and outside to locate the young lord and young lady.

They found them on the back lawn beside a crystal-blue pond. The little lordling was a few years older than her eight years. Imogen recognized that at once and was awestruck to find herself in the presence of an older, obviously well-heeled lad.

He held a fishing pole and was bossing his younger sister on how to properly hold hers whilst their governess snored beneath a tree. The young Lady Thirza was a few years younger than Imogen, but seemed vastly more sophisticated in her fancy dress and perfectly arranged ringlets.

"Lord Peregrine! Lady Thirza!" the maid escorting Imogen called out.

Both children whipped their heads around at the sound of their names.

The maid motioned to her. "This is Miss Imogen, the new vicar's daughter. Your mother bade you keep her occupied whilst the adults have their visit."

Their gazes fastened on Imogen intently.

"Occupied?" The little lordling looked affronted as he uttered the word.

"Indeed." The maid pushed Imogen toward the siblings. "Now play together."

The maid turned then and left them even as the boy further complained, "We're not *playing*. This is fishing. It's manly business. I didn't even want *her* here." He pointed a damning finger at his sister.

Thirza stuck her tongue out at her brother and then turned a discerning eye—much too discerning for a six-year-old—on Imogen. She looked her up and down. "You're ugly," she offered. Not meanly, just in that very matter-of-fact way that belonged to children accustomed to galling honesty.

Imogen's face burned. It was only mortifying because of the beautiful boy there to bear witness. He did not reprimand his sister or rush to Imogen's defense and that was all the more crushing. Instead, he smirked as though amused by his sister's insult.

Imogen mistakenly thought perhaps he would stick up for her. Foolishly so. She did not yet know the manner of boy he was. That was soon revealed, however, when she picked up a discarded fishing rod, presumably belonging to the snoring governess, and joined him beside the pond. For several moments they fished, their lines disappearing in the placid waters.

It was not long before she felt a pull on her line.

"I've got a fish!" she cried, grappling with her suddenly bowing rod. She reeled feverishly, hoping she didn't lose her catch in the process.

It was as she was reeling in her fish, a grand writhing silvery thing, that she noticed she was the only one excited on the bank of the pond. The little lordling and his sister watched in grim silence.

Imogen triumphantly lifted her fish over the ground of the bank and held it up in the air, proud of her prize and eager to show it to them and have them look at her with respect.

"Girls don't catch fish," the young lord accused.

Imogen frowned, her elation ebbing. "But . . . I did."

"Perry has never caught a fish that big," his little sister volunteered, nodding in the direction of her brother. "I didn't even know there were fish that big in there." She leaned forward and peered into the pond as though she could see into its depths.

The young boy flushed bright red. "You're stupid," he snapped at his sister. "Of course there are big fish in there. I've caught them. Many *many* times."

She commented by sticking out her tongue again. That must be a common reaction from her when it came to her brother.

"I am certain it was just beginner's luck," Imogen mumbled, and she wondered why she should even say that. She'd fished before when they summered in Brighton and often caught fish. She should not apologize because she had done something well. Where was her pride?

"I'm certain you are correct," he countered. "Girls can't fish."

She lifted her fish higher, unable to feign meekness any longer. "Well, apparently I can."

His nostrils flared. "Where did you say you moved here from?"

"Hereford."

"As in the cow?" His nostrils slightly flared as though scenting something foul.

"Yes." She nodded.

"Never heard of it," he announced, and for some reason she felt a stinging rejection in those words and she knew—this boy did not want to be her friend. She was not of their ilk. How foolish she had been thinking these golden children would become her bosom friends.

Imogen's eyes started to burn treacherously. She told herself that she would not surrender to tears in front of this vicious little girl and boor-ish lad.

She held out the fish in a gesture of goodwill toward the boy. "Would you like to keep it?"

His face reddened and he reeled back as though she had most grievously offended him. "I don't want your stupid fish."

He tossed his rod aside and stalked away.

"Now look what you've done," Thirza accused, propping her tiny fists on her hips. "You've made him mad. He doesn't want to fish anymore. Who will bait my hook for me now?"

Imogen shook her head, marveling how things had gotten so ugly. "My apologies. I did not mean to. I was only trying—"

Before she could finish, the little girl lunged toward her, hands stretched out. The flats of her palms made hard contact with Imogen's chest, slamming into her.

Suddenly Imogen was propelled backwards, arms flailing like a windmill. It did no good. She plunged into the pond.

It wasn't very deep, especially so close to the shoreline. She was able to stand.

Soaked and sputtering, her best Sunday dress plastered to her body, she scrambled to her feet and held her arms out at her sides.

Thirza laughed shrilly, her ink-dark curls bouncing. She bent over and held her stomach as though it made her belly ache.

The young lord stopped his retreat and turned back around. He watched Imogen with twitching lips. Unable to keep his mirth at bay, he burst out laughing, too.

The racket woke up the governess from her nap. She lumbered to her feet, wobbling for a moment until she gained her balance. Blinking herself awake, she smoothed her hands over her voluminous skirts. "What is happening here?" Her gaze lighted on Imogen. "Who are you?"

Imogen didn't respond. She could not.

Speech was beyond her. The sting in her eyes was too much. The tears began to roll unchecked down her face. She cried. Her tears blended with the droplets of water covering her face, so her weeping wasn't too noticeable. There was that at least.

"Who are you?" the governess demanded again, and Imogen shook her head, unable to speak the words burning through her.

No one.

She wasn't anyone. Not anyone that mattered to this girl and boy.

It was her first lesson upon arriving in Shropshire, and one she never forgot.

Chapter Six ❧

$\mathcal{P}$erry stood outside the double doors of the retiring room where Emily Blankenship had vanished and tried not to feel like an unwanted suitor.

He shifted his weight, shuffling on his feet as he waited for her to emerge, ready to ask her for the next dance as he had planned to do when he first spotted her.

He'd seen unwanted suitors before at balls. Hapless, spotted-faced young men loitering outside the ladies' retiring rooms. Desperation wafted around them in an invisible haze, and he'd always felt sorry for the lot of them. Didn't they know any better? Desperation never won a heart. He winced. And yet here he was.

He'd never thought to count himself among the ranks of unwelcome and hapless suitors. Never had he imagined he would be undesirable to the fairer sex.

As he lingered outside the doors, he fixed a mild smile to his face and ignored the curious looks sent his way from ladies entering and leaving the room.

He thought back to Emily Blankenship's face when their gazes had locked across the crowded room. She had bolted at the first sight of him—as though he was a contagious disease. As though one glimpse of him had turned her stomach. Her sister, who was forever at her side, was nowhere in sight either, and he could not help wondering if she was hiding in some corner, afraid to come out because of him.

Bloody hell.

It was as though he was trapped in some other cosmos. One in which the most common and ordinary ladies were diving into potted ferns to avoid him.

He cringed. Except this was not another cosmos. This was his reality. This was his life now.

It had to be the bloody rumors. Both Misses Blankenship had been friendly with him after church. More than friendly. The rumors were the only thing that made any sense. Nothing else had changed.

Clearly he needed to exercise his charm and win back their favor. If that meant addressing concerns over these bloody rumors, so be it.

His hands opened and closed at his sides. Someone was ruining his life with this damnable slander. He had thought nothing could get worse. How much lower could he descend than losing his title, his fortune, the bulk of his friends, *and* the lady he had been courting? The lady he had actually liked and thought liked *him* in turn had faded from his life faster than a wisp of smoke.

But apparently he could sink lower. Evidently he had.

He stared at the closed doors to the retiring room, feeling very much like one of those unwanted suitors from memory.

He had to find out who was behind this sabotage, and he had to put a stop to it or look elsewhere for an heiress, which meant leaving Shropshire and imposing on the few friends who still spoke to him. That brought forth a weary sigh from deep in his chest. He recoiled at the very notion of living off the generosity of the few friends left to him. It was difficult enough living with his mother—even if she was responsible for the situation in which he now found himself.

But you don't mind taking advantage and living off the generosity of a debutante's dowry.

He shifted on his feet and rubbed at his chest—at the sudden gnawing ache there. It suddenly felt as though his lungs were too small, too tight. He sucked in a gulp of air in an effort to expand them.

He didn't know why the act of courting and marrying for financial security should give him pause or discomfort. Marriages were formed upon such factors all the time. He should feel no compunction. That was the way of the *ton*. It was the way of everyone everywhere. Even humble yeomen married based on such reasoning.

One's rank, family name, finances and attractiveness were always negotiating tools. *Hellfire*, those had been the same deciding influences he took into consideration a year ago when he was still the Duke of Penning and had begun his courtship of Lady Circe. He winced. When he still possessed the wealth that went along with the title.

Now he felt decidedly . . . *less*. He had little to offer. His ego could only convince himself so much that his handsome face and charm were enough. There was reality . . . and the humility of the past year serving as a mirror, showing him the truth of his irrefutable reflection.

He glanced around, feeling suddenly inconspicuous where he stood. Indeed several eyes were trained on him. He'd felt the stares all night. As though he were a bug pinned beneath a glass dome. A specimen for public inspection. They were more than curious. They were critical and judging.

He had the sneaking suspicion that if he approached another lady, she, too, might run for the hills—or in this case, the retiring room. This was an altogether alien experience for him and not a little demoralizing. Rejection, he realized, was a lowering thing. It did not feel great. Not great at all.

He fought the impulse to leave. That would be cowardly and defeatist. He was unwilling to give up. He couldn't do that. If he left, it would be as though he were declaring all the rumors were true.

He decided to duck out of the ballroom for a breath of fortifying fresh air. A brief respite and then he would return to the ballroom.

Perhaps while he was out there, it might occur to him how to overcome these blots on his name—and how he might find the culprit responsible for them and put an end to this rubbish once and for all.

THE BALL WAS in full swing, perhaps even growing more crowded with every passing moment. The Blankenships truly had invited everyone. Imogen and Mercy were now pressed along the far wall. Relegated. Forgotten. But not, apparently, completely invisible.

"Oh! Hello, there, you two!" Mrs. Berrycloth exclaimed as she spotted them. She waved at them from several yards away. She wove through bodies to arrive breathlessly at Imogen's side.

"Good evening, Mrs. Berrycloth," Imogen and Mercy greeted the widow in unison.

The lady had traded in her black mourning

weeds for a less dreary gown of dark plum. The neckline was quite daring, displaying an abundant amount of cleavage.

"Enjoying yourself?" Imogen inquired, trying not to stare overly long at her mesmerizing décolletage.

"Indeed, I am. I just took a turn about the dance floor with one of Mr. Blankenship's guests. A barrister from London." Mrs. Berrycloth clutched her side. "I haven't been so exerted in ages. I am out of practice, it seems."

"Would you like me to fetch you some punch to help refresh you?" Mercy asked.

"Oh, that's kind of you. Thank you, Miss Kittinger."

Mercy slipped away to retrieve a drink for the widow.

"It is good to see you making merry, Mrs. Berrycloth," Imogen offered.

"Thank you, m'dear. I was happy to cast off my widow's weeds. It has been long enough." The widow had been thrice widowed, so she clearly knew what it was like to endure the constraints of mourning. "I've been looking forward to this ball. I've always loved to dance even if the late Mr. Berrycloth couldn't countenance it."

Her late husband had been a prosperous merchant almost twice her age. Imogen had never seen him dance at these things. Indeed not, he usually ate and played cards. All sedentary activities. He had not shared any of his younger wife's more energetic interests like dancing.

"The Blankenships' ball was auspicious timing then."

"Indeed. What of you, m'dears? No dancing for either of you? You two ladies should not be hiding here among the potted ferns."

Mercy returned then with punch in hand and answered, "Oh, I must keep a sharp eye on my sister. If I'm off cavorting, who will look after her?"

"Hmph." Mrs. Berrycloth looked Imogen up and down, assessing her in her modest gown. "And what of you Miss Bates?"

"Oh, I'm not much for dancing." At least not since she was a blushing ten and eight. She had been more adventurous then . . . up for anything. More the fool she.

"What? You are still young. I'd been married twice by the time I was your age and had not even met the late Mr. Berrycloth yet." Mrs. Berrycloth lightly swatted her. "You have plenty of time. You should be twirling about on that dance floor instead of fraternizing with all the old dames and wallflowers."

Imogen shook her head with a small laugh, not bothering to point out that she *was* a wallflower. Unapologetically so. Well, she *had* been a wallflower. She supposed she did not qualify anymore. Not at her age.

Now she was simply an aging spinster. But that was fine and well with Imogen. Her life had purpose and meaning. She had freedom. More freedom than most. So many wives had none of those things. They had only what their husbands allotted them. No freedom. No choices.

Husbands. It should not be that a woman counted herself fortunate if her husband was a good man. If he was a man of honor, a man who didn't neglect or abuse his wife. A woman should expect those very fundamental things as her due and not count herself lucky.

Indeed, in a perfect world there should be no husbands like Mr. Henry.

"Let me locate a partner for you, Miss Bates," Mrs. Berrycloth pressed, standing on her tiptoes and scanning the crowd for a likely candidate. "Ah, I think I see young Halston without a partner at the moment. He does have very nice teeth, and that's not something every gentleman can boast—"

Imogen shook her head vehemently. "No. That's not necessary. I am quite content as I am."

"Why, Mr. Halston should count himself lucky to partner with you. Your teeth are lovely, as well—"

"That is neither here nor there, Mrs. Berry-cloth," Imogen said without heat and offering a gentle smile, intent on giving no offense but determined that she not be intimidated into dancing. She was much too old for this nonsense. "I have no wish to dance. With him or anyone. It's not for me, I am afraid. I am quite settled in my life." Imogen often found herself saying such things at these functions. It was tiresome. She was constantly attempting to convince the world around her that she was happy as she was—a woman without a husband. Such an entity could exist—such a *person* could exist. It existed in her.

"Well, that is true as long as you have your dear papa. What happens when he's gone?"

Imogen felt the words like a sharp uncomfortable pinch. She looked at Mrs. Berrycloth in disbelief. No one had ever been so bold as to ask her that before. "Well, I—I," she stammered, disliking contemplating such a thing.

"I've had three husbands. I know well the ephemeral nature of life. Especially for a gentleman advanced in years."

"I—I—"

"No one lives forever."

"Well, yes. Of course." She knew that. Better than most. She'd already lost her mother in a horribly sudden manner.

One day Mama had been enjoying herself

amid her favorite pastime, happily toiling in the garden, and then a fortnight later she had taken to her bed, feverish from a festering wound. An accidental cut on her hand from her gardening shears had resulted in a fatal infection that brought about her demise.

It had been arbitrary and senseless and horrible. There was nothing anyone could do to save her. They could only sit by her side and watch her die.

Life, Imogen had learned then, could be as volatile as the weather. So Imogen was not blind to the impermanence of life. Indeed not. She knew how fragile the threads that made up one's existence could be.

"I do hope you have made plans for your future, Miss Bates. I only say this out of concern."

Imogen started at the remark, her thoughts reluctantly drifting to her future.

She would receive a small inheritance from Papa, but he was not a wealthy man. It would not be much. Perhaps just enough to keep her in genteel poverty—as long as she did not live to the ripe age of one hundred. She winced. Or fifty.

She supposed she could take employment as a governess or a teacher. She would have to do *something*. It was vastly unfair. She would lose her home. The vicarage would go to the next vicar. Her throat tightened at the thought. When she lost Papa, she would lose everything. Not only her beloved father, but her home. Her way of life. All would be forfeit.

Hopefully Papa would not be leaving her for a good while. She made certain he did not exert himself, overseeing all of his affairs for him and encouraging him to rest at every opportunity so that he did not suffer from another fit.

Hope also throbbed in her chest that Papa would find favor with the new Duke of Penning. The appointment of the vicar was completely at his discretion. The Duke of Penning not only selected the vicar, he could force him to resign.

Not that anyone knew when His Grace might arrive. There were rumblings that the man lived in Newfoundland working in the cod trade or in Greenland mining for iron. There were several stories, all unsubstantiated. An agent had been sent abroad to find him many months ago. Everyone waited with bated breath to see what manner of man he would be once he was located and appeared—especially as so many people had their livelihoods tied to him.

"Oh, there are many fine gentlemen about tonight. I'm sure any number of them could tempt you." Mrs. Berrycloth's eyes glittered and stopped to rest somewhere across the ballroom.

The skin at the back of Imogen's neck prickled. She followed Mrs. Berrycloth's gaze, already knowing what she would find, knowing what—or rather *who*—had captured the lady's most ardent attention.

Imogen sighed. The widow fixed her attention on Mr. Butler with clear admiration as he cut through the packed crowd, his long strides purposeful. Imogen's own gaze lingered on him, on his handsome features set in grim lines. Anyone else would look off-putting wearing such a moody expression, but he still managed to look handsome. Still compelling. She gave a slight shake of her head.

No doubt he was about claiming his next waltz with an eligible young lady who met his criteria for marriage.

Mrs. Berrycloth continued, "I must confess, it's nice to see His Grace out and about at village functions."

"Hm. Yes. But he's not the duke anymore, is he?" Imogen felt like she would be making that correction all her life.

"Oh, indeed, but what are we supposed to call him?" Mrs. Berrycloth sniffed. "I can't imagine calling him anything else. It feels rather . . . impolite."

Impolite?

"Mr. Butler," Imogen supplied. "We're supposed to call him Mr. Butler now."

Mrs. Berrycloth swatted her arm with her fan

and giggled. "Oh! Can you imagine? I could not do that. It would seem so rude."

"It *is* his name," she grumbled, annoyed at the widow's interest in Mr. Butler. She certainly wasn't behaving as Emily Blankenship had been. Evidently the recent rumors had not reached the lady's ears. It was difficult to imagine she would not care.

"I saw him earlier in the week and promised him a dance tonight."

"Indeed?" Mercy sent Imogen an amused look.

The widow nodded gleefully, as though she had managed a great coup. "What's more . . . he suggested we take an afternoon stroll one day soon."

Mercy's grin to Imogen seemed to say: *you did not run off all matrimonial prospects.*

"Oh. Did he now?"

The gentleman worked fast. Imogen had not realized that he had cast his web so wide as to include Mrs. Berrycloth. She fought down a derisive snort. But of course he had. The lady had her own fortune. That made her a viable candidate. She gave her head a small shake. Apparently she needed to work quickly, as well.

"Mrs. Berrycloth," Imogen began, "would you like to step out for some air with me?" She motioned to the double doors leading out into the gardens. "You look like you might enjoy a refreshing breeze."

"Oh, am I perspiring?" With a look of dismay, she waved her fan over her face with more vigor. Before Imogen could put her at ease, Mrs. Berrycloth was looping her arm with Imogen's and guiding them out to the veranda. "We can't have that. I don't want to appear red-faced and discomposed."

"Mercy?" She turned to her friend. "Care to join us?"

"I'll stay here. Grace is dancing a little too closely with a certain young man for my tastes. I best intervene."

"You do that." Nodding, and smiling sweetly, she and Mrs. Berrycloth advanced to the veranda.

At her first sweet inhale upon emerging outside, Imogen felt much improved. The air was cooler and less pungent than in that stuffy ballroom, to be certain.

"That is more like it, Miss Bates. Excellent suggestion. Much better." Mrs. Berrycloth descended the steps toward the burbling fountain. Imogen kept pace alongside her. The widow sent her a mischievous wink. "I can't look less than my best for my dance with the duke." She looked rapturous at her own delusional words and pressed a hand over her impressive bosom as though her heart threatened to explode from her chest. "La, I never imagined that would happen. He is such a beautiful man."

Imogen nodded numbly. It was like they were speaking two different languages. "Mr. Butler," she corrected automatically. The woman had to understand a lauded nobleman was not pandering to her.

Mrs. Berrycloth shrugged and glanced back toward the house, clearly eager to return for her much-anticipated dance.

"Are you not concerned?" Imogen began.

"Concerned? With what?"

"His recent fall . . . in Society."

Mrs. Berrycloth waved a hand. "Oh, pish posh. He's still a gentleman, and a very handsome one. Virile from all appearances. I cannot tell you how very important that is. After three marriages, it ranks as *very* important to me. A man's . . . er, stamina in certain areas can be very valuable. Trust me. Have you seen him astride a horse? Those manly thighs of his? Oh. My." She cut Imogen a meaningful look and then waved herself with her fan more vigorously, her skin flushing all over again. "Forgive me, Miss Bates. You must think me perfectly brazen. I sometimes forget you're still a maid. You're so very mature and self-assured."

Mature and self-assured. Translation? A spinster.

"I would not know about that," she murmured.

"His undeniable virility aside, there is much to recommend him. His mother *is* a duchess. His father *was* a duke. Perhaps his pockets are empty, but mine are more than deep enough for the two of us."

Bold words, but true enough . . . even as much as Imogen loathed to hear them. Mrs. Berrycloth was not as rich as the Blankenships, but she was quite well set. The notion of Mr. Butler and the lovely widow together unsettled her. Her stomach felt as though she had eaten something offputting.

Evidently Mrs. Berrycloth had not heard the rumors Imogen started.

Or could it be that she did not mind that he wore a wig and sported extra toes and kissed like a toad? Perhaps his manly thighs were enough for her?

Evidently Imogen needed to exert more influence.

"I thought you would be more discerning, Mrs. Berrycloth, given Mr. Butler's . . . condition, but I applaud you for your tolerance."

She stopped waving her fan and looked at Imogen sharply. "Condition?"

Imogen nodded doggedly, her mind working quickly to come up with another affliction to toss upon Butler's head in case she had heard the others and they did not deter her. "Yes. Um. It's a little bit of a delicate matter. I dare not speak of it."

"Oh, you can share with me." Mrs. Berrycloth sidled closer. "We are well past shyness. Speak freely."

Imogen hedged. "I'm afraid it's most unpleasant. I dare not repeat it."

"Tell me, please. What is it?"

"It's dreadful to say, but . . . Mr. Butler suffers from excessive . . . flatulence."

Chapter Seven ❧

*H*ad those words really just come out of Imogen's mouth?

She glanced around as though someone else was standing nearby and had uttered the incredible claim. But no. It was only the two of them. Imogen and the Widow Berrycloth.

Mrs. Berrycloth blinked as though she had misheard. "I beg your pardon, Miss Bates?"

"Oh, indeed. Poor Mr. Butler has met with physicians, herbalists . . . an unbalance of his humors, they all say." She shrugged again, unsure of the nonsense she was spouting, but she had sat beside Papa as he attended to several of the elderly members of the community and this was a frequent complaint they had lodged.

"Flatulence?" Mrs. Berrycloth demanded as though seeking clarification on the point.

Imogen nodded and continued, "Nothing can be done." She waved her hand in rapid little circles, hoping she did not look like someone lying through her teeth, even as she was. "He's lost a great deal of staff over it. All of Penning Hall reeked of rotten eggs when he was in residence. Now his mother's staff at the dower house endures it. The dowager duchess had had to double their wages to simply keep them on."

"Good heavens. How dreadful." Mrs. Berrycloth breathed deeply, her nose wrinkling in revulsion. "I had not heard."

"Yes, well, when he was a duke it went unspoken, out of deference. I'm sure you can understand that." It was amazing how the lies tripped off her tongue. Imogen had never lied as much in her entire life as she had in the last week. Who knew she had it in her?

She should be alarmed at this dishonest side to her nature, but she felt rather . . . euphoric. She had always been so very good—with the exception of her slight misstep with Fernsby. Although she didn't count herself as *bad* for placing her trust in him. Merely young and foolish.

This. Doing *this*. She felt wicked.

"But now that he is no longer the duke . . ." Imogen shrugged. "He has no such protection. Everyone knows. It cannot be hidden."

"I see." Mrs. Berrycloth expelled a shaky breath. "Well, thank you for sharing with me. This is good to know. Good to know, indeed. I am in your debt."

Imogen inclined her head and pushed down

the small niggle of disquiet working through her belly, attempting to banish it from existence.

She was helping women like Mrs. Berrycloth. Vulnerable women like the widow who would not question Butler's motives with any degree of scrutiny. They deserved better than being used for their wealth so that they could line the pockets of an undeserving man.

Whether they knew it or not, they needed protection, and Imogen was that protection. That was her role. With Papa not quite himself and Mama gone, it fell to her to look after his flock.

"Glad to have been of service."

"Oh, dear though." Mrs. Berrycloth covered her lips with her gloved hand. "I've promised him that waltz . . ."

"Hopefully he will not er . . . transgress whilst you dance," Imogen offered with a sympathetic cluck. "Although it is my understanding that he has little control over his body's . . . blunders."

"Oh!" Mrs. Berrycloth shook her head resolutely, pressing both hands to her flushed cheeks. "I simply cannot. I must make my excuses. Or hide."

"The ballroom *is* crowded," Imogen pointed out as though hiding from him were a very reasonable solution. "Perhaps you can elude him."

At the edge of her consciousness, nipped the

awareness that she might be taking things a pinch too far. Certainly he was a wretched man, but with each lie, with every fabrication, she felt herself slipping deeper and deeper into a hole.

And then she reminded herself that this was the same lad who laughed at her and scorned her and called her ugly things and didn't have time for the residents of Shropshire until he had found himself penniless and desperate.

"Yes, of course. I will simply avoid him. Or find myself occupied should he approach me. That should not pose too difficult . . ." Her voice faded as a figure suddenly emerged from around the fountain. A man.

They both froze as the gentleman stepped directly into the path of light blazing from the windows of the Blankenships' house, throwing his features into stark relief.

Imogen's lungs seized, unable to draw air. Had their very conversation conjured him?

Breathlessly she watched as Mr. Butler stopped before them.

"Ladies." He greeted both of them, but his eyes held fast on Imogen with an alarming intensity that she felt in her bones. Who knew such a frosty gray could make her feel so warm? As though she were seated too close to the fire.

"Oh! Your Grace . . . er, that is . . . Mr. Butler. Good evening to you. A fine night, is it not?" Mrs.

Berrycloth prattled on shrilly as she dipped in a quick curtsy that was not necessary and totally ludicrous. "And an even finer ball. The Blankenships know how to properly entertain, to be sure. How splendid that you were able to attend and see for yourself what you have been missing all these years."

Would the woman not cease her chatter?

"Miss Imogen and I were just taking some air," she added.

Apparently not.

On she went whilst Imogen struggled to find her own voice, finally arriving at something to say. "It's perfectly fragrant out here this close to Mrs. Blankenship's lovely gardens. I must speak with her gardener and learn all his secrets."

"Indeed," he murmured. "It is a fine night to indulge in fragrant air and *sparkling* conversation."

Imogen did not miss the emphasis he placed on the word *sparkling*. All the while he continued to stare at her—at Imogen—as though Mrs. Berrycloth were not even present.

Stare?

It might be fair to say he was *glaring* at her and she felt the intensity of those gray eyes like a poker to her overheated skin.

She resisted fidgeting and looked back at him with a lift of her chin, recalling that it never served to show weakness. She knew that was the precise moment that predators attacked, and for some reason, right now, Peregrine Butler very much reminded her of a predator—or certainly of an animal ready to pounce.

Mrs. Berrycloth looked back and forth between them, obviously sensing the tension. She cleared her throat. "If you will excuse me. It's growing chilly." She turned then and fled, abandoning Imogen like a soldier bolting at the first sight of a skirmish.

Imogen knew she could make her own excuses, too. She could flee. Propriety alone would recommend she do that. Although it was not outright scandalous behavior for her to remain. They stood within the light. Anyone could step out on the veranda and peer down at them. But she was the vicar's daughter. She held herself to a higher standard just as everyone else in the shire did. She really should go inside. And yet she was planted in place.

He said nothing for several moments and neither did Imogen. She willed him to speak, to reveal what he had or had not heard in her conversation with the buxom widow.

The intensity in which he stared at her implied that he'd overheard everything. She couldn't help herself. She took a sliding step back, away from him and the blast of his knowing and withering gaze.

"So," he finally said. "You're the reason everyone has been treating me like a bloody leper."

She gulped. "I beg your pardon?"

A muscle ticked wildly in his handsome jaw. "I think you heard me perfectly well, Miss Bates. You have been spreading lies about me."

Apparently she no longer had to envision what the conversation with him would be like when he confronted her about the rumors. She didn't have to wonder. Now he knew, and now they would have that very fraught conservation. She had been correct. It was no easy matter.

"Who? Me?"

"Yes. You, you conniving little witch." He advanced on her like a predator in the night.

She resisted the urge to run and held her ground. He wouldn't dare do anything with people—

She yelped as he seized her hand and pulled her around the fountain, into the shadows and out of the arc of light swelling from the house.

She tugged her hand free. "Unhand me!"

He promptly released her and she rubbed her gloved fingertips together as though she felt him through the fabric and on her skin.

His gaze, impenetrable as ever, cut through the dark. "You have never liked me, and this is clearly how you've chosen to exercise your vendetta."

"Vendetta?" She laughed nervously. "Absurd. Do not be so dramatic. I assure you, I have no vendetta against you, Mr. Butler." She lifted her chin sharply. "Now if you'll excuse me—"

"Oh, no. This conversation is long overdue."

She sent a wary glance toward the house, partially obscured by the fountain. When she looked back at him he had started counting off on his fingers. "I'm bald. I have a few extra toes. I'm a terrible kisser. And now it seems I have excessive and chronic flatulence."

She shrugged and crossed her arms. "Who is to say if any of that is . . . *untrue*?"

He blinked. "I say." He patted his chest fiercely. "I do!"

She laced her gloved fingers demurely in front of her. "I'm sure your charm will shine through and you will lure some young lady to the altar."

That silenced him for a long moment. He settled back on his heels and squared his shoulders as though digesting this. "Who's to say," he began, echoing her words, "that is what I am trying to do?"

Was he claiming that he wasn't on the hunt for an heiress?

"Everyone," she countered. "That's what *everyone* says. You're on the search for a bride, for an heiress, and everyone knows it. Given your circumstances, your agenda is clear."

"My circumstances?" he repeated, his eyes narrowing. "You speak of my loss of fortune?"

Now it was her time to count off on her fingers. "Fortune. Title. Home. All property and honors therein." She cocked her head. "Am I leaving anything out?"

He shook his head. "I've forgotten just what an impertinent chit you are."

"Only to you," she reassured sweetly. "Everybody else thinks me a perfect delight."

"And why is that? What did I do to deserve your dislike?"

She scoffed. "Please. Do not act as though you have been kind to me all these years and I'm just this . . . this bully. Our animosity is long-standing and dual-sided."

It was his turn to cock his head at her in challenge. "Animosity? I can't claim such an emotion when it comes to you. I can only characterize any feelings toward you as . . . indifference, Miss Bates."

Indifference? That stung.

He added, "I confess I don't give you much thought at all."

The sting sharpened.

Did he have no memory of the horrible things he said to her—about her?

Clearly *she* was thinking about him too much. Whenever they were in the same room, Imogen's gaze was drawn to him, and now, thanks to Mrs. Berrycloth, she couldn't cease to contemplate his manly thighs. And he felt only indifference toward her? *Wretch.*

Suddenly she was heartily glad of all her meddling. Evidently her occasional stab of guilt that she was perhaps taking things too far with her sabotage was misplaced.

She regretted nothing.

He continued, "I need you to stop spreading lies and change the minds of those who are laboring under these delusions you've woven."

She tsked. "That might be tricky."

He took a step toward her, backing her deeper into shadows. "I don't care if it requires Herculean effort. You owe me—"

"Owe you?" Outrage flared through her. "I owe you nothing."

"You owe me the truth."

She rolled her shoulders, squaring herself in front of him. "I cannot attest to the *un*truth of any of these allegations."

"Oh, that's rich." He laughed roughly, looking off to the side as if searching for patience before facing her again.

She adopted an innocent look, blinking with exaggeration. "I think it a fair point."

He grabbed fistfuls of his hair and tugged on the locks hard enough to make *her* wince. "See?

Real! My hair is bloody *real*. You are welcome to pull it yourself."

Her palms tingled and she curled her hands into fists at her sides to resist his irate invitation. The last thing she would ever *ever* do was lay hands to him.

"Not necessary. And very well," she acknowledged with a shrug. "I suppose I can attest to that, if you insist. If anyone should put the inquiry to me I will tell them your hair *appears* quite real and you are not bald."

"And as for my feet . . ." He stepped back and bent, reaching for his shoes.

"What are you doing?" She peered down at him curiously.

He looked up at her, a fiery glint in his eyes. "I want you to have no doubts, Miss Bates. You may count my toes."

"That's really not—"

It was too late.

He had one shoe and stocking off, and then the other. "See there. Count them. Ten toes. Now all the superstitious tattle can cease regarding the number of my toes. Let us put that one to rest."

She peered down at his bare feet in the gloom. They were surprisingly nice feet. Long. Lean. Clean. Nails neatly trimmed. Until this moment she did not know that attractive feet were so very significant. And yes, there were indeed ten toes.

Not that she expected to see any differently. She had spun the rumor from pure imagination. "Indeed," she murmured. "I see that."

He spread his arms wide at his sides. "And as for my chronic flatulence. I have now stood here for some time with you and have not given offense. I am quite certain you invented that particular rumor on the spot just now with Mrs. Berrycloth."

Truer words had never been spoken, but she dared not admit such a thing to him. She would never confess. Never apologize to the wretch.

She did not consider herself a stubborn person. To anyone else, she would admit wrongdoing, but not to him. Not to this man. For some reason she was intractable when it came to him.

You would need to put a bag over her personality. Perhaps that was the reason.

"And," he continued with a great breath, "I can assure you, I am not a terrible kisser."

Fire flamed his eyes, a burst of light in the night, and she recognized that this one point on the matter of his kissing prowess stung more than all of the other rumors about him. *Of course.* His ego could not tolerate the belief that a woman might find him—or his lips—less than desirable, less than skilled. Vain peacock.

And so very predictable.

She crossed her arms over her chest. "Ha," she coughed out, the single sound brash and defiant.

He flinched. "I beg your pardon?"

"I said 'ha.'"

"Yes, I heard you." He shook his head as though trying to make sense of what was happening. "What does that mean?"

"Oh, did that sound not capture my complete disbelief on the matter of your kissing expertise?"

His eyes narrowed.

She continued, "You must confess, there is no way I can ascertain the truth of this. I can do nothing to dissuade others from believing this particular allegation—ack!"

In one smooth move, he reached out, closed his hands around her arms and tumbled her against his person.

His mouth claimed her lips before she could form a more coherent exclamation.

He was kissing her.

Despite the physical onslaught, she understood his motivation and it was *not* an overwhelming desire for her. Of course not. He thought to kiss her to prove himself an adept kisser. That was clearly his mercenary goal. Well, he could stuff that notion. She would not be swayed . . .

He deepened the kiss, his lips slanting over hers, and the pressure made her belly flip.

Blast it.

Imogen knew a thing or two about kissing, too. No one would ever think it of her. Not her father, not any of the residents of Shropshire— especially not Mr. Butler. By his own admission, he never thought of her at all. He certainly never thought of her lips.

Indeed, she knew enough about kissing to know that he was a good kisser.

It had been years, but there was a time when she, in fact, had frequent practice. She kept that part of who she was a secret. She had buried it so deep that sometimes she even forgot that part of herself ever existed. A deliberate ploy, of course. She didn't want to remember that particular part of her history.

But in this moment, she remembered.

Kissing was like breathing, it seemed. One never forgot how to do it.

As his mouth moved over hers, she felt a stirring in her blood, a definite sputter and crackle to life that prompted a reaction she could not deny.

It had been too long.

That's what she would tell herself later.

He was too handsome. His mouth too hot, too persuasive, too addictive.

My life too lonely.

She melted against him, leaning into him, immediately and achingly aware of the firm pressure of his chest against her breasts. He brought his other hand up, burying it in her hair, mussing her coiffure, but she did not mind. Suddenly that breach seemed the smallest of concerns as shivers of pleasure eddied through her.

She parted her mouth on a sigh . . . or perhaps it was no sigh at all and a deliberate opening of her lips. An invitation so she could have more of a taste of him—so that he could have more of a taste of *her*.

He accepted by sliding his tongue into her mouth, slow and languorous as though he were savoring her. Her tongue met his and giddiness swelled through her at the first touch.

He tasted of warm whisky.

She knew from the one glass she had snuck on the evening of Winifred's wedding. She'd been staying at her uncle's house for the grand occasion. After the ceremony she had found herself alone in a room with a decanter and tray and she'd poured herself a drink, needing the fortification, and perhaps because she was seeking a little numbness, too. He tasted of that dark and spicy whisky now . . . and *man*. Tempting maleness. All her womanly places quivered in response.

She dove into the kiss—into him, bringing her hands up to clutch his jacket and yank him even closer, however impossible that may be. They were already crushed against each other. So close she felt the pound of his heart against her. So close no air even passed between them. She was no longer certain where her body ended and his began and still she wanted more.

She kissed him with fervor and pent-up longing, not even realizing until this moment that she had missed this in her life. Passion. Intimacy. The discovery and learning of another's taste— the texture and shape of another's lips.

Except this felt better than she remembered. More unrestrained. More desperate. Hungrier.

She'd never felt *want* like this. Never felt a need that shook her to her core.

It was impossible to stop. Impossible to resist.

She would not even try.

Chapter Eight ❧

$\mathcal{P}$erry was kissing the vicar's daughter.

The only thing more shocking would be if he were kissing the good vicar himself.

Contrary to what he said, Perry was not indifferent to Imogen Bates. He never had been. Quite the opposite. Just as she did not like him, he did not like her.

Even before he'd heard her speaking those ridiculous lies about him there had always been this . . . *tension* between them. Whenever she was in his orbit his stomach grew unsettled. His skin prickled and the back of his neck felt tight. He had assumed it was dislike.

Perhaps there was more to it though because he was kissing her hard, like he was a man starved for this woman.

But then he supposed liking someone was not a prerequisite for intimacy. At least for some gentlemen. Historically, he rather preferred to *like* his partners—or to at least find them unobjectionable—before kissing took place.

Evidently there could be exceptions, and Imogen Bates was one of them.

In the before times, when his life had included a dukedom, he was not usually so free with his passions. He did not kiss just anyone. Contrary to his reputation and what his own mother seemed to think of him, he was judicious where he spent his passions. He cared not to contract the pox, after all. Many a nobleman was riddled with it from far too many peccadilloes of a less than discerning nature. It was Perry's instinct to be more cautious.

And in this new life, shagging had been the last thing on his mind. He'd spent the last year wading through the quagmire of his lost life, trying to make sense of what had happened. He'd only recently thrown himself into the task of finding an heiress.

And yet Miss Imogen Bates triggered his ire.

Learning she was responsible for the rumors circulating should not have come as a surprise. He had no enemies in Shropshire. Only Miss Bates, of course. She never hid her distaste for him. Not when they were children and not in adulthood.

True, he may not have been decidedly warm toward her. There was the time that Thirza shoved her into the pond and he had laughed. Not well done of him, but they'd been children then. He winced, recalling also when she'd caught him saying those less than gentlemanly things about her in the conservatory. He hadn't been a child then. Just an arse.

Of course, she was the one spreading tales of him. Who else? He would have eventually landed on the conclusion that Imogen Bates was his saboteur. In time. Once he ran through all the possible suspects in the shire.

And yet she had gone too far.

Now he had gone too far and hauled her against him.

He'd acted without thinking. Nothing else could explain his impulse to kiss her. He should have restrained himself. It was reckless. He should have behaved better. She'd done nothing to entice him. Quite the opposite.

He generally liked cheerful and good-humored women. Lusty women whose big hearts matched their passions.

Miss Bates was not that.

She never smiled. In fact, more often than not, a scowl graced her face—at least in his company.

Desire had not propelled him to kiss her. His temper had gotten the best of him.

And yet every pore, every fiber of his being was humming and vibrating, consumed by this kiss and proclaiming him a liar. Whatever this had started out as, it was all about desire now.

Nothing could account for her ability to kiss like a well-seasoned paramour.

Her hands fisted in his jacket, no doubt ruining Thurman's efforts. The man had taken great pains to press his clothing this evening. He'd made certain that Perry left the house impeccably attired. "You might not be a duke anymore, but that does not mean you face the world looking like a vagabond," the old butler had said.

Her fists twisted, pulling his jacket tighter and bringing him closer. She was surprisingly forceful. And skilled. Her tongue knew precisely what to do.

He tightened his hand in her silky hair—somehow his hand ended up in her hair. It was as if his body—and his mouth—had a will of their own.

She made a breathy little sound at the back of her throat. He growled and kissed her harder. He never had a kiss like this before. It was deep and hard and soft all at the same time. She angled her head side to side as though she could not get enough of him—as though she wanted to gobble him up, eat him alive.

Then—astoundingly—she nipped at his lip with a tiny little snarl.

Lust shot straight through him in a hot spear. His cock went rock hard, straining against his trousers, and before he could check himself he was pushing his hips into her, loathing her voluminous skirts, loathing all their bulky garments.

Where had the genteel and demure Miss Bates gone? Perhaps she wasn't real.

He knew something about leading a fake life. Perhaps this was the real and true Miss Bates and that other creature was merely the facade.

Her fists unclenched the edges of his jacket and her hands slid beneath. She stroked her palms over his chest as though desperate to get through the layers of his vest and shirt to his skin. He could understand the impulse. He felt the wild need to touch her under her clothes with his hands, his mouth . . . to learn the texture and taste of her body.

She arched and pressed against him like she wanted to crawl inside and take up space alongside his bones. Her feverish lips kissed him with a moan purring in her throat.

If he didn't pull away from her now this would get out of hand.

It was already out of hand. He already had to fight the urge to drag her into the nearby rhododendron bushes.

He pulled back with a ragged breath to gape at her where they stood in the shadows. The night swelled around them, the sounds of the orchestra a distant melody. The swift burbling of the fountain matched his rushing pulse.

"Where did you learn to do that?" he rasped.

Her lips moved, but nothing came out. She had a pretty mouth. Especially kiss-bruised and blush-pink as it was now. It was wide and full-lipped, only the slightest dip at the center. He'd never noticed before. He'd only ever seen her frowns when he looked at her. Evidently there was a lot more to her than he had ever realized, and he was beyond intrigued.

Her fingers drifted to those lips now. "Wh-what?"

"Where did you learn to kiss like that?" he clarified, feeling as though he had taken a blow to his chest and couldn't catch his breath.

Something flashed in her eyes—a bright wave of emotion before a wall dropped down and shielded her gaze. "*You* kissed me," she got out, neatly avoiding his question.

"And you kissed me back." Quite thoroughly and quite well.

"I—I—" she stammered, a rare moment when he had never seen her at a loss for words.

He studied her, scanning her face and then looking her up and down, missing nothing, and yet feeling as if he wasn't seeing her fully. There was more to her than he ever realized. She had hidden depths. What other surprises did she hide? He wanted to know. He wanted to know them all.

"Imogen?" a female called out across the garden. "Are you out here?"

Her head whipped in the direction of the voice. "Mercy," she croaked out. Her hands flew to her hair. Proof of his recklessness. It had tumbled loose from its pins.

He liked it that way. He'd never seen it down. The honey-brown waves flowed wild around her shoulders. She was dangerously enticing.

"Imogen," Mercy called again, her voice more insistent.

Thurman had mentioned Mercy Kittinger as a possible candidate in his hunt for an heiress. The Kittinger family was one of the few independent farmers in the area, and they owned the largest tract of property outside of the Penning lands. Mama had not loved the notion, wrinkling her nose and muttering about never dreaming her son would wed a lowly yeoman's daughter.

"Imogen?" Miss Kittinger called again, a touch of impatience entering her voice.

They both looked in the direction of Mercy and then back at each other. He imagined the panic crossing her face closely mirrored his own.

He did not relish being discovered in a compromising position with Miss Bates. Even if he could overlook their incompatibilities, she was no heiress. Not even close. She was a country vicar's daughter—a vicar who lived at the whim of the Duke of Penning. Up until a year ago, that man had been him, so he knew precisely how little she had to her name. She would bring nothing to a marriage. *Nothing save her dangerously enticing person.*

Giving his head a swift shake, he looked down at his hands. He still touched her. His palms flexed on her arms as though verifying they were in fact his hands—that *he* was in fact touching her and she was not some illusion. He marveled at how very strong she felt, her biceps solid and firm. What did the vicar's daughter do with her time so that her arms were not frail or soft?

Coming to his senses, he released her, dropping his hands to his sides and taking a perfunctory step back, trying not to consider how she would be no shrinking violet in bed. Not based off that kiss. She would be a full-hearted participant and up for some vigorous love play if her behavior from moments ago was any indication. He'd been the one to end the kiss, after all.

He'd frequently heard among gentlemen that wives were for duty and mistresses for fun. It was difficult to imagine Miss Imogen Bates as anything other than a very proper wife. However, now it was also difficult to imagine her as anything but a very fiery and eager bedmate.

She had not stepped back from him. He held

up his hands, showing he had released her just in case she was unaware of that point. She did not move immediately. She looked up at him as though she feared—or hoped?—he might pounce on her. Again.

"What am I supposed to do?" she finally whispered, motioning to her hair. "I'm a mess. One look at me and everyone will know. I need to slip away."

"I don't see how that is possible."

She released a small sound of frustration.

He continued, "You and Miss Kittinger are good friends, are you not?"

"Yes."

"Do you trust her? With your confidences?"

"Yes. Of course. What does that signify?"

"I can't help you with your hair, but I imagine she can. Yes?" He looked down at her, patiently awaiting her response.

She considered that for a moment, her hand reaching up to fiddle with her luscious locks. "Y-yes. She could repair it."

"Then you should emerge and ask your friend for help."

She bit her lip and his gut twisted at the sight. He knew she did not intend for it to be erotic, but he could only recall what it felt like to have those lips and teeth on him. He recalled the texture and sensation and taste and he knew he needed to remove himself quickly from Miss Imogen Bates.

"Imogen, where are you?" Miss Kittinger's voice was closer now and more demanding.

"She is here to save you," he murmured. "Go now." He took another much-needed step back from her and nodded his head in the direction of Miss Kittinger where she roamed in the path of light around the fountain. "Step out to greet her. Hurry on. I will wait until you both have gone inside."

"And you will say nothing . . . tell no one of . . . this?" She motioned between them.

He stiffened. Did she think him totally lacking all honor? When he was the duke did he have a reputation for going about the shire and ruining young maids? Many a nobleman used their position and power to that advantage, but he had never been one of them.

"Go to your friend," he said tightly, his jaw aching from the tension. "Miss Kittinger will assist in making you presentable." He could not help himself from looking her up and down and thinking how very much he would like to make her *un*presentable.

Miss Bates blinked and snapped to action. Nodding in agreement, she started to turn away.

"Oh, Miss Bates," he heard himself saying.

She looked back warily over her shoulder. "Yes?"

"You and I are not finished."

Her brown eyes snapped, and he wondered how he had missed how very lively and lovely they were. Her eyes weren't merely brown. They were exceptional—a tiger's eye brown.

"This . . . er, what happened here was a singular occurrence." She stabbed a finger to the ground between them, marking the spot where she had kissed him as though their very lives depended upon what she was insisting. He could not help but wonder though: who was she trying to convince? Him? Or herself? "Do not mistake that it will ever happen again."

He inhaled and resisted arguing with her. It was his natural impulse—to tell her there would be *more* kisses between them, but that was just a ridiculous impulse. Unreasonable and untenable. All the *uns*.

She was correct, of course. This would not ever happen again. Even though she had only whetted his appetite, it could never happen again. "When I said we are not finished . . . I was not speaking of our kiss."

"Oh." Even in the gloom he detected the flush of embarrassed color on her cheeks.

"You will spread no more lies. You owe me my reputation." She'd spread these wretched rumors about him. The responsibility fell to her to correct them. "I want it back."

"Oh." Her chin went up a fraction. "Well. Best of luck with that."

Frustration rushed through him at her flippant reaction. "You need to help me," he insisted.

"I don't see how I can do anything for you." The confidence of her words seemed belied by the uncertainty he read in her expression.

"No?" The familiar anger bubbled up inside him. He took a careful breath. The last time words became heated between them they ended up kissing. "You will think of something."

"Don't rely on that," she returned.

"Oh, but I shall." A strange thrill raced through him at her challenging words. "You will do the right thing, Miss Bates. You're too good a person not to do the right thing."

Her lips twitched. "I'm far from a saint, Mr. Butler."

"Of that I am very aware," he retorted.

"Then I don't understand where these high expectations of yours are coming from."

Following those haughty words, she left him then.

Her utter temerity should have infuriated him. And it did. But she also aroused the hell out of him.

He stood behind the fountain, peering through

the fall of water, watching the blurry shape of her as she approached her friend. Mercy Kittinger made a gesture of exclamation and touched Miss Bates's lovely fallen hair.

If she were mine, I'd have that hair loose and flowing and tangled on my pillow every night. I would grab a fistful of it as I covered her body with mine . . .

Bloody hell. He was hard as a post.

He reached down and adjusted his cock against his trousers and took a deep, bracing breath, forcing himself to think of normal things—anything except the suddenly arousing Miss Bates.

This was *not* what he had intended for this night.

He'd never imagined himself standing alone in the night at a country ball, struggling to overcome an unwanted arousal for an unwanted female.

A few more words were exchanged and then the ladies' hazy forms turned and disappeared somewhere deeper into the gardens where Miss Kittinger would doubtlessly repair all of Imogen Bates's glorious hair back into its usual confinement.

He had the mad urge to follow and watch her and he called himself ten kinds of fool. She'd shocked him and now he was under some manner of temporary infatuation. There was only one cure. He needed to throw himself into the task of settling on one of these local heiresses and begin courting in earnest. With any luck, he could be betrothed before the first leaves turned in the fall.

He had intended to make significant progress this night. Both his mother and Thurman would be exceedingly disappointed in him. *Hellfire.* Perry was disappointed himself. But he could not yet summon forth the will to venture back into that ball and charm the ladies he had intended to court—all ladies, thanks to Imogen Bates, who were now avoiding him. He could simply slip away for home. He needn't even return to that ballroom.

He inhaled the crisp night air until his erection subsided and he felt his composure return. Suddenly it occurred to him that if he left now, Imogen Bates would win this battle. He didn't want to be at war with her, but it seemed they were. Without his wanting it, a war had somehow started between them.

He might not have started it, but he would not lose it. He was not defeated. He was not running away. He came here tonight to mingle with the heiresses of Shropshire, and he would do just that.

He was going back inside that ballroom.

Chapter Nine ❧

"What happened? Were you accosted?" Mercy demanded, her eyes afire, ready to fight for Imogen.

"What?" Imogen blinked from her distracted and whirling thoughts as they walked deeper into the gardens for more privacy. It took everything in her not to turn and glance over her shoulder in search of Mr. Butler. "Accosted? No, no. Not at all."

If anything, Mr. Butler might feel as though *she* accosted him. Certainly he had initiated the kiss, but she took over from there and led the way.

"Then what happened to your hair?" Mercy's gaze scanned her face and hair worriedly.

"It simply fell," she lied. "There was a fierce wind."

Mercy shot her a dubious look and then glanced around them. "There was a gale-force wind and we somehow did not notice it inside the house?"

Imogen shrugged weakly. She could scarcely pay attention to her friend. She was too busy reeling from what had just transpired with Mr.

Butler—what she had done to Mr. Butler. *With* Mr. Butler. It was scandalous.

She was a perfect scandal and she could not forgive herself. She knew better.

She had vowed never again. No more romantic peccadilloes. She had thought herself above such needs and desires. She had thought herself stronger than that. One heartbreak a lifetime was enough as far as she was concerned.

Heartbreak?

The thought jarred her. What had occurred tonight did not involve the heart. Nothing had changed regarding her feelings toward Mr. Butler. Er, nothing other than the disconcerting knowledge that she now possessed.

Peregrine Butler smelled good. He tasted good. And he possessed the most intoxicating lips. So intoxicating that she knew she could never kiss them again. Never taste them again. One time she could chalk up as a mistake. Twice would be a grave character failing.

She needed to forget all about it—pretend as though this night had never happened.

Mercy stopped and forced them to sit down on a bench. Imogen went willingly, numbness stealing over her as she stuffed away the emotions of the evening.

The stone bench was cold and immediately seeped through her gown. She didn't move or speak as Mercy attacked her hair. She was grateful to have Mercy contend with it for her. One thing she did not have to think about.

Mercy cleared her throat. "If you tell me not to worry, I won't—"

"Then don't worry," she hurriedly supplied.

Mercy huffed a breath, clearly unconvinced with Imogen's quick reply. "If something happened . . . you know you can talk to me, yes, Imogen?"

"I know that. Of course." And she did, but she was not ready to discuss what happened. Not even to her friend. "Nothing happened. Let's just set me to rights and go back inside. We don't want to leave your sister unsupervised."

Mercy stared at her for a long, searching moment before nodding and finishing her hair. "I suppose all that experience tending to Grace's hair served me well. There you go." She patted the sides. "A fairly decent chignon considering I didn't have a brush to work with."

Imogen stood up from the bench, nodding vaguely, not even bothering to touch her hair with her hand to verify if it felt intact. She and Mercy fell into step together. As they reached the fountain, Imogen scanned the area for a glimpse of Butler. She didn't see him. Perhaps he went home. That seemed likely considering the heiresses he was stalking were less than receptive. What reason did he have to stay?

Her chest eased and lightened a bit at that prospect as they ascended to the veranda. She would not likely see him again this night. There was that. There would be no avoiding his gaze and fighting back a flush of heat if she stood in proximity to him.

The ball was still very much underway. She immediately spied the whirling couples through the glass French doors. The flash of colors and the lively music seemed in direct opposition to her mood.

Still, she loathed the idea of going back inside and pasting a smile on her face—mingling with everyone like nothing was amiss. Like nothing shattering had just occurred.

She sucked in a breath and rejoined the masses.

Everything in her yearned to slip around the house and hop in a carriage and take flight for home. She longed to lock herself away in the comfort of her bedchamber. The only problem was that they had not taken their own carriage here tonight.

They had accepted the gracious offer from the baroness to ride with her and her daughter this evening. Imogen was well and truly stuck. She could not walk home. It was dark and much too far, even if she knew every road and path in this shire as well as her own face. Doing so would be overly dramatic and only alert Papa and others that something was amiss.

Well and truly stuck.

Moving through the bustling ballroom, she was immediately assailed with all the scents and sounds of the Blankenship ball. The sweat from so many bodies crammed in one space mingled with cloying colognes and perfumes and the rich smell of congealing food.

"Shall we refresh ourselves with a drink?" Mercy asked.

Imogen nodded in agreement and followed Mercy, single file, through the crowd.

A quick sweep of the room and she spotted Papa deep in conversation with Gwen Cully, the local blacksmith. She had taken over her family's smithy as her father was deceased and her uncle was getting long in years and not quite up to the task anymore. She had worked alongside the men in her family for many years, ever since she could walk. No one in Shropshire blinked over her role in a male-dominated enterprise.

The Blankenship sisters were dancing.

The baroness was at the center of a group of ladies who were engaged in an animated conversation. Imogen could guess what—or rather *who*—might be their topic of discussion. She continued after Mercy, surveying the ballroom as she went.

And her gaze collided on him.

Mr. Butler was *still* here. Bodies quickly obscured him, and she lost sight of him, but she had spotted him. Her eyes had not deceived her. He was still here.

She stopped hard in her tracks, not even moving when someone jostled her from behind.

"Pardon me."

She didn't even turn to see who addressed her. She could only stare across the room, searching for another glimpse of him, starkly handsome in the bright light of the ballroom.

She might be rattled over what transpired and battling a chronic blush, but in that brief flash he'd seemed as composed as ever. She peered through the crowd, trying not to look conspicuous in her quest to locate him.

A crack split the crowd, and she spied him again through the opening. He was mingling with several gentlemen. No ladies in their midst. She smiled slightly. Apparently he was still a pariah among that gender.

One of the men conversing with him turned, and she was granted a full view of Mr. Blankenship, the only other gentleman in attendance who was dressed as richly as Mr. Butler. His color palette might be more flamboyant, but there was no doubting his peacock-blue jacket threaded with gold was costly.

Butler was speaking. Something he said struck Mr. Blankenship as the height of amusing. The older gentleman tipped his head back and laughed uproariously, clapping Butler on the back jovially. It dawned on Imogen then that it did not matter how unsavory she made him in the eyes of the ladies. If the papas, in this case Mr. Blankenship, liked him, then that was all there was to it.

Heiresses had fathers who decided upon the husbands for their daughters. Imogen winced at the unfairness of that. Luckily, she was no heiress. But that meant Mr. Butler only had to win over the papas.

Butler's gaze locked with hers across the ballroom, and there was such knowing smugness in his smoky gaze that she felt a fresh wave of indignation sweep through her. Understanding passed between them.

She narrowed her gaze on him. He knew a father would not care about the rumors she had started. The things she had said would be deemed trivial and, sadly, not serious enough to dissuade a father.

Mercy lightly touched her arm, capturing her attention. "Imogen? Are you well? You're looking pale. Can I get you anything?"

"Oh. Um. The crowd is a bit of a crush. Perhaps some ratafia would refresh me."

"Of course. Wait here. I'll be but a moment."

As Mercy disappeared into the press of bodies, Imogen faded back against the edge of the ballroom, taking position alongside the wallflowers and widowed dames—one dame in particular whom she knew to be a salacious gossip, even greater than any of the Blankenship women.

There was one queen of gossip in every town, and in Shropshire that was Mrs. Hathaway.

"Mrs. Hathaway," she greeted.

"Ah, Miss Bates. Not taking your spot on the dance floor this evening?"

"No, not tonight." Or ever again.

"Just as well. I've counted and the ladies present far outnumber the gentlemen. Not ideal. Not ideal at all. Shropshire must work to even these odds."

Imogen nodded as though in agreement.

"Perhaps when the new duke arrives he will have brothers," Mrs. Hathaway added hopefully.

"Perhaps," Imogen murmured, not bothering to point out that the previous two Dukes of Penning had never deigned to grace any of the local fetes. Why would the new duke, once they hunted him down—or his possible brothers—be any different?

Whenever he returned from Newfoundland or Greenland or wherever he was, he would be just as socially distant as previous dukes. If he had brothers, they would be remote, too. It was the way of the aristocracy. They were all pompous prigs. The baroness was singular in her willingness to socialize with country society.

"It's a shame about Mr. Butler though." Imogen cleared her throat, relieved at how normal her voice sounded. "He has had a most difficult year."

"Indeed. His parents' sins are no fault of his," Mrs. Hathaway generously admitted. "I am glad to see him settling into the happy arms of our little hamlet. Long overdue, I say."

"Oh, yes." She paused, struggling with her next words. "And then there's the other thing. Such a shame."

Mrs. Hathaway abruptly ceased fanning herself and pinned her cloudy-eyed gaze on Imogen. "What other thing?" She blinked. "What *first* thing?"

Apparently the rumors had not reached the great keeper of rumors. That was a strange bit of irony.

"Miss Bates?" Mrs. Hathaway prompted. "What is it?"

Imogen hesitated, momentary doubt seizing her. She had a flash of Mr. Butler's face as he asked her to restore his reputation, insisting she owed him that.

Between the dancing figures, she spotted Mr. Butler still chatting with Mr. Blankenship. They talked with their heads bent close together. They looked like the closest of acquaintances, allies, and it was galling. She doubted Butler had ever talked to their host for the evening for any significant length of time before he was forced to move in with his mother and pay court to women he would have considered far beneath his notice a year ago. Imogen recognized this so clearly. Why did no one else?

Mr. Blankenship was talking now, nodding and motioning eagerly toward the dance floor. Imogen tracked his attention directly to his daughter, Emily. She was finishing dancing with her partner, curtsying lightly before him as the song drew to a close. Imogen's head whipped back to gauge Butler. He smiled, nodding as he said something in turn to Mr. Blankenship. The sight made her stomach clench.

Splendid. She needn't hear their words to know. Their conversation was about young Emily. Mr. Blankenship was probably giving his daughter away to Butler right now—lock, stock and barrel—and, of course, Mr. Butler was accepting. Moments ago he had been kissing Imogen, but now he was across the room negotiating marriage to another.

Over my dead body.

Hot emotion swept over her. With indignant heat burning a fiery maelstrom in her chest, she leaned in beside Mrs. Hathaway and began speaking in hushed tones with great relish, catching the lady up on all she had missed . . . and adding a new story about Mr. Butler—perhaps the most creative one of all—with grand flourish. The *pièce de résistance*. A story that would have any papa snatching up his daughter and keeping her far from the clutches of Mr. Butler.

By this night's end Peregrine Butler would be the most ineligible man—to daughters *and* papas alike—in Shropshire.

IMOGEN SAT AT her dressing table, vigorously brushing her brown hair until it crackled. Thankfully, they had not stayed at the ball much longer after she had whispered those words to Mrs. Hathaway.

Those words.

She winced. She could not even bring herself to say them in her mind. It was difficult now to even contemplate them in the peace and security of her bedchamber.

She had wanted to start a rumor that would chase off prospective fathers-in-law and not simply repel prospective brides. Imogen suspected she had now succeeded at that. Oh, very well. Beyond her wildest dreams she had succeeded at that. No man worth his salt would want his daughter to marry Mr. Butler now. She had seen to that.

Thankfully, she had not lingered to see the ramifications of her efforts. Papa had grown weary and the kindly baroness insisted they depart before he overtired himself.

Lowering her brush, Imogen tapped it anxiously on the surface of the dressing table.

She stared at her reflection in reproach until she could endure it no longer. She looked away from herself and fiddled with the various perfumes and creams littering the surface. Most of them had belonged to her mother. Imogen only used them sparingly, as when they were gone they would be gone forever. Just like Mama was gone from her. Imogen wanted them to last.

Silly, she supposed. They were inanimate things, but sometimes, inhaling the fragrances, it was like Mama was still with her. Talking and smiling. Imogen would have a flash of her so clearly in her mind, bending over her knitting or working in the garden or bringing baked goods to a neighbor. For a moment it felt real. It felt like she was right beside her.

Imogen wondered if they would have had the kind of adult relationship that begged confidences. It was difficult to imagine confessing to Mama her actions from this last week. She would not have approved of Imogen inventing rumors. Mama had been unfailingly honest. She'd lived as she preached—or rather as Papa preached. And now as Imogen preached since she was the author of his sermons.

Imogen frowned, thinking how her actions would disappoint both her parents. Perhaps she had gone too far. Especially that last fabrication she had told to Mrs. Hathaway. And then there was the other thing that had transpired this very night.

How could she have kissed him?

You didn't kiss him. He kissed you.

"And then you kissed him back," she accused her reflection as though the Imogen Bates in the mirror was someone other than herself.

But tonight she did feel like someone else. She felt like she was gazing at a stranger.

It had been a long time since she put her lips to a man's, and she had assumed the last time would be the *last* time. She'd never thought to do it again, and especially not with someone so wholly inappropriate.

She'd vowed never to make that mistake again. Never to put her lips where they did not belong—and they definitely did not belong on Peregrine Butler.

A knock sounded at her door and she bade enter, glad to put an end to those particular thoughts of the past. No more. She'd finished with it years ago. She'd made peace with herself and those days when she had been foolish enough to believe in a scoundrel's words.

"Good night, my love." Papa shuffled in wearing a robe and mismatched slippers. She was certain he was not aware of the color of his slippers. His eyes were not what they used to be even with the benefit of his thick spectacles. He leaned down to press a kiss on the top of her head. "What plans have you for the morrow, daughter?"

"I was thinking of working in the garden."

The garden was long overdue her attention. She would never be as attentive to it as Mama had been, but Imogen did what was necessary to tend it and keep it from perishing. There were some cabbages, beetroot and leeks that needed gathering and Imogen knew they would be delicious in their dinner tomorrow. There would be enough for a few vegetable pies. Doubtless a few of their congregants would enjoy their culinary labors.

Gwen Cully had her hands full with her uncle bedridden these days. She would doubtlessly appreciate a day when she did not have to come home from toiling in the smithy to then prepare a meal.

"What of you, Papa? What are your plans?"

"Well, I wanted to catch up on some correspondence and then I was thinking of calling on Mr. Gupta. He mentioned receiving a new book on the fall of Rome that I would very much like to peruse."

"Lovely. Do you need someone to—"

He patted her shoulder. "I am not so infirm I cannot walk myself. It is scarcely a mile."

Imogen resisted correcting him that it was a little farther than that. She knew it was important to not make him feel feeble in body or mind. If she were in his situation, she would like to maintain some of her independence, too. It was a tricky game they played—he asserting his independence and she trying not to offend and overly curtail him.

"You could take the gig," she suggested.

As much as she did not love him operating conveyances—his reflexes were not what they once were—it was a small carriage and it would be a short drive. Better that than him walking such a distance.

"Daughter, I am able to walk," he insisted with an indignant wobble of his head as he stared down at her. He had shrunk a bit, but he was still tall enough to look down at her even when she wasn't seated.

"With a cane," she gently reminded him. "You walk with a cane, Papa."

"Dr. Merrit said it was important to continue

walking if I wish to recover more of my mobility. Did you not hear him say the same thing?"

"Very well, Papa." She relented, noting his flushed cheeks and not wanting to cause him distress. Although she had also heard Dr. Merrit warn him to not overexert himself. There was no sense in arguing with him.

With a mollified nod, he bestowed another kiss on her head, his warm breath rustling her hair. "Off to bed with you now," he directed as he had done when she was a little girl. It gave her heart a pang, for in many ways he was more child than she these days.

"Good night, Papa."

He closed the door after him and she headed for her bed. Slipping off her robe, she slid beneath the counterpane she had already turned down for the night, happy for the comfort of her bed.

Once settled, Imogen blew out a breath and stared into the dark, fixing her thoughts on the morrow and the tasks ahead of her, mentally checking them off one by one and deliberately keeping her mind from straying to the evening's ball and Peregrine Butler and the taste of his lips on hers.

Chapter Ten ❧

$\mathcal{P}$erry spotted the good vicar slowly ambling down the lane outside of Shropshire and paused astride his horse.

The older man leaned heavily on his cane as he advanced, both of his gnarled hands gripping the brass head for support.

Perry grimaced. *Advanced* was a gentle euphemism. He was not making much progress at his current pace.

Dismounting from his horse, he held on to the reins and hailed the vicar, tipping his hat as he called out a greeting.

The man broke his focus from his shuffling feet and looked up, his expression lighting with delight when it landed on him. "Oh, good day to you, Mr. Butler." His rheumy-eyed gaze skipped to the horse beside Perry. "Out for an afternoon ride on that fine beast of yours? It's a fair day for that."

"Indeed it is, sir."

After a restless night, Perry had risen early. He had tossed and turned. Fraught with the memory of the prior evening's events, he'd scarcely slept. Not only did he discover who was spreading rumors about him, but he caught her in the act—and then he kissed her.

He had kissed Imogen Bates.

He still felt it in his gut. Deep in his blood. He had kissed her as though she was his to kiss and hold. As though there was not hostility and long-standing aversion between them. As though she were not a prim and gently bred lady but instead a hot-blooded lover. The kind of lover you took in broad daylight and cover of night equally. Without modesty. Without caution. With only wild abandon.

God, he had been too long without female companionship of the intimate variety. That was the only explanation. For no other reason could the painfully straitlaced vicar's daughter ever entice him. *Hellfire.* She'd looked down her nose at him since the day they first met.

Ironic, of course. She was a humble vicar's daughter whilst he had been a duke's son. And yet she had somehow always made him feel lacking. A lad in mismatched shoes with spots on his face. She could wither him with a look even when they were children. It had made him uncomfortable. Rank alone demanded he feel superior. And yet in her presence he never had.

He should have felt no desire for her.

Oh, she was not unattractive, but no ravishing beauty either. He'd seen far more eye-catching women in London ballrooms. Her large brown eyes were fine enough. They'd been luminescent in the gardens. Following their kiss, though, those eyes had gleamed as if lit from flame.

Upon rousing from his bed, he'd dressed and departed the dower house.

He'd spent most of the morning at the local tavern before remounting his horse and riding aimlessly, lost in his thoughts. But he didn't bother saying any of that to the vicar. Indeed not. The pious man would think he'd been at the tavern as a patron, there to drink—and it was much too early in the day for a respectable gentleman to spend his time in a tavern.

Perry could not very well explain he was there for something else, something more. That reason was too elusive, too outrageous even for him to wrap his thoughts around yet.

Hellfire.

He didn't know what he was doing at the tired tavern, surveying the derelict place, talking to old Mr. Compton, the owner, asking him all manner of questions. He could only think that as far as taverns went it was a humble establishment . . . and the only one in Shropshire.

In a village that was bustling and becoming more metropolitan with each passing day, The Hare and The Basket could be more.

It *should* be more.

Perry knew about first-rate establishments. He'd spent all of his life in them. As a customer, of course. As a patron. Never the proprietor, but he'd certainly known his share of proprietors, and he could still recall the best ones. The ones who greeted him at the door, who saw to his needs with charm and easy grace and style. Several of them he had called friends. He'd liked them. He'd respected them.

All of this he thought about as he had sat in The Hare and The Basket and considered the many ways in which it could be better—the ways it could be made into a premier attraction for the denizens of the shire and even beyond.

He shook his head, dismissing those notions as he smiled at the vicar. Such thinking was fanciful and eccentric. No good member of the *ton* went into trade. His mother would be scandalized to know he was even thinking along such lines. Marriage to an heiress was supposed to be his way out of his troubles, as she was wont to tell him. A gentleman did not so much as dabble in commerce.

And yet it could be argued Perry was no longer a member of the *ton*. He realized that was the very thing at stake here—his place in the world. He'd been assigned a place at birth, but now that was gone and he had to decide where he fit.

He glanced down the lane in the direction of the vicarage. "Are you heading home, sir?"

"Yes. Yes, I am. I'm just returning from a delightful visit with Mr. Gupta." He pulled out a leather-bound book that he had tucked inside his wide jacket pocket and brandished it in the air. "The man is in possession of an enviable, ever-growing library and always so kind to loan to me from it."

"Mr. Gupta is indeed a well-read man." Perry nodded. Looking ahead, he gestured down the lane. "Shall I accompany you home?"

The man straightened his hunched shoulders with a touch of righteousness. "I don't need an escort, young man. I am quite able to stand on my own two legs. They are not yet completely useless."

"Of course. I simply always enjoy your company. I intended to ride past the vicarage on my way home at any rate. It's lovely at dusk, the light gilds the ivy covering the stone of your cottage."

The vicar's expression softened. "Ah. You've noticed that, too? It *is* lovely. You know, that was exactly how the house looked when I first clapped eyes on the place all those years ago. We'd arrived just as dusk settled. My dear wife was beside me. Of course Imogen, too. She was such a precocious child. She took one look at the house and declared it home." The vicar sighed and paused for a long thoughtful moment, shaking his head as though clearing it of that tender reverie. "Very well then. Thank you, lad. Let us walk together. You remind me of your father. He always did enjoy a lively discussion."

Together they walked on, moving at the vicar's crawling pace. Perry's horse nickered impatiently and tossed his head as they strolled.

Perry and the vicar kept up a steady conversation. The man mostly talked about Roman history, the topic of the borrowed book currently in his possession. Perry noticed he did tend to jump from topic to topic a little erratically, without much transition. Perry had never noticed this about the man before, so he could only surmise it was a development of age and his recent health woes.

The combination of walking and talking seemed to labor his breathing. Perry frowned in concern at the man and slowed their pace further.

What was his daughter thinking letting him wander so far from home? Anyone could see he was not up to the task. They reached the cozy vicarage in twice the amount of time it would have taken Perry were he walking alone.

The housekeeper greeted them both at the door and he suspected the lady had been looking out the window, hoping to spot her employer returning home in the waning day.

She tsked as she helped him out of his coat. "You should have been home an hour ago. You promised to be back in time for dinner and the hour is nearly upon us."

The vicar inhaled deeply. "Oh, my. That does smell heavenly, Mrs. Garry. I am famished." His gaze shot to Perry. "You must stay and join us."

"Oh, I have no wish to intrude."

"I insist."

The housekeeper looked at him expectantly, smiling in welcome. He was certain Imogen Bates, wherever she lurked, would not smile so welcomingly when confronted with him. No doubt she would have words to say that did not echo her father's kind invitation.

Perry's lips twitched as he imagined that. His last glimpse of her had been across the Blankenship ballroom. Her eyes had glinted at him in challenge.

"Yes, thank you," he heard himself saying. "I think I should enjoy that. I should enjoy staying for dinner very much indeed."

IMOGEN PLACED HER last beetroot in her overflowing basket and pressed a hand at the small of her back, rubbing the tight area as she stretched. She had tended the garden well into the afternoon, pulling it free of weeds before gathering two baskets of vegetables.

Mrs. Garry had arrived earlier to collect the first basket so she might reap its rewards and get Cook started on the vegetables for their dinner.

Hefting the last basket indoors, Imogen left it in the kitchen for Cook, and then took herself upstairs to wash and change her clothes for dinner.

Papa, she assumed, was having his afternoon nap. She knew his walk must have tired him, although he would never dare to admit it.

When she emerged from her chamber to check on him it was to find his room empty. He must have already roused himself for dinner and was waiting downstairs for her. It was a familiar routine.

Patting her freshly tidied hair, she descended the narrow stairs, humming lightly. Mrs. Garry was just passing through the small foyer with a tray of Papa's favorite claret. He often liked to indulge in a glass before dinner, and she thought it did help take the edge off some of the ache in his joints.

"Ah, there you are, Miss Imogen. Dinner is almost on the table."

"Thank you, Mrs. Garry. I take it Papa is in

the parlor?" she inquired as she fiddled with the lace fichu tucked inside her bodice and started for the double doors.

"Yes. They're in there," Mrs. Garry called as she vanished into the dining room with the tray.

Nodding in satisfaction, she strode toward the room before Mrs. Garry's words penetrated. Imogen stopped hard in her tracks.

They?

Had they a guest?

Her curiosity piqued, she resumed her pace, entering the parlor where she once again froze.

There, seated across from Papa, sat Mr. Butler, his arm flung along the settee's back with casual arrogance, as though he was accustomed to making himself at home in her tiny parlor.

Her throat squeezed tight.

"Ah. Miss Bates." Those devilish eyes of his alighted on her. He lifted to his feet, ever the gentleman. At least superficially. He had not behaved as a gentleman with her in the Blankenship gardens. "Lovely to see you again."

She opened her mouth, but no words emerged. Words strangled in her throat.

"There you are, daughter," Papa said, the sound of his voice, when she could not find her own, sweet music to her ears. "I've brought us a guest for dinner."

"Ah. I . . . see that," she managed to get out as she hastened to her father's side, offering him her arm as he clambered to his feet.

"I happened upon your father coming home, Miss Bates," Mr. Butler offered.

She cut him a sharp glance. Was that judgment she heard in his voice?

"Dinner is on the table." Mrs. Garry arrived just then, hovering in the threshold.

"Let us eat. I am famished," Papa declared, moving ahead of them in his eagerness.

Imogen hung back to demand of Mr. Butler, "What are you doing here?"

"It is as your father said. He invited me to dinner." Mr. Butler canted his head and looked down at her in disapproval. "You really should mind your father better. He was struggling to make it home today on his walk."

She fought against the burning flash of guilt. Alongside the guilt, her resentment stirred that he should criticize her care of her father. Except he was right. She should not have permitted Papa to walk himself to Mr. Gupta's. She had known it was too much for him, but it was impossible to tell him that and she let Papa persuade her, hating to treat him like the invalid he so desperately resisted becoming.

"I don't need your instruction on how to care for my father."

She started for the doors, intent on following her father to the dining room. The quicker they ate, the sooner this whole thing would be over. The sooner Mr. Butler could take his leave and go home.

His hand on her elbow stopped her and sent a jolt of awareness through her. She sucked in a breath and turned to face him, yanking her arm away from his grasp. "Don't touch me."

"I was only attempting to escort you in to dinner. It is the polite thing to do."

"Oh." Well, now she felt silly. She sniffed and attempted to look more composed. "We don't stand on such formalities here, Mr. Butler. You needn't escort me anywhere."

He held up both his hands in the air as though attempting to pacify an unpredictable animal. "Very well. I meant no offense."

She glared at him. He stared back, looking decidedly composed. She suspected he was enjoying himself—enjoying her discomfiture. Alone like this, she could only think of the last time it was just the two of them together, and this did not feel like such a grand idea.

The air between them crackled as though a storm was imminent. Imogen swallowed against the impossibly large lump in her throat.

Her gaze dropped to his lips and lingered there, marking their shape, their color, recalling their pressure, their taste. Struggling with mortification, her gaze flew back to his and in his eyes she read his awareness.

He was remembering, too.

With a ragged breath, she tore her gaze from him and looked longingly to the door through which Papa had just passed.

Of course, that intimacy was there, hovering between them like a fluttering moth, impossible to ignore.

He gestured for her to precede him. "After you."

With a single dignified nod, she ventured forward, wishing he would not follow, but knowing he would. He was here. No changing that now.

He was in her home and they were about to dine together in some bizarre alternate reality where the former Duke of Penning was happy to fraternize with her small, humble family. With *her.*

Chapter Eleven ❧

*O*nce they moved into the dining room, Mr. Butler held out her chair for her. Of course, with his unfailing manners he would do that. There might have been cross words between them, but he would always extend her courtesy. He might have been stripped of his noble birthright, but his nobility ran deeper than rank, deeper than his name. Deeper than skin. Imogen realized this of him, even as she was loath to admit it to herself. He had his redeeming qualities.

She stiffly sank down and seated herself, positioning her body on the edge of the seat, her spine as rigid as a slat of wood, careful that they not come into contact again.

Mr. Butler took his seat and joined them, bowing his head as Papa said grace over their meal. Imogen could not help from studying him as Papa blessed their food, watching him undetected and marveling at his presence in their modest dining room.

"We should have done this a long time ago," Papa declared as he snapped his napkin and lowered it to his lap. "It is so nice to have you here permanently in Shropshire."

She winced at her father's rather obtuse if kindly intended remark. The only reason Mr. Butler was in Shropshire was out of necessity. He could not help it. He had lived in London before his change of circumstances, and he doubtlessly would prefer to still be *there* and not stuck *here*.

Mr. Butler murmured his thanks as Mrs. Garry took the initiative to serve Papa from the large vegetable pie. Steam wafted up into the air as she cut through the flaky golden crust and placed a generous slice of the savory goodness on Papa's plate, then on each of theirs.

It was simple fare, but delicious. No multiple courses for them. Imogen could not help but think he was likely accustomed to more sophisticated meals boasting several courses.

"This looks scrumptious, does it not, Mr. Butler?" Of course it did not occur to Papa to be self-conscious of their humble meal, and it should not affect her either. "You cannot do better than vegetables picked this very day," he declared as he dug in with his fork.

"No, sir, you cannot," Butler agreed.

"Nicely done, Imogen," Papa praised. "Your mama would be proud that you've kept her garden flourishing."

"Thank you, Papa," she returned, her cheeks afire.

"Are you responsible for maintaining the garden, Miss Bates?"

"We all contribute to it, Mr. Butler."

Papa waved his fork at her. "Do not be modest, daughter." He looked to Butler. "Our dear Imogen does most of the work, and this meal is the product of her labors."

If possible, her cheeks stung hotter. Butler was not like her papa. He likely thought her as lowly as a field hand for her efforts. Men of his ilk did not deem it genteel for a lady to dirty her hands, and she was certain he thought little of her.

Except his expression did not reflect that. Mr. Butler looked at her almost in admiration and she lowered her gaze to her plate, telling herself it must be her imagination. As furious as he had been with her last night—kiss notwithstanding— he would not look at her with any form of approval or warmth. He thought her a menace.

She had not forgotten his parting words, warning her to mend the damage she had done. *You owe me my reputation. I want it back. You will help me, Miss Bates.*

Those ominous and vaguely threatening words did not match the way he was looking at her right now. She swallowed thickly.

If he knew about her conversation with Mrs. Hathaway he would absolutely not be looking at her in such a manner. Indeed not. His gaze would be murderous.

The sight of him cozying up to Mr. Blankenship had filled her with a surge of complicated emotions. She'd reacted without thinking, the taste of his punishing kiss like fire on her lips. The kiss might have started out as a punishment, but it had turned into something else. It had turned into a kiss that she delighted in and seized and took ownership of for herself. It had fueled her in some bewildering way.

Her face hotter than ever, she took a much too big bite and chewed, glad for a reason to abstain from conversation.

They fell into companionable silence as they ate. Mrs. Garry left them and there was only the scrape and clink of cutlery and glass for a good few minutes. Thankfully Papa still very much possessed an appetite, and he very much enjoyed his food, almost to the point of gluttony. Not that his lanky frame gave any hint of that.

Imogen studied Peregrine Butler beneath her lashes as he sat in the chair across from her. The chair her mother once occupied. It had been empty a long time now. Usually it was just Imogen and Papa in this dining room, at this table, except when they accepted one of the invitations extended by members of his flock and dined out.

Lately, of course, they accepted fewer of those invitations given Papa's condition, and they rarely ever invited anyone into their home anymore. Except for tonight. Papa had taken it upon himself to break custom.

And yet it felt nice to have a third person at their table again. Even if it was Mr. Butler. His body nicely filled the usually empty space.

Butler patted his napkin at his mouth. Only crumbs remained on his plate. "Any time you want to invite me over to reap the benefit of your labors, Miss Bates, please do not hesitate."

Her cheeks warmed at the compliment. He had certainly never sat across the table from a lady who had harvested with her own two hands the meal he ate. Now, contrary to her early self-consciousness, she felt a twinge of selfish pride to be unlike what were doubtlessly scores of females in his life.

"Of course, Mr. Butler. You are welcome whenever you choose," she said and strangely the words did not even stick in her throat.

He motioned to the pie at the center of the dining table. "Might I?"

"Oh." She blinked. "Of course." Before she could move to assist him, he was lifting up from his chair and helping himself to another slice of the savory pie.

The warm pleasure she had felt in her face now spread even further throughout her.

Until she recalled that one final wicked rumor she had whispered about him to Mrs. Hathaway. It would have made its way through town by now.

Her pleasure dashed, suddenly the food she had just eaten settled like stones in her stomach. Observing him last night with Mr. Blankenship, she'd had a knee-jerk reaction. Very well. An *overreaction*. Now she could acknowledge that.

Perhaps nothing would come of it.

Perhaps Mrs. Hathaway would say nothing. It was an unlikely hope.

Imogen closed her eyes in a long, pained blink as she reflected on the impulsive words she had uttered to the town's biggest gossip.

Thankfully Papa was engaging Mr. Butler in conversation and neither gentleman noticed anything untoward in her expression. She was simply relieved to be spared the burden of carrying the conversation all by herself.

She listened with half an ear as her own thoughts whirled and twisted through her. She caught only snatches of their discussion. Papa's topics ranged from theology, to history, to the upcoming fall fair and which farmer might win the prize for the best sow.

She knew she should better monitor what was being said in case Papa lost his train of thought and needed her to step in to keep him on track. Usually, she was more diligent about doing that very thing . . . but then a distraction the likes of Peregrine Butler was not usually in the vicinity.

The dinner might not boast multiples courses, but Cook had prepared dessert and they indulged in a refreshing raspberry flummery.

"Now I must come back," Butler declared with relish as he tucked into the creamy custard. "This is bliss on a spoon."

Papa twirled his spoon in a small circle. "Cook is a marvel. She could work in any household in the land."

Finished with dinner, they rose and retired to the parlor. Imogen almost expected Butler to take his leave at this point, but he lingered.

At Papa's request, Imogen settled before her harp and began to play. Most ladies played the pianoforte, but her mother had taught her the harp, and although she was not nearly as proficient as Mama, she could adequately strum a tune.

She played the solo from Donizetti's *Lucia di Lammermoor*, closing her eyes as she often did whilst she played. Upon the last chord, she opened her eyes and found that Papa had dozed off in his wingback armchair.

With the music fading in the room, his soft snores could be heard over the crackling and pop of the fire. His head lolled against the back of the chair and his mouth sagged open. She smiled fondly at him.

"He's tired," Butler offered up unnecessarily.

She turned her attention to Butler. He stood near the fireplace, one hand resting on the mantel. A small fire crackled in the hearth, casting light on his dark trousers.

"Yes," she agreed. "He did not manage a nap today as he usually does."

"That walk took him some time."

It felt like a jab and she scowled. Squaring her shoulders, she defended, "My father is a very independent man."

"He needs tending."

"He is well tended, I assure you. I take care of him in a way that does not rob him of his dignity," she insisted.

He stared at her in silence, his scrutiny intent and she couldn't fathom his thoughts. She looked back at her father napping in his chair.

After some moments, Mr. Butler's voice reached her. "He said you're of great help to him."

She must have missed that remark when she was woolgathering at dinner. "Of course. Why wouldn't I be? I am his daughter."

"And your mother is gone," he added.

She nodded, feeling a little awkward. Butler's eyes were far too keen on her. "He needs me."

"Did she help him with his sermons, too?"

She tensed and cut him a sharp look. How did he know of that? Had Papa mentioned that? Oh, she really ought to have paid closer attention. She and Papa had discussed how no one in the community should be alerted to her involvement in his sermons. People had to believe Papa was the same man he had always been. No one could think his episodes of apoplexy had affected him in the long term and made him less than able to perform his duties.

"No, my mother assisted in other areas though. She was a much better gardener."

"And you're the better writer?"

She swallowed and shifted uncomfortably, unwilling to answer that. "Er. I also help Papa with his paperwork." In truth, she did all of it for him these days. His bookkeeping had been a mess before she got her hands on it.

His gaze skimmed her face. "I'm sure you do. You're quite the enterprising lady, Miss Bates. You do it all."

She lowered her gaze, certain he was ridiculing her now. "Please don't mock me, sir."

"I am not mocking you. Rare is the individual as productive as you are." Her cheeks grew warm under his regard—until he said his next words. Then the heat was the result of an altogether different reason. "I am certain once you put yourself to the task, you shall have no problem dismissing the rumors of me you started."

She shook her head. Of course.

"Is that why you are here?" she hissed, sending a quick, wary glance to Papa. "Did you even *accidentally* happen on my father? Or was that a ploy?"

"A ploy? You think I stalked him?" A corner of his mouth kicked up and she ignored how rakishly handsome he looked. "If I wished to see you, I needed no ploy to do it."

She shot a worried look at her father. Thankfully, he still snored on unawares. "I think you have one purpose here and that is to have me do your bidding," she rushed to say, her voice a feverish hush on the air.

He laughed lightly, shaking his head. "Have you ever done anyone's bidding, Miss Bates? You don't strike me as a biddable sort."

"I listen to my father." She sniffed.

No one else was due her deference as far as she was concerned.

"I might not be your father, but it is my hope that you will do the right thing of your own accord."

Well, if that did not make her feel riddled with guilt.

As though sensing he was being discussed, Papa suddenly snored loudly enough to wake himself. He jolted in his chair, sitting up and looking around wildly as though he had forgotten his location.

Imogen quit her seat before the harp and hastened to her father's side, resisting looking at Mr. Butler as she glanced to the clock on the mantel. The hour was growing late. She should see Papa to bed. Sound enough reason to put an end to this most unusual of evenings.

She doubted such a thing would ever happen again. She could not imagine another time when Peregrine Butler should take the time to dine with them, no matter how much he claimed to enjoy tonight's dinner. He had his agenda and she and Papa were not part of that.

She was not part of it, and she would do well to remember that and cease her interference in his plans. Yes, she had a change of heart. Borne of desperation and self-preservation, she'd changed her mind. She would leave him be, and he would then have no reason to seek her out.

If he wanted to marry a lady for her dowry and that lady was agreeable to being so manipulated, then so be it. He would not be the first man to do so—nor would the lady in question be the first to marry for reasons that had nothing to do with love and respect.

"Papa," she whispered so as not to startle him. She placed a hand on his shoulder and gently squeezed.

His eyes flitted to her face and she watched as awareness filtered back in. "Imogen? Oh. What time is it?" he asked as he glanced to the clock.

Mr. Butler's clothes whispered as he moved away from the hearth. "Time for me to take my leave. I'm afraid I overstayed my welcome."

"Oh, never say!" Papa took her arm and rose to his feet. "You're welcome to stay the night, Mr. Butler, so you don't have to ride home in the dark. We always keep our spare room prepared for guests."

Imogen felt her eyes go wide. Peregrine Butler in the bedchamber next to hers? She tensed, forcing her gaze to remain fixed on her father so she did not turn to gawk at Mr. Butler.

"Oh, I could find my way home blindfolded, and even if I could not, my mount knows his way home. He's well trained and could find his way to the stable through a blizzard."

Papa did not look convinced, but he nodded, and motioned for Imogen to move in Butler's direction. "See our guest out, Imogen. If you'll forgive me, Mr. Butler, I'm going to start up the stairs for bed. Thank you for joining us."

"I had a marvelous time. Thank you."

Mrs. Garry, who had undoubtedly been listening at the door, appeared in the room ready to take her father's arm. Imogen and the housekeeper had grown increasingly concerned at his maneuvering on the stairs and tried to be there when he ascended or descended.

Mr. Butler looked to her expectantly, arching an eyebrow as they were left alone in the parlor.

"This way," she murmured, gesturing ahead as though there was any great mystery as to the location of the front door.

She marched through the small foyer whilst Papa finished ascending the stairs alongside Mrs. Garry and disappeared from sight.

"I trust you can find your way to our stable," she said rather curtly as she pulled open the front door for him.

He hesitated before crossing the threshold. "It's a short stroll. Why don't you walk with me, Miss Bates?"

She peered at him suspiciously, her hand flexing anxiously around the edge of the door.

He gestured for her to precede him out into the evening.

Surely Papa did not mean for her to see him to the stable? It was not necessary.

The corner of his mouth quirked in a smirk. "Afraid?"

"Ha. You don't intimidate me, Mr. Butler." At least not very much.

She swept ahead of him into the night. He stepped out after her, shutting the door behind them. They walked around the house toward the stable at the back.

"It's very dark out." She glanced up at the moonless night. Visibility was low. She hated to ask the question, but felt compelled to do so. "Are you certain you do not want to accept my father's offer to stay the night?"

"Do you want me to stay the night, Miss Bates?"

His deep voice felt like velvet on her skin. "I only ask out of concern."

"Pity. You needn't fret though. I'll make it home safely."

Nodding, she crossed her arms tightly over her chest as they advanced on the stables, her steps hard and quick.

She sent him a curious glance, wondering why he should want her to accompany him. Why did he not simply take his leave? He had never sought her out before. He'd resented all the times she had been foisted on him when they were young. Was it so he could harangue her further about her rumormongering?

"Is this where you berate me further to restore your reputation, Mr. Butler?"

Why else would he want to be alone with her?

"No need to go over that again. I trust you will

do the right thing. You're the vicar's daughter. A good Christian." His eyes seemed to be laughing at her now. "Of course, you will do the proper thing."

She bristled. "I never claimed to be a saint. I'm not without flaws." In her experience some of the most righteous people possessed the greatest flaws. She had always marveled at that contradiction.

"No, you're not a saint," he agreed, and she bristled even further, stopping hard outside the stables. There was no need for her to go beyond this point with him. He could fetch his own mount himself.

She turned to face him. "Here you are." His expression was difficult to read in the darkness.

He stopped, inclining his head in acknowledgment. "It's been diverting."

"Diverting?" she snapped. "Certainly not my company? You once called me sanctimonious. You said I had the personality of a rotten lemon."

"Ahh. That was not well done of me." The levity in his voice vanished, replaced with a hint of embarrassment. If she wasn't so annoyed, she'd enjoy his seeming contriteness. "I'm sorry for that."

She blinked, startled. Was he apologizing?

"I was young. It's not an excuse, but I am sorry for any pain or discomfort I caused you."

This was unexpected.

Who was this man?

She did not know what to say, but then that was fitting as she did not know him any longer.

Perhaps she never had. Perhaps everything she thought about him had been wrong.

She shook her head and then stopped to nod jerkily. It was as much acknowledgment of his words that she could offer. "Take care riding home, Mr. Butler."

There. Those words seemed safe.

Turning, she fled back through the dark to the hulking shape of her house, still hugging herself when she reached the sanctuary of her bedchamber. She lowered her arms to undress and slip into her nightgown. At her dressing table, she sank down on the bench and began taking down her hair.

A knock at her door made her jerk. "Who is it?"

Papa's voice called out and she released a shaky breath that turned into a hoarse little laugh. She was being silly. Had she expected Mr. Butler to give chase? Her heart raced a little at the prospect, imagining him following her and bursting inside her chamber. With another shake of her head she told herself that no part of her thrilled at the notion.

"Come in."

Papa shuffled into the room. "Did you see Mr. Butler off, Imogen?"

"Yes, Papa."

"He's such a nice man."

She forced herself to nod in agreement. "Yes, he is."

"Such a shame all the misfortune to befall him."

Her stomach twisted in on itself as she considered how disappointed Papa would be with her if he knew of her recent actions. Her reflection in the mirror looked pale. "Did you need something, Papa?"

"Oh, yes. I was in bed and then I remembered the letter." He lifted a trembling hand, stretching it toward her, a piece of foolscap she had not noticed when he first entered the room clutched between his fingers. It shook on the air between them. "It came some days ago, but it slipped my mind."

She smiled indulgently. A great many things slipped his mind.

"What is this?" She stood from her seat and took it from his fingers.

"Your cousin, Winifred, wrote to us."

At the mention of Winifred's name, her stomach heaved yet again. Not that a letter from her was anything dire or even rare. She wrote to them a few times a year. Papa was her sole uncle, after all, and Imogen her only cousin.

They had been close once. Before Winifred married.

She began reading, skimming over Winifred's neat scrawl regaling them with her busy social calendar and Maynard's many achievements at school. It was difficult to fathom. Winifred was only a year older than Imogen, but she had a seven-year-old son. A son that had been away at school ever since he was out of leading strings.

"I apologize for being so remiss, m'dear. I'll have Mrs. Garry air out the lavender room tomorrow so it is ready for them."

Imogen snapped her attention from the letter she was only halfway finished reading to gape at Papa. "They're coming here?"

"Oh, yes." He waved at the letter. "Read on. You will see. You will see."

She looked down at the letter as though it had turned into a serpent in her hands. "Winifred is coming here—"

"Yes, she and her husband are traveling north to Elgin and intended to stop over for a night or two."

"Or two . . ." she whispered.

One night she could endure, but two full nights? What would she do with herself? How would she interact with them? How would she sit across the table from Edgar multiple nights and behave as though he was not a wretched excuse of manhood?

Her mind roamed frantically, seeking some solution, some escape.

Perhaps she could take herself off elsewhere.

Perhaps she could be gone before they arrived. Desperate thoughts and all impossible. She could not leave Papa. She could go nowhere.

She looked down at the letter again and tried, not very successfully, to focus on the words scrawled on the page. "Did she say when they are coming?"

"Ah, yes. As I said I was very thoughtless." He tapped the side of his head. "You know me these days. I'm afraid I'm quite forgetful. The letter when it arrived . . . oh, let's see. When was that?" He looked toward the ceiling of her bedchamber as though the answer was inscribed there. "Two weeks ago?"

She sputtered, "Papa! Two weeks ago?"

"Yes, m'dear. Read on," he directed. "They arrive tomorrow. Won't that be lovely?"

Chapter Twelve ⋘

A scream rent the air and jolted Perry awake from a pleasingly dreamless sleep. He looked about wildly in confusion, scrubbing two hands over his face as he tried to recall where he was.

The chamber, though finely appointed, was not his bedchamber at Penning Hall. The space was much smaller and lacking the deep masculine hues of mahogany and deep blue damask. His dressing room at Penning Hall was larger than this bedchamber.

He eyed the several paintings and delicate figurines of cherubs throughout the room, and then he remembered where he was. *Cherubs.* He shuddered. His mother was quite enamored of bloody cherubs. They were all over her house.

It all rushed back.

He was in a guest bedchamber in his mother's dower house.

The scream that had interrupted his slumber ended, but now a flurry of footsteps sounded on the stairs. They drew closer, pounding down the corridor. With grim acceptance, he knew they were headed toward his chamber.

He'd selected the chamber located at the back of the house, a room tucked away at the end of a corridor—for what little good it did. He thought occupying the most remote bedchamber might make him less conspicuous in the house. Almost as though he wasn't here at all, in his mother's dower house, relegated to a chamber that vomited cherubs.

It had been many years since he resided under the same roof with his mother, but he had not forgotten what it was like.

When he finished at Eton, he'd moved directly into his own house in London. A proper bachelor's residence. It was what was done, and make no mistake, both he and his mother preferred it that way.

He loved his mother, and she loved him, but it was easier for them to both love each other when they weren't living under the same roof. He suspected it was that way for a great many grown children.

Except Imogen Bates.

If appearances could be believed, she reveled in living with her father. They doted on one another. He'd be surprised if a cross word was ever spoken between them. It wasn't natural. He resisted the voice inside him that called that admirable and told himself it was simply further evidence that she was not quite right.

His mother had her friends and diversions and interests, and—at the time he completed his studies at Eton—his sister to still usher out into Society. She had been happy to see him out on his own and not underfoot.

The only thing that had saved her from total despair when he lost his title and moved back in with her was that Thirza was still the wife of the very powerful and well-connected Earl of Geston.

The door to his chamber burst open unceremoniously, striking the wall with a bang.

His mother strode in, her wild gaze sweeping the bedchamber.

He scrambled to pull the bedding up to his waist. She might be his mother, but he was not in the habit of exposing himself to her. He could not recall the last time his mother had even seen him in the altogether. Quite possibly, she never had. There had been wet nurses and nannies in his life from day one. She likely had never done more than hold him and bring him out at parties to show off the heir. Laughable now when he considered how he had never been the true heir.

"Peregrine!" she exclaimed, and then he noticed that her stormy eyes were red-rimmed and fraught with worry. "How could you have not told me?"

"Told you . . . what?" He gripped a fistful of sheets at his hip and shook his head in confusion.

"That you—you are afflicted!"

"Afflicted?" What was she talking about? He searched his mind. Did she know of his kiss with Imogen Bates and the advent of his inconvenient desire for her? It was certainly an affliction.

"You have the pox!"

"The pox?" he barked. "I haven't the pox. Where did you hear such rubbish?"

She ignored him, pacing back and forth at the foot of his bed, her hands gesturing fiercely in her agitation. "Here I am, working most diligently to secure a match for you that will keep you respectable and get you into a home of your own and back in the *ton*'s good graces. Granted it won't be what you once had, but it will be better than nothing, which is what you have now. The pox, Peregrine!" she wailed. "No one will want to marry off a daughter to a pox-riddled penniless bastard."

He flinched. It was the truth. Ugly as it was to hear. Well, except the part about the pox. That was unequivocally *not* true.

Usually his mother spoke with more delicacy. This only proved her level of outrage.

"Mother," he began carefully, the tension in

his jaw making his teeth ache. "Hear me well. I do *not* have the pox."

"Well, that is what's being bandied about Shropshire."

His hand clenched tighter around his fistful of sheets. "Who is saying this?"

"Cook's assistant went into town to procure some fish for dinner. She overheard it in the shop. She said several people were talking about it. She came home at once and told Cook. And then Cook told Thurman." She waved her hand in a rapid little circle. "Thurman told me because that is how tittle-tattle works, my dear. Nothing is secret. *Nothing* sacred." Her arms stretched wide at her sides. "Now here I am demanding an explanation for what it's worth."

He closed his eyes in one hard blink.

This had Imogen Bates stamped all over it. It was definitely her handiwork.

Yesterday he had thawed toward her. He'd enjoyed himself with her. The meal had been one of the most pleasant dinners he'd enjoyed in a long time and that had everything to do with her.

He liked her.

He liked the way the candlelight had played over her skin and hair. He liked her voice. He liked watching her hands as they worked her fork and spoon. He liked a great many things about her and he especially liked that soft mouth of hers.

He had spent most of the evening envisioning kissing her again. It had taken everything in him not to pull her into his arms outside of the stable. He had barely been able to restrain himself. It had taken all his will to let her go without attempting another kiss.

Forcing himself back to the present, he chased off thoughts of kissing the thoroughly vexing and troublesome Imogen Bates.

"Peregrine," his mother trilled. "I'm waiting for an explanation about this scurrilous rumor. You must suspect who started it."

Indeed he did.

Either this was a previous rumor Miss Bates had started, which she knew about when they were together last night, or she had roused herself this morning and got an early start on making more trouble for him. Either way, it was unacceptable. Either way, he felt betrayed.

With no thought to his mother's sensibilities, he flung back the counterpane and launched himself from the bed, diving for the armoire holding his clothing.

"Peregrine!" Mama cried in outrage.

He ignored her and hastily dressed. He'd become proficient at dressing himself. His valet,

Carter, had remained at the Hall as part of the Penning staff, awaiting the arrival of the *true* Duke of Penning. That hurt a little less every time he thought of it. He wondered if some day it would cease to hurt altogether? Would he look at his life with contentment and not think of it as a loss at all?

His mother released a mollified breath as he pulled up his trousers.

He repeated his earlier words. "I do *not* have the pox."

"You are certain of that?"

"I would know more than the local fishmonger, believe me," he snapped. "Trust me. I am not so afflicted."

His mother exhaled in relief and sank down on the edge of the bed. She rubbed the heel of her palm against her forehead, threatening to dislodge the turban covering her hair. Mama was a creature of habit. Her hair was never visible before the dinner hour, at which point her maid would arrange her artificially darkened strands in an elegant fashion.

"Why are people saying such things about you?"

He opened his mouth and closed it, reluctant for some reason to cast Miss Bates to the wolves—or in this case—to his mother.

His mother had always been fond of the Bateses.

Especially the vicar. Imogen's father would engage Perry's father for hours on the subjects of history, philosophy, theology. The two of them could find pleasure discussing what they considered to be the best breed of sheep. Mother always appreciated the vicar's ability to keep the duke preoccupied. That appreciation extended itself to Imogen Bates. He hated to dash her perception of the young woman. His mother had no clue of the deep river of deceit coursing through her.

But he knew and he would never forget and be taken in by her soft eyes and mouth again.

He knew and he intended to put a stop to her mischief once and for all.

Grabbing his jacket, he slid it on, forgoing the usual vest and cravat. He strode toward the door.

"Peregrine!"

"My apologies, Mother." Dutifully, he turned and pressed a quick kiss to her cheek.

"Where are you off to in such a state?" She waved a hand over him in disapproval. "Look at yourself! You're still a gentleman and should conduct yourself accordingly and dress yourself as one."

He resisted the urge to argue with her. He knew many did not consider him a gentleman anymore.

"Is it not obvious?" he asked instead. "I'm off to find the culprit responsible for these rumors

and put a stop to this nonsense once and for all."
For what it was worth. He needed to act quickly.
Before it was too late and she had chased away
all marital prospects for good.

Mama wagged a finger at him. "No fisticuffs."

He snorted, imagining himself engaged in
battle with Imogen.

Of course, his mother had no notion the culprit was not a man.

Suddenly the image of him locked in battle
with Imogen took on a decidedly amorous twist.
In his mind they were locked and entwined, but
they weren't fighting. Indeed not. They were
rocking together in a frenzy of lust. He gulped
and shoved the unhelpful image aside.

"Of course. I won't be violent." Violence had
never been part of his nature. "I promise."

Although keeping his hands to himself might
prove a challenge now that he knew she had better uses for her mouth than spreading slanderous lies.

But keep his hands to himself he would.

He'd softened toward the lass last night. He
would not be so foolish again.

IMOGEN KNEW THE moment her cousins arrived.

The more dramatic side of her nature believed
she sensed it like a change in the air: a slight
dropping in temperature or shift in the wind

that raised her skin to gooseflesh. She shivered and rushed to the window, peering out the crack through the sheer curtains.

Indeed, they were here, despite all her wishing to the contrary and that letter they sent proclaiming that very intention. Their fine carriage came down the lane like a fateful zephyr.

Papa's sister, Aunt Bernadine, had married well. As she and Uncle Hugh had been blessed with only Winifred, they'd left their very prosperous haberdashery business to Winnie—or rather to Winnie's husband. Not that Uncle Hugh was deceased. He merely gave little attention to the business these days.

From Winnie's letters, Edgar managed their half dozen haberdashery shops, overseeing the day-to-day running of operations whilst Uncle Hugh spent his days poring over puzzles and his evenings dining and playing cards at his club.

She watched as the conveyance lumbered its way toward her house, her throat thickening as it did.

The carriage stopped with a creak of wheels.

A stone lodged itself in her throat as the driver hopped down to open the door for her cousins to descend.

They were here.

Imogen took a gulping breath.

She would have to face them and be normal

around them. Whatever that might be. She was not even certain what constituted normal. How did one behave *normally* after everything that had transpired?

Eight years had passed, but she had not forgotten. The pain had subsided, but the lesson had been learned, and, truth be told, there was still the abiding humiliation.

She watched the carriage, exhaling heavily, waiting for them to emerge.

The driver opened the door and held a hand up to her cousin. Winifred descended gracefully, lovely and elegant in her traveling gown of cobalt blue, a driving cap covering her golden curls. Edgar, her wretched husband, followed.

Imogen sucked in a sharp breath, bracing herself.

She'd seen them only once since their wedding day and that was when Imogen and Papa traveled for Aunt Bernadine's funeral two years ago. The visit had been thankfully brief. They had not even stayed overnight, instead staying with one of Papa's friends from his school days. They had not wished to burden their grief-stricken relations—much to Imogen's relief.

But now they were here, and she knew. There would be no hiding. No escape.

This would be unbearable.

Chapter Thirteen ❧

A London trip, 1841

𝓘mogen fell in love on the summer of her eighteenth year during her annual trip to London to visit Aunt Bernadine's family. Summer trips to Aunt Bernadine were customary.

Falling in love was not.

It happened on the third day of her visit. She was with Winifred in Hyde Park, joined by several of Winnie's very fashionable friends. Their dress, their manners, their many stories that always seemed to involve people and places she had never heard of made her feel less than . . . *less.*

Imogen struggled not to look so very immature and unsophisticated in their company. Hopefully no one noticed her for the fraud she was.

Her cousin was quite popular, she soon learned, and was never short on companionship. Her drawing room was always full to the brim and Winnie never went anywhere without a small army of friends hanging on her every word.

It had not always been that way. Imogen's visits to London had not always been like that. When they were little girls, it was just the two of them. They spent their days playing together, frolicking in the garden and making floral wreaths from the tulips and lilacs and lavender.

Occasionally a maid would take them to the park or the subscription library, but Imogen never had to compete for her cousin's attention. She never had to beat out others. She'd had Winnie all to herself. She missed those days fiercely.

If becoming an adult meant forgetting your friendships and all the little things you liked to do in favor of talking about parties and dresses and boys, then Imogen longed to stay a child who wove floral coronets forever. That, she thought, sounded like heaven.

Now Winifred was a debutante and apparently quite the sought-after one, from the perpetual crowd surrounding her.

Imogen watched from the fringes of every room as Winnie and her friends entertained each other. She watched, battling loneliness, missing her cousin, but she valiantly tried to adjust to this new reality.

She attempted to follow the conversations, focusing on their words and trying to summon the interest to care. But it was difficult feigning interest in the new millinery shop that opened on Bond Street boasting some choice riding caps.

It was in the midst of this discussion that Edgar Fernsby first sidled beside Imogen in the park. "I wager you never knew such a variety of riding caps were in existence?"

Once she overcame her astonishment that one of Winnie's set had singled her out for exclusive attention, she found her voice.

In fact, over the following days Mr. Fernsby continued to single her out for his sole and flattering attention. Perhaps even more astonishing was that Imogen regularly spoke back, quite at ease in his company. It felt natural talking to him, natural becoming his friend.

Remarkably, his interest in Imogen didn't wane. He strolled alongside her at the back of Winnie's group of doting friends as though she were the most fascinating person in the party.

He began to call regularly at Winnie's house, each time fixing his attention on Imogen, inquiring after *her* health. He was intrigued by everything about her. Her hobbies and interests. Her favorite books and flowers and foods. The names of her pets. No one ever took such an interest in her before. At least no gentleman.

Edgar Fernsby returned again and again to Uncle Hugh's house, flattering her with his company until she realized the unbelievable truth. He was *courting* her.

He joined them at the theater and the museum and at the park. He was as constant as the stars and when one evening he coaxed her into slipping from Winnie's drawing room amid the musicale Aunt Bernadine was hosting for two dozen guests, she obliged him and followed him into the dark and empty library that smelled of leather and parchment.

She should have known better, but she did it anyway. She trusted him.

When he kissed her against the double doors, she permitted it, reveling in the moment, in the warm fuzzy sensation that swept over her.

After that evening they were sneaking kisses whenever they could. Behind potted ferns. In Aunt Bernadine's garden. In a dark alcove at the theater.

All very discreet, of course. They made sure of that. She thought him very considerate to keep her reputation in mind.

Kissing became like breathing. Something she needed every day from him. It was their secret. A luscious little gem she held in her hands, cupped between them like fairy dust. The secrecy of it all was part of the thrill. That much she knew.

He spoke of them spending the rest of their

lives together and she was eager for Papa's visit in less than a month to collect her. At that time Edgar would reveal his intentions to her father and ask for his blessing. That was the plan. It was decided. They had discussed it. He had proposed. She had accepted.

It was happening. Before the year was out she would be a married woman. She would be Mrs. Edgar Fernsby. Imogen only wished her mother was alive to meet her dear Edgar—to see her so blissfully happy. Mama had always said one day would arrive when Imogen found her perfect partner. Imogen had had her doubts, but clearly Mama knew what she was talking about because Imogen had found him.

She'd had no notion when she left to visit her cousin for the summer that she would meet the love of her life. Her young heart was bursting from the newness and unexpectedness of it all. She saw stars and hearts and rainbows in everything. Which would explain why her maidenly reserve was nonexistent. Nothing had prepared her for such an ardent suitor or his cajoling words. She'd never been the object of any man's lusts.

Perhaps it was because her father was a vicar. Gentlemen tended to steer clear of her. Or perhaps it was her provincial existence that did not boast an abundance of suitors or even potential suitors. She was unaccustomed to such an assertive gentleman.

A few afternoons before Papa was set to arrive, Imogen and Edgar found themselves alone in the garden. A common enough place for them in their interludes.

Edgar kissed her and the pressure of his lips on hers grew more and more insistent and coaxing.

She gave a feeble protest as his hand pawed over the front of her gown, her fingers circling his wrist. "Edgar, I don't think . . ."

"It's all right, love." His gaze fastened on her face, his eyes reminding her of a pleading puppy dog. He brushed his thumb down her cheek. "Don't you trust me?"

"Of course. Yes."

"Then let me make you feel good."

She released her grip on him and let him touch her at will. He wanted to *and* she did love him . . . and trust him. She wanted to please him. They were going to be married, after all.

Pinning her against the tree, his hand found its way beneath her skirts and he fondled her between her thighs. His fingers unerringly found the slit in her drawers. It was wicked, but not . . . unpleasant. She wouldn't say his awkward strokes were making her feel good though. Not as he promised.

"Ahh, there, there, my love," he panted in her ear, increasing the pressure of his fingers until he probed inside her. "You feel splendid."

She winced, inching away from his touch. "Ouch."

"Beg your pardon," he murmured, sliding his fingers out from beneath her skirts. "Let's try something else, eh?"

"Something else?" she queried, slightly relieved for an end to that bit of awkwardness.

"It's my turn," he said with a waggle of his eyebrows, taking her hand and guiding it to his manhood.

With a quick glance around, he hastily freed himself of his trousers.

"Edgar?" She looked around nervously. "Are you certain—"

"It won't take long. I'm almost there, love." He guided her and showed her how he wanted her to move her hand up and down the length of him.

He wasn't very large. She didn't know what to expect, but he was far from intimidating even as he grew slightly in size at her ministrations.

"That's it," he encouraged, dropping his hand away and leaving her to her rubbing and stroking of his rod. His breathing grew erratic. "Oh, I've dreamt of you touching me like this, my love. I knew you would be brilliant at it."

With a groan, he spent himself and she wrinkled her nose in distaste at the sudden wetness coating her palm and fingers.

He quickly removed a handkerchief from his pocket and tossed it to her as he tucked himself back inside his trousers.

"That was brilliant, love," he said in approval, nodding as he tidied himself.

Strangely, she did not feel brilliant.

They returned inside. Separately, of course, for the sake of discretion. But he did not look at her the rest of the evening. She tried to meet his gaze, but he avoided her eyes, and she could not help wondering if she had perhaps been less than brilliant.

In fact, he stayed away the next couple of days. No calls. No joining them for their walks in the park or for tea.

Papa arrived and Imogen grew desperate to see Edgar again. Perhaps he had confused the date of Papa's arrival?

His absence was worrisome. Beginning to fear that he had fallen ill or to injury, she entrusted a letter to a servant with instructions to deliver only to Edgar at his residence.

When the servant returned, he assured her that he had placed it directly in Edgar's hand.

She had no choice but to wait.

Just as she had no choice but to leave with Papa

as scheduled two days later and return home to Shropshire.

For days, for weeks, she foolishly looked to the horizon, staring forlornly out the window, wondering what could have happened and searching for Edgar's figure to appear to fulfill his promise of marriage.

It was two months later when they received the news.

Word reached them via a letter from Aunt Bernadine. Winnie was betrothed.

To Mr. Edgar Fernsby. They would wed at the end of the season.

A bit of Imogen died that day.

Her heart most certainly broke, but so did something else inside her. Her last bit of childhood, the innocent inside her that believed in things like love and happily-ever-after and blind trust.

Mama had been wrong. There was no perfect partner waiting for her. She would never be so foolish to believe that again.

Chapter Fourteen ✤

*A*s Imogen peered out the window and into the yard, her grip on the filmy edge of the sheer curtains tightened until her knuckles ached. A fingernail poked a hole through the fabric, rending it, but she couldn't be bothered to care.

Edgar Fernsby was here. He had dared to come here.

Blast it. She released the curtain and stared through the crack, scrutinizing Edgar as he stepped into the midmorning light. She searched for the differences in his countenance, if any, that time had wrought.

He had not changed very much . . . and yet he had.

His skin was pallid, and the luster was gone from his eyes. She could detect that even from her window.

He lifted his hat and smoothed a pale hand over his head. His hair had thinned and rested somewhat limply against the shape of his skull.

She knew without touching that those strands would feel wilting and not at all as they had once beneath her fingers, silky rich and thick.

Mr. and Mrs. Fernsby stood side by side, a fine pair in their lavish attire—and something seized inside her. A wash of panic. A bitter taste coating her mouth. A tremoring up and down her body.

"No," she whispered, stepping back from the window.

She did not want them here. *She* did not want to be here. She could not do this. She could not face them. Not yet.

Panicked, she darted in multiple directions in her small bedchamber, like an ant seeking escape from the rain, before returning back to the window and looking down again.

They were gone. They had advanced on the front door. Any moment they would be inside her home. A knock sounded from the bowels of the house. Soon Mrs. Garry would let them inside and she would call up for Imogen to come down.

No, no, no, no.

Yanking the curtains wide, she pulled open the window, more grateful than ever for the wall of ivy covering the front of the vicarage. Hiking her skirts up to her thighs, she straddled the windowsill, casting aside any sense of modesty. These were desperate times. She would not endure an entire day with Winifred and Edgar. She would have to face them eventually, at dinner, but she could avoid them during the day. For now, *eventually* could wait.

A glance down confirmed her cousins had already entered the house.

It was now or never.

As though to hammer that home, Papa called to her from belowstairs, "Imogen!"

She stretched one slippered toe until she found a trellis hole, reminding and encouraging herself that she had done this before—when she was a child.

Her pulse jumped against her throat and she hurried her descent, carefully staying to the right of the front door, but to the left of the parlor's wide mullioned windows. It would not do at all to be spotted climbing down the trellis like a hoyden escaping her cage. Even if she was.

She did not give herself time to consider the madness of her actions. Papa would simply think she had slipped from the house to complete an errand without them noticing. Mrs. Garry might wonder how she had not noticed Imogen departing, but she would never believe she had done anything so rash as to slip out her window.

Dropping down on the ground, she shook her skirts back into place and then dusted her hands on the fabric, carefully wading through the front flowers, trying not to crush them as she stepped up beside the window.

She was careful to remain out of sight as she peeked into the parlor.

Papa was standing at the hearth beside Mr. Fernsby and Winnie was seated on the sofa, speaking in a lofty manner to Molly as she tugged off her velvet gloves. Molly was their occasional maid who helped out Mrs. Garry a few days a week. She looked a little apprehensive as she faced the full force of Winifred.

Imogen could not hear her cousin's words but she could surmise she was instructing the girl on some matter or another. Perhaps instructions for their bedchamber, or the tea service yet to be served to them. Winnie had always excelled at bossing others around.

"That was quite the most singular way I've ever observed someone exit a house."

Imogen spun around with a gasp to find Mr. Butler standing not two yards behind her, his head cocked at a curious angle as he studied her.

"Do you never announce yourself?" she hissed, hopping clear of the window, again taking care not to stomp on her flowers.

He first surprised her in the Blankenship gardens, then in her very own home, and now here again. She had never seen so much of him before, day after day after day. The man needed to wear a bell around his neck.

"I thought I just did."

She cast a worried glance over her shoulder, fearful she might be detected by the occupants inside her house, then stepped hurriedly forward, determined to put as much distance between herself and her cousins as possible.

Oh, she would have to face them. She knew that. But it didn't have to be now. And it didn't have to be like this. If she could minimize all time spent with them until they departed, the better for her. It would mean less time pasting a pretend smile on her face.

Mr. Butler dogged her heels as she circled the vicarage and opened the side gate that cut through the vicarage cemetery.

It wasn't as morbid as one might think a cemetery to be. It was full of blooming rosebushes and flowers, and a beautiful old oak tree sprawled at the center of the graveyard. As a child, when she first moved here, she had climbed that tree and sat high in its branches, looking out in awe at the vicarage and the surrounding fields and trees, the myriad rooftops in the nearby village, and the distant smoking chimney at the Henry farm.

The cemetery grounds were very green and well tended. Fresh vases of colorful blooms sat at several of the graves. Papa saw to that. Well, rather, he once saw to that when he had remembered to do such things. Now she remembered to do it, and the task fell to her along with the rest of her increasing duties.

The gate had a longer than usual delay before it clanged after her, and she sent yet another worried glance over her shoulder to confirm she wasn't being followed by Fernsby—an irrational fear perhaps, but she felt the flash of it, nonetheless.

Indeed, she was not being followed by Edgar.

Mr. Butler was there, passing through the gate after her, his handsome expression cast into grim lines.

"Are you stalking me?" she demanded.

"As you are fleeing and not stopping for a much needed discussion, then yes. I am following you. Indeed, I am."

She felt herself scowl. "Go away."

The arrival of her cousins made fresh the humiliation she had thought she buried years ago. She needed to find someplace to lick her wounds in private and compose herself.

Mr. Butler's presence did not help in that endeavor.

She had scarcely spent any time in his company whilst he was a duke, but now that he was plain and simple Mr. Butler he was everywhere. She could not escape him. As soon as she had the thought another intruded. *There was nothing plain or simple about this man.*

He had kissed her and she had kissed him

back and she had never felt as alive as she had in that moment when his mouth had locked on hers.

Shaking her head, she was determined to put that behind her. It was an aberration. A thing that had simply happened in a flight of temper. It didn't mean anything.

She wove a path between tombstones and stone crosses and crypts. "Why won't you leave me be?" She felt an odd mixture of dread and elation at his persistent attention. It baffled her and she clearly was not in a state to make sense of it.

"I want to know everything. No more evasions. No more lies."

Everything? All her truths? That gave her a jolt of alarm. The pulse at her neck gave a skittering leap.

Because the truth was this: Kissing Peregrine Butler had brought forth feelings and sensations she had never felt before. Not even when she was ten and eight and believed herself in love. Even besotted as she had been all those years ago, a kiss from Edgar had never made her feel as splendid as she had felt with Peregrine Butler and that was dangerous.

Longing was dangerous. Especially for a firmly committed spinster who had no hope of developing anything lasting with the likes of Mr.

Butler. He was after one type of female. And she was not after anyone.

She could certainly never tell him all of *that*.

Shaking her head as though that would perfectly clear it, she demanded, "What do you mean?"

"I want to know *all* the bloody rumors you've been spreading. I don't want to wake up in the morning to any more surprises."

He was here because of that. Of course. He knew of the latest rumor. She winced.

"Don't you have somewhere else to be? Charming unsuspecting heiresses?" *And their papas.* Yes. She'd prefer he do that if it meant he left her alone. She felt too vulnerable right now . . . too raw for this.

"I would love to be doing that very thing, however, you've made that a difficult endeavor." He sounded angry now.

She winced again. She had put a bit of a crimp in his agenda. She should not have said that thing to Mrs. Hathaway. She knew that now. In truth, she'd known it the night she did it. In her bed after the Blankenship ball, staring into the dark, the truth, the wrongness of her actions, had found her.

Shaking her head, she reached the back gate to the cemetery and passed through it, every stride taking her farther and farther from her house and the wretched Mr. Fernsby. The knot in her chest gradually eased.

She lengthened her strides for the line of trees ahead. They loomed like the Promised Land.

"Miss Bates, would you please stop for a moment?" he bit out in exasperation behind her.

She kept going. She spent a good amount of her time on foot. Rarely did she take a horse or carriage anywhere when on her own. Not a day passed when she did not walk from one end of this shire to the other end. The fact that he could keep up with her brisk pace illustrated that he was fit in his own right.

"You realize you have no coat on? The day is rather chill."

She glanced down at herself, realizing he spoke true. There was a bit of chill to the air, but she could not summon the will to care. She would not go back home for anything. At least not until much later. Not until she must.

"Where are you going?" he pressed.

She shook her head slightly. *Away.*

Away was all that mattered.

Why had they come? They'd never done so before and she knew from Winnie's occasional letters that they had vacationed in Scotland before. Never before had they stopped in Shropshire en route north. She'd assumed it was Edgar's good sense keeping them away. Given their history, it was the prudent thing to do. This visit was not prudent *at all*.

It was only two nights. At least according to Winnie's letter. Perhaps less than that once—*if*—they realized Papa was not himself. Prolonged social engagements could be awkward with Papa. He grew overtired and repeated himself, forgetting what had already been spoken. For that reason Imogen was selective about what invitations they accepted and scarce was the occasion when they hosted overnight guests.

Larger, short-lived events like the Blankenships' ball where Papa was no single individual's sole focus worked best. She didn't want it bandied all over the shire that her father was incapacitated in any way. The new duke could arrive any day and word could reach his ears that Papa was less than whole. On his whim, they could be ousted. Then where would they go? What would become of them?

"Miss Bates!" Her pace did not slow. "Imogen!"

She halted at the sound of her Christian name on his lips. It was a first. She didn't realize he even knew her name.

She turned slowly, staring at him.

He held his arms wide at his side, and she realized he had eschewed a few articles of clothing himself. He was without his vest and cravat and merely wore a shirt of white lawn beneath his jacket that opened in a V at his throat, revealing an enticing glimpse of very firm-looking skin. Such a rebuff to propriety felt a lapse even for him.

"Yes?" she asked with impressive equanimity.

He shook his head, and then glanced around them. "What are you doing out here?"

Various answers barreled through her mind.

Running away. Hiding. Shirking my duties as daughter and hostess.

All true, but none she would admit to him. That would only lead to more questions, and answers, if revealed, that would make her appear vulnerable.

She turned back around and resumed walking. "I'm not doing anything. Merely taking a stroll. What did you want? Why were you calling at my house?" she asked even as she knew the answer. He was here because he'd discovered what she had said to Mrs. Hathaway.

He fell in beside her. "Where are you off to in such haste? And why did you flee your house through a second-floor window?"

"I departed through my bedroom window so I did not have to take the stairs." It was both the truth and unrevealing.

"Why?"

She opened her mouth and closed it, determining she did not have to explain herself to him. Then, for some reason she did not understand, she volunteered, "We have houseguests."

"And that requires escaping through your window?"

"For these particular guests, yes."

"I am intrigued. Who are your guests?"

"My cousin and her husband."

"And they are so very terrible you must flee through windows?"

"I felt compelled."

He nodded. "Ever intriguing."

He could well remain intrigued. She was not about to unveil that sordid bit of history to him. "What did you need from me, Mr. Butler?" A redundant question perhaps. She knew what he wanted of her, but she did not know how to undo what she had started.

His gray eyes smoked over. "You know what I need of you. This new rumor of yours is spreading through the village like brushfire. Do you know how I learned of it?"

"I haven't any notion."

"My mother."

She winced. *Oh dear.*

He continued, "My own mother confronted me. Woke me abruptly this morning screeching to the heavens that I have the pox."

"Oh." She felt almost amused imagining that

scene, visualizing the very grand duchess confronting her son in such a manner.

He was not so amused.

"Oh," he echoed, and then made a sound of disgust. "How many rumors did you start, woman? I thought we had talked over them all. You made no mention of this one last night. What else need I be braced for?"

"Who says I'm the one who started it?" she asked, even though the question rang lamely to her own ears. Right now she felt raw and vulnerable. Prey cornered. By her cousin, Winifred, by Edgar . . . and now by Peregrine Butler. Survival demanded she defend herself.

"And who else is out there starting rumors of my person?"

She shrugged. "I cannot claim to know."

They entered the woodland, leaving the fields behind them.

Her family collected their firewood from these woods. She used to accompany Papa and Mrs. Garry's nephew, Lewis, to accumulate wood for their supply, but now it was just Imogen and Lewis. Every couple of months, they took the cart and cut down what they needed.

"Don't play coy with me, Miss Bates. We know it's you. Are there more rumors I need to be girded for?"

She shook her head, appreciating that this was

an admission of sorts that she had fabricated the pox rumor. She accepted that. It would be her last untruth. Truly. She was finished with this scheming.

He exhaled. "Well. Good. I'm glad to hear that." He winced. "I mean not *good*. My reputation is virtually ruined." His gaze narrowed on her. "But that is what you set out to achieve, is it not?"

She nodded. "It is. I thought it important to protect the ladies of this community."

"Protect them? From me?" He stepped closer and the breadth of his chest struck her as so very broad and solid looking. Not merely in appearance though. She knew he was solid because she had felt that chest. Against her. Against her palms. Crushing her breasts. "Because I am such a despicable person?"

"Not . . . despicable," she replied.

"Oh? What am I then that makes me so very unsavory?"

"You're insincere," she snapped, disliking being pressed on the matter.

"Insincere?" he echoed. "That is my greatest fault?"

He lifted a hand and she flinched.

He hesitated, awaiting her tacit consent, holding his hand midair. She released a breath and he continued, bringing his hand toward her face and wrapping his fingers around a tendril that had fallen loose from her pins. She knew her hair must be an untidy mess given her recent exertions.

His touch was gentle on her hair as he tucked it behind her ear. She shivered as his fingertips grazed the tender skin below her ear. Goosebumps broke out all over her body and she shivered.

"Have I been insincere with you?" His fingers lingered, tracing her earlobe.

His deep voice rumbled between them, rubbing along her skin like a caress. She supposed not. He had been many things with her, but not insincere. Her mind flashed back to their time in the garden and the kiss and the way his mouth had felt over hers.

Her gaze dropped to his lips, recalling the taste of him, the texture, the pressure of his mouth and tongue and teeth. Nothing about that encounter had felt insincere. It felt as real and as honest as anything that had ever happened to her.

"Have you nothing to say?" That appealing mouth of his curled into a slow, languid grin.

She moistened her lips, but still did not speak.

He continued, "Astonishing. I did not think it possible to silence the garrulous Miss Bates."

She found her voice and said, "Your reputation is not ruined." Even though she did not fully believe that herself, she needed something to say and it felt like she should try to reassure him at the very least.

"Oh, but I think my prospects in all of Shropshire are officially dashed, much thanks to you." The annoyance was back in his voice—if it had ever left him at all.

"Can a man's reputation ever truly be lost?" She shook her head, grabbing a fistful of her skirts and starting up a steep incline. He kept stride with her. "It does not work that way for your sex. In my experience, nothing can happen so grievously to a man's name that it can't be repaired."

She'd seen it time and time again. Men pardoned for infractions simply by the grace of their gender. The same tolerance could not be applied to females. It was the same everywhere. She had seen it even in her beloved Shropshire. Women were not even granted full rights under British law. That alone spoke volumes on the inequitable treatment of women.

"Spoken like a true bluestocking."

"I'll take that as a compliment. A woman needs keen intelligence to secure herself even a fraction of the rights men have for simply being born."

"You hardly seem a woman subject to oppression. There are not many women your age with independence and the respect of her community . . . *and* no pressure to be a wife and mother."

"I suppose I *am* fortunate," she agreed lightly. "At least as long as my father lives I am fortunate. My well-being merely depends on his ability to conquer death, after all." She forced her eyes wide, blinking up at him. "Perhaps he will live forever, and I will have nothing to fret over."

Mr. Butler's expression looked decidedly less confident at that.

With a smug lift of her eyebrow, she pushed on ahead.

He followed, trailing after her through the sudden thickening of brush until they broke out into a small watering hole. He made a small sound at the lovely little spot that she had discovered years ago on a walk.

"What is this place?" he marveled.

"My pond."

"Your pond?"

"Indeed. It's my special place."

"But it's on my land." He didn't know the place, but he knew it was on Penning property.

"No," she said slowly. "It's on Penning land. Not yours."

He released a breath, looking both chastened and annoyed. "Very well. Trust you to correct me on that matter. This is Penning land. Not my land. The point being, how can it be *your* special place?"

She shrugged. "Am I not permitted to think of a place as special to me? You can't toss a rock without hitting Penning land." She moved, climbing up a very large slab of granite that jutted like a shelf from the pond. "The very house I live in was built by the seventh Duke of Penning, *your* great-grandfather. Almost everything around here is dependent on Penning." She sat down, very correctly arranging her skirts over her legs.

He dropped his long length down beside her.

She surveyed him beneath her lashes, and then she heard herself asking, "You miss it?" She was not sure why she cared. She should not be bothered to care.

He bent his knee and propped his arm on it. "Miss it? What precisely?" He glanced out at the placid waters thoughtfully. Not so much as a ripple marred the serene surface. "Let's see. The land? The house? The myriad servants? The deep pockets? The friends? The parties? The ladies eager to line up for courtship?" He sent her a derisive look. "I could go on, but it would only bore you." He snorted and nodded. "Of course I miss it. I would be a fool not to."

"But you'll settle for marriage to either of the

Blankenship girls or the baroness's daughter?" she asked in an almost perfectly normal voice. "That will make you happy?" She didn't know why she was asking after his happiness. It had never mattered to her before. She was simply curious now, she supposed. No more than that surely.

"Happier than now." His eyes glittered as he leaned back on one elbow. "I would have readily accepted a match with either of the Misses Blankenship or the baroness's daughter, once she is officially out. But now I should be so fortunate to gain a dinner invitation from either of those families, much less a blessing in marriage."

"My fault," she acknowledged.

"The rumors have done what you intended them to do." He stared at her intently, and she struggled to defend herself against the accusation in his eyes. In his mind, she was clearly a manipulative little witch. "Tell me. Why? Why are you *really* spreading such stories?"

The question asked so softly, so intensely, unnerved her.

He saw through her.

He did not accept her earlier explanation. He believed she was motivated by more than her need to protect the ladies of Shropshire.

And he would not be wrong. She had other reasons.

Because you would need to put a bag over her personality.

He had crushed her as a child with his words. That sting had stayed with her all these years. She let it influence her. She had not considered that he might have changed.

His unexpected apology had lessened her ire, however—just as it had caught her by surprise.

She could not answer him, though. Not without revealing more of herself than she wanted. She did not want him to know just how much he had hurt her.

But he stared at her intently, waiting for an answer, so she clung to the only explanation she had ever given, even if she was not so convinced anymore. "These girls deserve better."

He absorbed that for a moment. "And you're responsible for seeing to the happy marriages of every girl in the shire? That is quite an undertaking."

"If I can help a girl avert a sad fate, then why should I not?" she snapped.

"And I'm that sad fate?" His eyes widened and then he tossed back his head in a rough, mirthless laugh. "Don't be reticent. Tell me how you really feel, Miss Bates."

"You're only after what they can bring you."

"And you don't think ladies look at me and evaluate what I might bring them? They weigh the advantages for themselves. Does not *everyone* contemplate marriage in terms of benefit?"

She stared at him in frustration. "Just because something is the status quo, does not make it right."

He shook his head at her in seeming awe. "You are quite the crusader, Miss Bates? You think to change the world?" The mocking glint in his eyes told her he did not mean that as a compliment—nor did he believe that she could change the way things were.

"Perhaps just this small corner of it," she shot back. "It's my duty to look after the people in this village . . . especially the vulnerable."

"I don't suppose it's occurred to you that I've fallen into that vulnerable category you are so very concerned about. Where's your compassion for me? Will you not look after me?" His voice lowered and softened a bit at that last question and a small shiver rushed through her.

"You?" She forced a caustic laugh and fought against that delicious shiver. "I don't think you are in requirement of it."

"And I don't suppose it has occurred to you that *I* might offer something in marriage."

"You? What would that be? You still live with your mother and it's my understanding that is not by choice."

The lines on either side of his mouth tightened

and she knew she'd hit a nerve. "You are well apprised of my situation. You are correct. I have no property. No wealth. No rank. And yes, I currently reside with my mother. But there are other things I can still offer."

"What, pray tell, can you then offer a wife?" She tried to hold a smile, but there was something in his face that made the curve of her lips falter and fade. The air between them felt positively alive, tight and crackling like the air before a storm.

"Pleasure."

Chapter Fifteen ❧

Pleasure.

The word dropped deep and thick, twisting on the charged air between them like a living, breathing thing, ready to sink its teeth into her if she drew too close.

She swallowed against the sudden tightening of her throat and glanced around, suddenly aware in a way she had not been before of how very alone they were. She'd brought him here, led him to her secluded little spot without truly giving any thought to how isolated they would be.

He elaborated, "I know about the giving of pleasure."

She opened her mouth and closed it, not certain how to respond to that audacious statement. She brought her knees closer to her chest, hugging them as his deep voice played over in her mind. *I know about the giving of pleasure.*

Of course, he did.

Heat swarmed her face. She understood what he meant by pleasure. He was speaking of the delights to be had in the marriage bed.

She understood that he arrogantly thought he could deliver to his wife physical gratification and that it counted for something and would make marriage to him worthwhile.

It stood to reason that a couple could not live their lives in bed. They had to surface and see to the duties of life. There were twenty-four hours in the day and not all could be spent engaged in intimacy. And yet he thought the *pleasure* he could give was enough.

Arrogant man.

She had experience with men who arrogantly believed they were the deliverer of all that was good in life. Well. In her case, it had been only one man. One man who promised her pleasure and forever and lied and was now currently drinking tea in her parlor.

Things did not always work out the way they should in life. Just because a person deserved good things did not mean they obtained them. She knew that for many women there were no delights in the marriage bed, much less in the marriage. Or whatever delights might be had in the marriage bed, it was not enough. Not enough to make up for the dissatisfaction of being trapped in a loveless union where the only escape was death.

Imogen could often look at the face of a wife and determine whether she was happy or not.

People generally wore their emotions on their face, in their body language. One's true state could not be hidden every moment of every day. No one was capable of that level of concealment. Her own neighbor, poor Mrs. Henry, was a perfect example. The broken woman was the appearance of abject misery.

What made Mr. Butler so confident that he could please a woman?

He kisses like a dream.

Blasting that voice from her head with a withering mental snarl, she said, "Men think that they know all about a woman's pleasure. *If* they even think about a woman's pleasure at all. Though I suppose you are at the head of the pack since you even bother considering it."

"I can't speak for other men. Only myself."

"I am sure every man thinks as you do."

"You sound like you speak from experience. Could this be why you're a kissing maven?"

She blinked, her face afire at his much too perceptive remarks. "A kissing maven?" Her lips twitched and she averted her gaze, smoothing her hands down her skirt-draped legs. Something to do with them—to keep them from trembling.

"Indeed." One corner of his lips curled seductively. "You are quite proficient. You do not kiss like a vicar's prim daughter. What would the

good people of Shropshire ever think of their demure Miss Bates if they knew?"

"And how should a vicar's prim daughter
kiss?"

His gaze dropped to her mouth. "Well, they
should all kiss like you, Miss Bates, but I doubt
they do." She gulped. Heaven save her from that
deep velvet voice. "More's the pity."

More's the pity.

"Oh." Her cheeks flamed, and she once again
averted her gaze, staring down at the toes of her
half boots peeping out from her hem.

"Shall I show you?"

Her gaze snapped to his face at this mildly
posed question. "Show me? Show me what?"

That crooked smile of his deepened. "The
aforementioned pleasure."

"Of course not," she snapped indignantly
at his indecent offer. She readjusted her arms
around her bent legs and shifted nervously where
she sat.

Her mind drifted to Edgar's attempt to show
her pleasure. He had promised to make her feel
good. Or some such enticement. A bold lie. It had
not hurt precisely, but it had been uncomfortable, and it had certainly *not* been pleasurable.

For some reason, unlike that time, she suspected there would be pleasure with Mr. Butler.

His eyes narrowed on her thoughtfully. "Because you don't believe in pleasure?"

"I did not say that." On the contrary. She believed he could deliver on the pleasure. His voice alone made her feel pleasantly flushed all over.

"Tell me something," he pressed, ignoring her weak denial. "Is it that you do not believe pleasure exists for a woman? Or that *I* cannot deliver it?"

She sputtered, her mind a wild tangle. This was a wholly inappropriate conversation, and yet they were having it. It did not help that his proximity sent her pulse racing and her limbs shaking. He smelled of soap and sunshine and freshly pressed linen. Who knew any person could smell so intoxicating?

Her hands clenched tighter in her skirts to keep them from trembling. She was looking at his mouth again, and she forced her gaze away, mentally upbraiding herself. Now that she knew the taste of his lips it was difficult to pretend otherwise.

The former Duke of Penning sat with her in her favorite spot weaving seductive words and staring at her like he could see beneath her clothes—and he *liked* what he saw. She could not have imagined it.

Him. With her. Like this.

He would not be here with her, if he was still the duke. It was a glaring truth. She could not feign ignorance of that, but right now he was very . . . distracting.

His index finger came to play with the hem of her skirts, ruffling the dirt-smudged fabric. Not touching but close enough to her ankle that her breath constricted in her throat. "I can make a wife very happy."

"In bed," she retorted. "You can make a wife happy in *bed*. There is more to happiness than what happens in the marriage bed."

He inclined his head. "Perhaps. But it is a very good place to start. It cannot be discounted. You think I can bring nothing to a marriage?" He paused a beat and she felt that silence swell between them like a giant balloon, ready to pop at his first touch. "Let me show you otherwise."

He inched his body closer, encroaching without touching, and making her wholly aware of just how much larger he was. And warmer. Or was that her body that felt suddenly overly warm in the chilly afternoon?

"Wh-what are you doing?" She could not believe she just asked that question, but as he was propositioning her she might as well be clear on the specifics of what the offer entailed.

Not that she was entertaining the notion. She was not. She was simply curious.

"I'm showing you. There are hundreds of ways to please a woman."

Hundreds?

Her mind raced. She couldn't get those words out of her ears. She moistened her lips, both tempted and overwhelmed at the notion of *hundreds*.

No. She gave her head a small shake. He could not entice her. She would not be taken in so easily. She wouldn't be duped. Not again.

"'Hundreds of ways' is rather vague, I fear." With an air of disinterest that impressed even herself, she moved to slide off the rock.

He grasped her wrist, stalling her. "What if I said I would begin by slipping my hand under your skirt and placing it upon your leg like this?" His hand dipped beneath her hem, circling her ankle.

She gave a little squeak and froze.

"Is that properly specific for you?" he murmured.

Oh. My. That was specific.

She nodded jerkily, her voice trapped in her throat, strangling as she absorbed the simple sensation of his hand on her.

Except there was nothing simple about it.

His palm radiated heat through the fabric of her stocking. She could feel the imprint of each of his fingers like a brand. What would it be like if she tore off her stockings so they were skin-to-skin?

If his hand didn't stop at her ankle? If he

touched her everywhere? She would likely go up in flame.

"Is it? Imogen?" he whispered her name and it felt like a full body caress. "Specific enough?"

This time she managed speech. "Y-yes."

She should keep moving away, sliding off the rock and putting distance between them, but his deep voice lulled her. To say nothing of his touch. He was scarcely making contact with her, but she was held in place, pinned to the rock.

The palm of his hand gently cupped the outside of her anklebone, fingers circling, gripping her there for a moment, radiating heat up her leg from that one point of contact.

He was not eager or greedy or hurried. There were no fumbling hands beneath her skirts, poking and prodding at her.

This was no ambush.

He stretched his body out beside her like a cat lazing in the afternoon sun, his fingers grazing slow circles around the bump of her anklebone. As though they had all the time in the world.

As though they had eternity on this rock.

The tips of his fingers began walking inward, starting a slow ascent up her stocking-covered leg. "And then I would proceed like this over your stockings, detesting that they're here to bar me, wishing for skin . . . looking for your skin, hungering for that first contact."

His voice was its own form of seduction, wrapping around her like silken chains, gently imprisoning her. He looked back and forth between her face and his ministrations as though gauging her willingness.

The air ceased to flow in and out from her lips, but she remained, loath to break free from her intoxicating bonds.

She went perfectly limp as he traveled up, reaching her knee, stopping when he arrived at her garters. He played with the ribbons holding up her stockings, murmuring, "Then I would touch you above your stockings. My fingers right here . . . on this delicate skin."

Her limp legs parted wider at this first touch on the inside of her thigh, at the pads of his fingers on her flesh.

She went from not breathing at all to breathing too much, too fast, too hard.

She pressed a hand over her galloping heart as he stroked the inside of her thighs.

"Then you would finally have my fingers on your soft . . . warm . . . skin," he breathed, trailing up the inside of one thigh, slipping through the loose legs of her drawers, and then back down and around to the fleshier outside of her thigh, giving her a firm squeeze that she felt right between her legs—a deep swell of pressure at her core that made her gasp.

Her skirts were rucked up to her hips. The afternoon sun beat down on her in her state of dishabille even as the chill air turned her skin to gooseflesh. It was indecent and decadent and she couldn't find the will to care.

There was no awkwardness. No shame. No discomfort.

Only shivers. Delightful shivers.

The pace of his caresses became agonizing and almost too slow, too gentle, and she wished he would move faster, wished his hands would grasp her . . . fondle her a bit harder. She wasn't glass. She wanted him to squeeze her flesh again as he just had done on her thigh.

She wanted more of that.

More of him and his magical hands.

"Next I might free you of these." There was no *might* about it. He quickly untied the waistband of her drawers, tugging them down her legs in one smooth move and tossing them aside. They landed above her head on her bed of stone. "And then I'll have you spread gloriously in front of me, so I can touch you and feast on you . . ."

Her entire body was humming and vibrating like it was possessed. It did not even belong to her anymore. It belonged to him. And she didn't even care about that—she was too overcome with the onslaught of his attentions to worry about that.

She flinched as his hand grazed the folds of her womanhood and he stilled, his eyes quickly scanning her face, reading her quick wave of tension. He retreated, moving his hand back to her thigh, stroking and kneading her flesh, winding her up again until she was panting. Until a gnawing ache pulsed between her legs.

His velvety voice continued near her ear, spiking fresh chills down her neck. "I would lavish kisses on all this sweet skin. Like this."

He dropped down, and she sighed in pleasure at the lingering kiss he bestowed on the inside of one knee, and then the other.

Yes. *Pleasure.* She felt it. Just as he had promised.

Just as he said he could deliver.

She continued to feel that pleasure as he settled between her legs and began raining kisses all over her thighs. Everywhere. The insides. The outsides. The undersides. He rolled her over and kissed the back of her knees—openmouthed kisses where his tongue licked her sensitive skin. Skin she never knew was so sensitive.

She was a wreck, discomposed and panting, flattening her palms against the cool stone.

"I'll kiss and touch you . . . all over." His hands drifted up the backs of her thighs, his broad palms finding the bared cheeks of her bottom, smoothing over the plump flesh and squeezing.

The pressure sent her over the edge. She moaned, tilting her hips, pushing up into his hands, brazen and shameless and not the least bit self-conscious because it felt too good.

Even with her small bit of experience all those summers ago, she never knew that intimacy could be like this, that it could be so . . . *intimate*.

He gripped both cheeks, kneading and massaging, sending sensation blasting through her. Her back arched and her fingers curled, nails digging into rock.

Moisture rushed between her legs and her moans broke into a hoarse, rattled cry that did not sound like her. It did not even sound human. She was something else, another creature born of primeval need and fierce desire.

He rolled her over. She fell limply onto her back, her bones reduced to pudding. She chased after her breath as little ripples of sensation eddied through her.

His hands slid around her hips and dragged her closer, bringing her to him like a feast to be devoured.

She lifted her head weakly, attempting to peer down at him.

His face was there, between her thighs, his gray eyes as dark and feral as a beast intent on its next meal, and that meal was Imogen. It was as disconcerting as it was thrilling. Her hand lunged for his head, her fingers diving into his thick hair.

"What are you . . ." She stopped abruptly, shivering as she felt his warm breath lightly blowing on her.

She squirmed and fidgeted, aware of how very wet she was down there—and that he could see that for himself. Mortified, she opened her mouth and choked out, "You should not do this." Men did not do this sort of thing. People did not do this. *Did they?*

He stilled, the breeze of his breath halting as he spoke. "Why shouldn't I?"

"It's . . ." She groped for the proper word and settled for the truth. "Embarrassing."

"Embarrassing?" he echoed, surprise lacing his voice. "There's nothing embarrassing about this pretty quim." He stroked a finger down her exposed flesh and she whimpered. "Or all the things I want to do to it."

She moistened her lips. Curious. Intrigued. *Tempted.*

"Like what?" she heard herself ask, the question coming from some place deep inside herself where secrets and long-buried longings dwelled.

What was she doing asking such a thing? It was practically an invitation.

She was inviting him . . . this boy she once despised who was now a man that she . . . well. She did not know what she felt for him now. It was suddenly very complicated.

"Like this," he answered.

Then his head went down, and his face was there, buried between her quivering thighs, his mouth directly on her, hot and ravenous, devouring her.

"Oh. My!" She arched her spine, using the flat of her palm to push up off her rock bed.

He flattened his hand on her abdomen, pinning her for his hungry mouth. The pressure of his lips and tongue on her was too much. His tongue was everywhere. Taking deep sliding licks on her sex, slow and savoring, before arrowing in on the little bud nestled at the top of her mound.

She had noticed it was sensitive before—when washing herself, but she had never given herself to exploration before. Clearly she should have done so because it was a marvelous button of flesh.

She cried out as his mouth landed on it, grazing with his teeth, flicking it with his tongue and then sucking deep until stars erupted behind her eyes and a fresh rush of moisture met his mouth.

He moaned in approval as she cried out, incoherent words bubbling up from her throat as a climax ripped over her. She gripped his head, her fingers tight in his hair, her legs splayed indecently wide for his head and shoulders.

He continued consuming her, his head bobbing relentlessly, pumping between her hands as his mouth devoured her.

"Mr. Butler," she pleaded.

"Perry," he growled, grinding his mouth deeper against her. The vibration of his name on her only sent her desire twisting higher.

"Perry," she gasped, her head lolling on hard granite. "Perry . . . Perry, Perry!"

She could do nothing as another swell overtook her, bigger than the one before. Tears rolled from her eyes as his mouth continued to hum and suck against her sex.

She writhed beneath him, seeking relief, an end to the delicious torment. It was elusive, but near. "I can't—" Her words died on a shriek.

He eased a finger inside her wet channel. Her inner muscles welcomed him, clenching around him as though welcoming him home. He curled his finger inward, stroking at some invisible patch of flesh while his tongue simultaneously laved and drew that little nub of pleasure into his mouth.

That was all it took.

She flew over the edge. A great wave crashed and broke free inside her and she was sobbing, shaking as she floated back down. Lethargy stole over her body. She melted into a puddle on the slab of rock.

He withdrew from between her legs, pulling her skirts back down.

He joined her on the rock, lying on his back beside her. "I told you."

Her blissful euphoria dissipated. She turned her head to look at him.

His countenance was one of supreme satisfaction and she felt a twinge of disquiet at that expression on his too-handsome face.

"You told me?" she queried.

"Yes. I know about the giving of pleasure."

His words dropped like rocks in her stomach. "So this was merely a . . . lesson?"

Mortifying heat rushed into her face. Well, he had done a splendid job making his point. She felt like a fool and had to resist the sudden urge to slap him. She curled her fingers into a fist, her nails cutting into her palms. Violence was never right.

He frowned, reading her expression and suddenly looking uncertain. "I . . ."

She did not wait for him to make up his mind about what to say next. She sat up abruptly, snatched her discarded drawers and scooted away from him, dropping down off the slab of stone with a slight *oomft*.

He said her name sharply. "Imogen."

She looked up at him, resentment riding high in her chest. "Thank you for the lesson. You are quite right. You do have something to offer. You proved your point quite skillfully. So much so, in fact, that I will make amends and put an end to all rumors at once."

He blinked. "You will?"

She nodded jerkily. *Anything to put a stop to these interactions. Anything to send you on your way, back to sniffing at debutantes and paying me no mind.*

"I will." *Somehow.* "Your bride-to-be is indeed lucky." She said that last bit with a heavy dose of scathing mockery . . . and a gnawing ache forming at the center of her chest.

His mouth opened and closed. Clearly he was at a loss for words.

Good.

She turned and left him like that. A haddock groping for words.

She started for home with a heavy sense of satisfaction at having the last word. There was that at least.

It was too soon to return to her house, but perhaps she could slip in through the back door and sneak into her bedchamber. Mrs. Garry would cover for her if necessary. Although coming face-to-face with Winifred and her husband no longer struck her as that horrible anymore. After what just transpired, it hardly seemed significant. Who cared what happened years ago? She had greater concerns in her life.

Shaking her head, she found a discreet place to stop and slip her drawers back on beneath her skirts. She tied the drawstrings with angry movements, telling herself this would never happen again.

First a kiss. Now *this*? It was beyond scandalous.

Clearly she needed to give Perry—*no*, Mr. Butler—a wide berth. He was looking for a wife and . . . well, she was not on the market.

Even if she was on the market, she would never meet his criteria. She blinked suddenly burning eyes and took a moment to rub at the center of her chest, wondering at the spreading discomfort there.

She would do as she promised and set matters right, clearing the path for him so that he could court all the blasted heiresses of Shropshire to his heart's content. He would have what he wanted. Somehow she would restore his reputation and then she could continue with her life as though none of this had ever happened.

Chapter Sixteen ❧

I will make it right.

Imogen repeated this mantra over and over in her mind as she marched from her house into the village with purposeful strides the following day.

She had promised Perry—*Mr. Butler*—and she intended to keep her word.

She had permitted herself to get carried away. She fully realized that now. Her hurt feelings in the past and overzealous need to protect the women of Shropshire had overruled her good sense and morals. She winced. She was no great arbiter of justice, and yet she had told herself she was right and he deserved all of her judgment and every bit of misfortune to befall him. That was its own form of transgression. One would think a vicar's daughter would know better and be more generous in spirit. Apparently no one was immune from turpitude.

Undoing what she had done was the correct thing to do. Not only for him, but for herself. Her conscience longed for that relief.

And there was another matter.

A not so insignificant matter.

If he could reclaim his reputation and once again be free of all the rumors she had started, then *she* would be free of *him*.

There would be no more tense conversations. No more staring across her dining table at him. No more turning around to find him there, charming Papa, or directly in front of her, or tromping after her—or seducing her on a rock.

She grimaced. Very well. Seduction had little to do with what happened between them on that rock. It made her sound unwilling and she had been a full participant.

He would have no reason to see her at all.

No reason to kiss her ever again. No reason to run his mouth all over her thighs and on . . . other parts of her body. *Heavens.* She needed to put it all from her mind.

They would be as they were before. Coolly distant strangers.

She swallowed thickly and let that whirl around in her mind for a while, like a marble spinning and looking for a place to land and settle.

No reason to kiss her ever again. Coolly distant strangers.

If that caused a twinge in her chest, she ignored it. She had long ago accepted that she would never know intimacy. No more than that brief tryst she had so foolishly indulged in with Edgar. She would never be a wife and she was content with that fate. In fact, it had been a great comfort knowing she would not have to risk herself again.

There was fear in putting herself out there where she could be harmed again. Cocooning herself in her familiar and beloved Shropshire, in her childhood home, in her frilly girlhood bed, in her cozy bedchamber with its faded rose wallpaper, away from all potential dangers made her feel warm and safe and cozy. Even if a small part of her would miss him, she was relieved.

She marched past the smithy shop, slowing her militant advance as Gwen Cully emerged out into the yard, carrying a bucket, lifting it as though it weighed nothing at all, and dumping the contents over the fence that bordered the smithy and her house. She was strong. Not just for a female but for a person.

Imogen supposed that was her birthright. She came from a long line of blacksmiths. Her grandfather and father and uncle. She'd been working alongside the men in her family ever since she could stand in front of a forge. She was easily the tallest woman in the village, towering over most men. She wasn't willowy tall either. She was solid. Sturdy. There was no mistaking she worked her muscles every day toiling at the anvil.

The villagers called her an Amazon. Often to her face and in her hearing, but they said it in a teasing manner as though that mitigated any potential sting. It was one of those things that made Imogen uncomfortable. No woman wanted to be broken down to a designation based on her appearance. As though they were all nothing more than their facades.

"Miss Cully. Good day to you," Imogen called out in greeting. "How is your uncle?"

Miss Cully looked up, wiping her forearm against her perspiring brow and smiling as she caught a glimpse of Imogen. They were of a like age. Whenever Papa had called on the blacksmith, Imogen had quite enjoyed accompanying him. She and Gwen would play outside. It was a decidedly different experience than when Imogen had tagged along with Papa to Penning Hall. Gwen would show her the inner workings of a smithy. The girls had laughed and gotten on well together.

Gwen wore trousers, but no one in these parts blinked an eye over it anymore. With her father gone these three years past and her uncle practically bedridden due to his poor back, she was the only blacksmith around, and Shropshire was glad to have her, nontraditional or not. When one needed something wrought from metal, they would accept anyone with the skill to do it, and Gwen had proven herself quite capable in that area.

"He is quite well. Resting right now. Thank you, and thank you for dropping off dinner last week for him. He loves your cook's biscuits."

"I will extend your compliments. She is quite proud of them, and always makes more than we could possibly eat. I will drop by with some more."

"My uncle will love that." She propped her empty bucket on the top rail of the fence and rested her boot on the bottom rung, showcasing the shapeliness of her calves and thighs. She was always so at ease with herself. Dressing in trousers was clearly second nature to her. "Any time you have more than you can eat, we're happy to reap the surplus."

Imogen nodded. "By all means. I will send them your way." She glanced from the bucket and back to Gwen. "Very busy today?"

"I'm repairing some copper wall sconces for up at Penning Hall. Miss Lockhart wants the place in order before the arrival of the duke."

"Ah." Imogen nodded. "Of course. She is a most diligent housekeeper."

"She is that. She has always kept me busy, but she has a whole slew of things for me to do after

I repair these fixtures." Gwen grinned. "No complaints, of course. I appreciate the business."

"You work too hard, Gwen. I don't suppose this is a good time to ask you to come and check on the gate behind our house. The latch is sticking. It might need replacing."

"Oh, I'll always have time for you. I'll come by later this week. Perhaps a little before dinner." Gwen grinned cheekily, shaking her head and tossing the shorter strands of fair hair back from her forehead. The pale wisps only fell back in place with a bounce. She wore her hair in double plaits and pinned them to the back of her head. It wasn't the tidiest arrangement, and it brought to Imogen's mind a Norwegian milkmaid, but Gwen somehow made it look fetching even with all the flyaway strands.

Imogen smiled. "That would be fine. You can stay and we will feed you and send a plate home for your uncle."

Gwen placed a hand over her heart. "You are far too good for this earth, Imogen Bates."

Imogen's smile turned shaky. She didn't think she could hold on to it much longer. "Oh, I don't know about that." She did not feel too good for this earth lately. Not at all.

Not even close.

As though Gwen's words reignited the sudden urge to get on her way and set matters to rights, she said her farewell with a promise to see Gwen soon.

Waving, she turned and took a bracing breath. Time to put her plan to action.

Imogen walked until her destination loomed ahead. She opened the little white gate and walked through it up the stone walk to the front of Mrs. Hathaway's house.

She stood before the door for several moments, letting the sunny yellow paint comfort and embolden her. *Promises have been made.* The demands of her conscience begged a resolution.

Taking a deep breath, she lifted her hand and knocked briskly.

She would blame it all on a misunderstanding. Indeed. She nodded once determinedly. That should work.

She would insist she had not said he had the pox. No. No. She had simply misheard. The ballroom had been too loud. What she had said was: *He has a bantam cock. He tripped on a clock. He has a head full of rocks. He needs new socks. He just purchased a red bantam cock.*

Certainly one of those things was plausible and only a little ridiculous. From there, Imogen would dive into another topic. She would regale Mrs. Hathaway with some bit of news or harmless gossip. Imogen's houseguests would be a topic of interest.

This was all about correcting the rumor she had started and moving on to another more interesting subject. Imogen could do it. She would fix it. And then she could move on.

Perhaps her life would return to how it was before she had tangled with Mr. Butler. They could go back to being nothing to each other.

As opposed to what?

What were they now?

She shook her head, shying from answering that question, but knowing, at the very least, that they weren't *nothing* to each other. They were definitely something. It was indefinable and complicated. But something.

She looked skyward, freezing as her gaze landed on a silvery spiderweb in the corner of the porch ceiling. Squinting, she stared at that web, at the large spider with its delicately thin legs dancing over the threads. That web, that spider, transfixed her. As did the smaller bug stuck in its snare, helpless to do anything other than let its fate play out. She felt an odd kinship to that small bug.

The door creaked open and she soon found herself being greeted by Mrs. Hathaway. "Miss Bates! How lovely to see you. Come in. Come in."

Imogen murmured a greeting and stepped inside.

Chapter Seventeen ❧

*T*he Hare and The Basket was the most crowded Perry had seen it in a good while, but he still found a seat. The long trestle table wasn't empty, but he did not mind sitting among strangers. There was no pomp and circumstance in his life anymore, after all. No reason to cling to airs. He was not due it.

He was not anyone extraordinary, and sitting among ordinary people felt rather normal—more normal than he felt sitting at his mother's table sipping a glass of Madeira as she schemed to get him back into the graces of high society. More *preferable*, at any rate.

This, he realized—sitting in a pub that had seen far better days—was somehow more fitting. It felt more aligned with who he was . . . who he had become. He was not certain when that had happened.

When had he become this man who felt more at home among the common denizens of Shropshire?

It was not as though he was invited into the

ballrooms and drawing rooms of the *ton* anymore. He actually felt some relief that he was beginning to acclimate to his new life. There was an ease and naturalness to moving about and navigating this new existence. No butler or valet or man of affairs hounding him and keeping on top of his schedule—making appointments for him without even his knowledge, telling him where to go, whom to meet, what to do.

His life was his own in a way it had never been.

A few local yeomen chatted at one end of the table, their rough, work-hewn hands moving on the air as they spoke and lifted their tankards of ale. He recognized them from about the shire. They nodded at him and he nodded back in greeting even as he lifted his ale and took a drink.

He was not one to drown his troubles in drink, but today he felt the urge . . . and he'd been so drawn to this tavern of late, contemplating ways in which to improve it, to make it the shining attraction that Shropshire deserved. All his visits here . . . the place was starting to feel like home in a way his mother's home was not.

His thoughts drifted back to Imogen Bates. They never strayed far from her lately. She had promised to put the rumors to rest for him. He was not certain how she would accomplish that. And yet he would not put it past her. The woman was the type of person who got things done. She exuded efficiency. She had made a promise and he believed she would keep it.

So why did he not feel more relieved?

It might be nice for everyone to know he did not carry a festering disease that would slowly erode his mind. Why was he not plotting his next move and narrowing down his list of heiresses? If his reputation was repaired as Imogen promised, then the baroness's young daughter would be the perfect choice and a great win indeed for him given he had not a penny to his name. The baroness had always liked him and she seemed more concerned with her daughter's happiness than with her marrying a well-heeled gentleman with deep pockets. And from the way the girl always giggled and blushed in his presence, he knew she was not averse to his suit.

If he put his mind to it, he could make the lass happy. It would not be that difficult. He would be doting and kind. He would eventually care about her. How could he not? He was not so heartless that he would not develop feelings for someone he lived with day in and day out. Someone with whom he shared a bed and who gave him offspring. Feelings of affection would be normal.

Except it did not seem that very urgent that he wed an heiress anymore. The burning resolve to do so, to find his rich bride and restore his life to a trace of what it had been before, was gone. He searched, probing around deep inside himself, but he could not find that desire anywhere anymore.

Suddenly he did not feel as though matrimony to an heiress was the answer to all his woes. He'd been fine enough for the last year. Very well. Perhaps not *fine*. He'd moped around for far too much of it.

This had not been the best year of his life. Losing everything would do that to a person. He'd faced the loss of everything he knew and was forced to move in with his mother. He could state unequivocally that grown men should not live with their mothers. He did not relish sleeping in her cherub-infested guest room. He had to rectify that and soon.

He was not a man without education and verve. He'd made good marks in school, and more than one of his instructors had praised him for his cleverness. He could do something besides attaching himself like a parasite to a woman and leeching off her for his livelihood. *Blast it*. Imogen had gotten into his head. Never before had he doubted himself or his plans. Now this was the only thing he could consider—an alternate method to support his way through life.

He could settle on something else, an enterprise of some sort. It was very bourgeois of him and his mother would hate it. Thurman would be appalled. His friends, both the remaining ones *and* the ones that wanted nothing to do with him, would all be entertained at his evolution. It would give them something to talk about over drinks and cards at the club.

In any event, he was well qualified to run an estate as a manager or acquire a position as a man of affairs or a secretary. If nothing else, he could use his own two hands and put himself to work. He looked around the tavern again consideringly, seeing it again for all it could be.

As scandalized as his mother and sister would be to see him reduced to actually toiling for his occupation, there was honesty in it. Integrity. He could be satisfied with himself at the end of the day.

It would feel better than sulking about and pining for his old life and plotting which woman to woo into marriage to save him.

Imogen had been right. It was all a rather unsavory business, this matter of bride hunting. There was no honor in it . . . and he was done with it. Finished. No more.

He exhaled a great breath. Suddenly he felt as though a weight had been lifted from his chest as he released himself from the notion that he must marry and marry soon.

In its place, an unfamiliar sense of energy bubbled up in his chest. He had never felt it before, but he suspected it could be . . . *freedom.*

He was free.

Free in a way he had never been as the lauded Duke of Penning, but he was now free as a penniless bastard.

"Another drink, sir?" A young barmaid approached to ask.

"That will be all, thank you."

Perry finished his drink and pushed up from the table. With a parting nod for the men who shared it with him, he marched for the door with a bounce and lightness to his step.

Now it did not matter what rumors were being bandied around the shire about him. Perhaps he could track down Miss Bates and let her know her efforts on his behalf were no longer necessary—or at least not so urgent. He wasn't after an heiress anymore. And . . . he would not mind seeing Imogen again.

In fact, he would enjoy the sight of her and the sound of her voice . . . the sensation of her skin. He shook his head at his presumption. He was perhaps getting ahead of himself. There was no guarantee she ever wanted him to touch her again. She was the honorable vicar's daughter. She was not the manner of female open to dalliances, and yet he had dallied with her.

And he longed to do so again.

Perry emerged from the tavern into the sunlight, blinking his eyes several times to acclimate to the decidedly brighter afternoon. It had been overcast and slightly drizzling when he entered earlier in the day.

"Ah, Your Grace. Good day to you."

Perry turned at the greeting to find Mr. Gupta approaching down the sidewalk.

Mr. Gupta was smartly dressed as usual, swinging a fine mahogany silver-headed cane. He'd moved to Shropshire a few years ago and opened a bathhouse that was an instant sensation. It serviced both ladies and gentlemen of the shire, with divided parts for each. Most prized were his soaps and shampoos. He had a steady stream of customers who entered his bathhouse for his alkali products alone. Perry's own mother was very fond of his almond shampoo.

He doffed his hat. "Mr. Gupta. Good day to you. And please," he corrected, "it's Mr. Butler now."

"Ah, yes!" He waved his hand in unnecessary apology. "I had heard of that, of course. I fear I will never commit it to memory. I shall try though."

"I'm certain when the new Duke of Penning arrives, you will be able to keep it properly straight."

"Oh, is your predecessor soon to arrive then? Have you heard?"

"No, and I am not exactly being kept apprised of such matters," he confessed, which was perhaps more than he should admit, but Mr. Gupta had such a genial manner about him that it invited confidences. Perry suspected it was because Mr. Gupta was in the business of making customers feel so welcome. Hospitality was his specialty.

Mr. Gupta turned and glanced up at the dilapidated tavern sign. "And how was The Hare and The Basket today? Was Mr. Compton up and about?"

"No, I did not see him." Now that he thought about it, that was unusual. Old Mr. Compton commonly stood before the counter directing his servers and calling out greetings to patrons—occasionally carrying out platters of food himself.

"That is a shame," Mr. Gupta mused with a sad shake of his head.

"Is something amiss with Mr. Compton?"

"Ah, have you not heard?" Mr. Gupta continued to shake his head. "He is not well. Took a fall and has not left his bed in days. Such a pity. I've heard that his daughter has started looking for someone to buy the business. She wishes to take her father and move them to live with her aunt in the south. Claims the cold and damp of our winters aggravate his joints."

Perry nodded and eyed the tavern with fresh appraisal. Perhaps that's why the inside of the tavern seemed shoddier than usual. Without Mr.

Compton's attentions, his daughter would likely struggle with the upkeep. It would fall into even greater shabbiness.

"I hope someone will soon take it off their hands," Mr. Gupta was saying. "A tavern is the center and heart of a village. It would do well with a fresh coat of paint and a little love to revive it."

Perry looked back at him and smiled, wondering if the man could see into his mind and the thoughts that had been circulating there of late. "Some people would argue that the heart is the church."

Mr. Gupta chuckled. "Do not tell our dear vicar I said that. Or Miss Bates."

"You secret is safe," he assured.

Mr. Gupta snapped his fingers. "You should take it over."

Perry attempted to school his features in equanimity. Clearly the man was a mind reader.

Mr. Gupta continued, "You could breathe life back into the place . . . refashion it as one of your most excellent gentlemen's clubs in Town with fine food, drink, cigars . . . a place for cards and games." His dark eyes glowed in animation. "You would know how it should be. With your charm and your knowledge of high society and culture, you would be natural at it."

Perry did not reply immediately. His mind rushed and turned over the notion of entering into business, of taking an industrious idea and making it a reality.

Was it too coincidental that Mr. Gupta should suggest such a thing? That he should give voice to the very thoughts Perry had been harboring? And immediately on the heels of Perry reaching the realization that he should do something with his life other than marry an heiress? If he had been seeking encouragement, he had found it through no effort of his own.

"I am no businessman," he replied cautiously, almost afraid to let himself hope.

"Perhaps today you are not. But you could be." Mr. Gupta shrugged. "You could be one tomorrow. As a lad in my village, I had no notion I would live in England and manage my own business."

"A very prosperous business," Perry complimented.

Mr. Gupta inclined his head in modest acknowledgment and pointed at Perry. "You never know where life may take you, but you must be open to opportunities as they present themselves. You must be ready to take the leap, or else you will go nowhere."

You never know where life may take you. Perry could not argue with that. A year ago he could not have contemplated himself this way—with nothing. *With no one.*

An image of Imogen Bates flashed through his mind.

He had no right to think of her except that he could not stop doing so. He held no claim on her. She was not his to ponder and yet he could not forget about the taste of her or her response to him or what it would be like to be with her fully . . . in all ways.

Mr. Gupta clapped him on the back, jarring him back to the present. "You should think on it, Your Grace. Er. Mr. Butler, that is."

Perry nodded. "I will." *I will continue to think about it.*

Still shaking his head, he tried to temper his mounting excitement. It clung, however. He could not stop churning over various ideas. Deep buttery leather chairs. Soft sofas by the fireplaces. A fine cook with a menu that brought people from all over the shire. Roasted pheasant with buttered turnips. Smoked oysters with herbs. Meat pie with the richest gravy, so savory one would be forced to lick the plate.

Mr. Gupta chuckled. "I see you are already thinking the matter over. Good for you." He nodded as though Perry had, in fact, already accomplished something. With a few more genial claps on Perry's shoulder, he started off down the lane, turning back with a jolly wave and calling out, "I look forward to seeing what the future holds for you, Mr. Butler. I am certain it will be quite extraordinary."

Extraordinary?

Perry had not thought so. He'd been in such a low state this last year, convinced a marriage of convenience was the only way to salvage his life. What a fool he had been. His life yawned before him. A blank slate. He could fill it in any way he wished.

Now he was beginning to hope . . . to believe.

Why not? Why could it not be extraordinary? Just because he was no longer the highborn Duke of Penning but merely the lowborn son of the late Duke of Penning? He could do anything— be anything.

Anything except be noble. Somehow that mattered a little less to him.

Perry continued, walking with a lighter step. He squinted, peering down the lane as someone emerged from Mrs. Hathaway's cottage.

Strange that a year ago he would not have known Mrs. Hathaway, not by name or sight, should he have encountered her on the street. He certainly would not have known which house was hers. Now he knew. It was the one with the scalloped trim and yellow front door.

Indeed, he knew where Mrs. Hathaway, widow to the late owner of the *Shropshire Gazette*, lived. He supposed when one married a newspaperman charged with dispensing all news throughout the shire, peddling the latest *on dit* would be as natural as breathing to her, even all these years after her husband expired and someone else operated the *Shropshire Gazette*.

Now he knew about Mrs. Hathaway and most everyone else in the shire. Attending church with his mother and venturing out to other social engagements in the village, he at last knew his neighbors.

He knew this town . . . and he liked it.

Strange how this place had become his home once he lost his home. Ironically, he knew Shropshire better than he had when he'd had a stake in it, when he had been charged as its lord with its prosperity.

The back of his neck prickled with premonition as the woman who emerged from the house started down the walk and turned onto the cobbled street. He knew her instantly.

She wore no hat. The sunlight struck her brown hair, gilding it in the afternoon. She was wearing a prim yellow walking dress, her steps smart, her hips swaying slightly.

How had he never noticed that about her before?

There was an undeniable sensuality to her. Now he noticed it. Now he at once recognized her across any distance. His body immediately reacted. His skin tightened, vibrating over his flesh and bones.

He would recognize her anywhere.

Now and forever.

He stepped forward slowly, enjoying watching her undetected for a moment. It was as though her feet scarcely touched the ground. She was in perpetual movement, a flurry of action—always in motion, always with purpose. He admired her as she went along . . . envying that purpose. Perhaps because he had just reached the conclusion that he wanted that in his life, too.

He opened his mouth to call out to her, stopping himself at the last moment from shouting her Christian name across the village. That would not do much for discretion. She would not appreciate it. He might as well take out an advertisement in the *Shropshire Gazette* proclaiming himself infatuated with the vicar's daughter. True or not, he did not need to let the entire village know it.

"Miss Bates!"

She stopped and turned in his direction.

Across the distance, her expression was unreadable, but he had the definite sense that she was *not* glad to see him. Her entire body stiffened ramrod straight and her chin went up a notch. It dawned on him then.

She had been coming from Mrs. Hathaway's home. Mrs. Hathaway. The town gossip. Following Imogen's promise to restore his reputation, he could guess why she would be calling on that particular lady today.

He fought back a small grin. He supposed he could inform her that there was no longer any urgency to the matter of salvaging his reputation.

He moved forward.

She held herself still, watching him approach until he was but a few strides away, and then she bolted like an animal startled from the brush.

That was unexpected.

"Imogen," he whispered loudly after her, still hoping for discretion. He jogged a few paces to catch up with her. A quick glance around revealed none of the few people walking on the sidewalks paying them any heed.

She continued walking, but his longer strides easily kept pace with her.

"Why are you ignoring me?" he asked.

"I'm not." She looked straight ahead as she walked, not sparing him a glance.

"You cannot even look at me."

She did not respond to that, instead saying, "Why are you pursuing me? I did as I said I would. Your name is restored. I . . . *handled* that most problematic rumor. The rest I do not think much of an impediment to you." She took a deep breath and continued, speaking with a slight edge to her voice, "You can go about your plans of courtship with no concern now. People will soon know that you are very marriageable. Now you can leave me alone."

"*Now* I can leave you alone?" He wondered if he looked as confused as he felt. "Did we have some manner of agreement? Am I not to look or speak to you again now that you have corrected all the rumors about me?"

If that had been the understanding, then he would never have agreed to it. He did not want to stay away from her. He would not.

She sent him a wary glance. "That is precisely what I thought. We have no reason for further communication now. I won't interfere with your quest any longer, Mr. Butler."

Mr. Butler was it now?

Yesterday he had her shouting his name to the heavens but now they were polite and stilted again.

"My quest?" She almost made it sound honorable, like a noble mission. Ironic considering he had decided to give up on it for that particular reason—because it was *not* honorable, and she had been very clear on that point with him. She'd made her opinion heartily known. He continued, "I have decided to put my matrimonial goals to rest for a while."

She fully looked at him then, her eyes widening. "What? Why?"

He shrugged. "I don't think I need an heiress, after all."

She shook her head. "Why?"

Because marrying an heiress would mean I'm done with Imogen Bates and I do not want to be done with her.

It was one reason—the first to pop into his head, but he knew better than to say it out loud. She did not strike him as receptive to his suit. Indeed not. She'd fled at the sight of him.

Suit? Was he actually considering courting Imogen Bates?

She continued walking, looking straight ahead as she spoke. "'Tis done. There is no need for us to communicate anymore."

Other than the fact that he *wanted* to communicate with her.

He shrugged with a casualness that belied his seriousness, keeping pace alongside her. "Why can we not interact? Who's to say we cannot?"

She shot a quick glance at him, her look one of horror. "*I* say." She pointed to herself. "*I* say."

"We cannot be friends then?" he asked with deceptive mildness, as though he was not hoping for more than friendship.

"Friends?" She shook her head, narrowing her eyes. "Is that what you want from me? Friendship?" Her expression hardened into something so very unlike her.

There had always been a softness to Imogen

Bates. Perhaps not conveyed to him, but he had seen it. A warmth and kindness she exhibited to others. As the self-appointed caretaker of Shropshire, she had a big heart and wore it for all to see. Except right now. Right now she tucked that heart of hers out of sight from him. "You never wanted to be my friend before. In fact you said I was a rotten lemon."

He winced and inclined his head once in acknowledgment. "The follies of one's youth."

"Not *one's* youth. *Yours.*"

He did not care for this wall she was hastily erecting between them. He wanted her soft and melting and pliant in his hands again. Not this prickly creature breathing fire at him. He wanted her kindness and smiles. He wanted to reach that tucked-away heart.

He inclined his head. "Very well. My follies." He held his arms out wide at his sides in apology. "Forgive me?"

She sniffed. Looked at him and away and back again, sliding him measured looks under her lashes with her big brown eyes. "You do not want to be my friend. You think me an easy conquest after yesterday's sordid little play."

"Sordid?" He pressed a hand over his heart as though wounded. "Bite your tongue, my dear. Dare not cheapen what we did. It is more aptly described as paradise."

At that praise, she looked away, her cheeks burning a fiery red.

"You're beautiful when you blush, Miss Bates."

"Don't say such things to me," she hissed, her gaze snapping back to his face.

"Why not?"

"Because it's not real. You don't mean it." She motioned between them.

"Oh, it's quite real. Your beauty is real. Yesterday was real." He nodded decisively, holding her gaze, willing her not to look away from him.

The color in her cheeks deepened. "Don't speak of that."

He took a step closer, enjoying the way the pulse at the side of her neck thrummed above her modest collar. The overwhelming urge to lower his head and place his mouth there, to cover that madly drumming skin with his lips and tongue, seized him. He resisted the impulse.

"Why not? It happened. It can happen again if we—"

"No." Her eyes widened, large with distress.

"What are you so afraid of?" he whispered, reaching out a hand and lightly brushing her elbow. "That it might happen again? Or might not?"

"It won't happen again," she insisted, stepping back from him.

"You're afraid," he pronounced, certain of that

even if he did not understand why. "You will not even consider it. You will not let yourself believe that you and I might—"

"There is no *us*. I don't know what game you're playing at—"

"I'm playing no game."

"Then you're a fool to think this might be anything . . . genuine." A small puff of outraged breath escaped her. "A year from now I won't cross your thoughts. You will be married to your rich wife and not here, not walking the streets of this village as though you are one of us."

He glared at her, anger stirring inside him. "If I don't belong here, where do I belong then? Not among the *ton*. I'm not a *noblesse* any longer. So you mean to say I don't even belong here in Shropshire? Shall I relocate to the bloody moon then? Perhaps there I will better fit in?"

She looked taken aback. Her hands flexed around her reticule. Shaking her head, she opened and closed her mouth several times.

"Oh! Miss Bates! Hello, there. Perhaps you can help us." A lady hurried down the lane, towing her gawky daughter along with her. As much as he had learned of Shropshire and its inhabitants over the last year, the identity of this woman eluded him. Not Imogen, however.

"Ah, good day, Mrs. Merrit. Miss Merrit." She nodded to each of them.

"I was just discussing the matter of lace gloves or linen for an outdoor picnic with my daughter. Can you weigh in on the matter? What do you think?" The lady looked down her narrow nose at Perry and then looped her arm with Imogen, tugging her away with a disdainful sniff, indifferent to the fact that Perry and Imogen had been in the midst of a discussion. A discussion that was decidedly unfinished.

The snub felt deliberate. No doubt the lady knew of the stories circulating about Perry and thought to save the vicar's daughter from the likes of him.

He remained where he was, watching helplessly as Imogen retreated from him down the lane.

He'd caught a glimpse of her relieved face before she turned away. She was undeniably glad to have been rescued just as their conversation was getting intense. She'd practically jumped into Mrs. Merrit's arms.

She thought it was over.

She thought they were done.

He stared after her for a long moment before turning away.

She would be wrong.

Chapter Eighteen ❧

*F*ortunately for Imogen she had thus far avoided her houseguests. Mostly.

She successfully occupied herself with tasks during the daytime and only had to endure Winnie and Edgar through the obligatory dinners. It wasn't too difficult a feat, and the benefit was twofold.

Not only did staying busy spare her from her cousins, but it kept her from moping around, overwhelmed with thoughts of Perry Butler. Imogen had not seen him in two days, and she hoped that meant he had given up on whatever strangeness had seized him the other day.

He had intimated that there was *something* between them. Then he had gone so far as to say that the notion frightened her. *Ludicrous.* They were no romance in the making. Indeed not. She would not be so foolish as to believe in that bit of fancy.

Casting aside such thoughts, she fixed her gaze on her cousin across the table. Winnie was in the middle of a story about one of her friend's daughters who eloped with an Italian painter.

At least these evening dinners weren't too miserable. Winifred monopolized the conversation, as she was wont to do, and never seemed aware of how little Imogen spoke.

Usually Imogen was able to eat and excuse herself shortly after dessert with no raised eyebrows.

In the mornings, she made a point to be gone before they rose for breakfast. Thankfully they were late risers.

According to Winnie's letter, they would only be staying two nights before resuming their way north, but it was starting to feel quite the prolonged stopover. Two nights had come and gone and they were still here. Imogen began to wonder: *When would they depart?*

Imogen knew the question had to be put forth. She had not anticipated they would stay this long. She needed to know there was an end in sight. Gathering her nerve, she asked, "How much longer do you intend to stay here, Winnie?"

She directed all comments to her cousin. She could not bring herself to speak directly to Edgar. Thankfully no one seemed to notice the snub. Oh, Edgar likely noticed, but Imogen did not care what he thought.

"Oh." Winifred lifted her napkin from her lap and patted her lips daintily. "Well, it's just been so lovely here." Her gaze darted to her husband.

"Have I not been saying how lovely it's been visiting with Uncle Winston and Imogen, Edgar?"

"Mm-hmm." He nodded as he chewed, lifting a forkful of cabbage and peas to his mouth. "Indeed. Indeed."

"It's going to be a struggle to tear ourselves away."

A non-answer if Imogen ever heard one . . . and that was perhaps the most concerning point of all. They seemed unable or unwilling to tell her when this visit might come to an end.

Mrs. Garry gathered Papa's empty plate, sending Imogen a meaningful and rather desperate look that seemed to say, *please tell me these people aren't going to be here forever.*

Imogen knew they added considerable work to the household. It was just Cook and Mrs. Garry tending to the house with occasional help from Molly and Mrs. Garry's nephew when he wasn't attending school.

Imogen pitched in when she could, but much of her days were spent executing Papa's duties. He no longer managed the number of visits to parishioners as he once did. Whenever he accomplished a call, it wearied him so much that he usually returned home to collapse in his chair by the hearth and nap for the rest of the day with Mrs. Garry doting on him, making certain he ate and drank whilst Imogen went about the shire seeing to his flock.

Mrs. Garry's distress at the imposition of their guests was understandable. It was difficult enough for Mrs. Garry keeping the house with only Cook and Molly to occasionally assist, but waiting hand and foot on Winnie went above and beyond her duties. Imogen winced. She would likely offer forth her resignation if she had to wait much longer on the demanding woman, longstanding loyalty to the Bates family or not.

"So you have no definitive departure date?" she pressed, determined to get an answer.

Papa frowned slightly. It was ill-mannered and apparently it did not escape his notice, even as absentminded as he was these days.

"My, my, coz. You sound almost eager to be rid of us." Winnie wagged her fork at Imogen in rebuke, sending tiny bits of ham and grease flying onto the tablecloth. She didn't even blink at the mess, merely fixed her gaze on Imogen.

"No. Not at all," she lied.

Mrs. Garry gave her a pointed look as she lowered a dish of bread rolls down before Papa on the table.

As Edgar's mouth was stuffed full of ham, the juices from which ran down his chin unchecked, he grunted in happy approval and snapped at

Mrs. Garry, gesturing for her to fetch him the steaming rolls. Imogen shuddered in distaste. He was revolting. What had she ever seen in the wretched man?

Mrs. Garry's lips tightened, but she said not a word. She waited for Papa to select his roll and then rounded the table to serve Edgar.

"What do you do for entertainment in your little hamlet here, coz?" Winnie asked, avoiding Imogen's original question regarding their plans for departure.

She exhaled, wishing Winnie would answer that question but realizing that perhaps she already had. Perhaps her silence on the matter was answer enough.

Imogen plucked agitatedly at the edges of her napkin on her lap. "Oh, I visit with members of the congregation. Help Papa with his sermons." No way would she admit to Winnie that Papa's mind could no longer track long enough to write a full sermon from beginning to end. It was what Imogen did. It was all part of pretending that Papa was still a man in full possession of himself. "I tend to the garden. Help Mrs. Garry about the place."

"Oh, it all sounds perfectly menial. How dreadful!" Winnie's pretty face pulled into an exaggerated grimace. "How do you abide it, coz? You really should have more staff to support you. It's uncivilized," she said as though that was a matter which Imogen could easily change.

Her cousin had only ever led a life of privilege . . . to such a degree that she could not fathom anyone living differently than she did. But then Imogen supposed that was the nature of privilege—the inability to empathize with other people and their lot in life.

Imogen nodded dispassionately, not at all inclined to explain her situation or how she far preferred this lifestyle to that of living in Town. "I am sure you will want to leave soon for far greener pastures that provide more diversions worthy of you."

"Oh, in good time. It has been much too long since we've had a visit. Remember the fun we used to have?"

"Yes," Imogen agreed. "We did have fun together." When they were girls. Before Winnie had married. "I do miss those days." Yet Imogen knew those days were gone. They could not go back to that time.

"How about we venture out tomorrow?" Winnie suggested. "I've been here nearly a week. Why don't you show me more of your dear little shire. You have a baroness here, do you not? And a duke? Where are these most exalted personages? I would very much enjoy accompanying you on your calls to them." She wrinkled her nose. "Not to that lady farmer you visited today."

Imogen took the gig and called on Mercy today. She had gone on the pretext that it was Mercy's birthday. That was next week, in truth, but no one contradicted her on the matter. Mrs. Garry did not question it; merely packed a sweet bread for Imogen to take her to her friend.

"Mercy Kittinger is my friend," she defended.

"You *should* be socializing more with the baroness or this duke."

"Well, the duke is not in residence." Whomever he was and wherever he might be. "No one knows when he will arrive." If he did at all.

"Oh, that is unfortunate. What of the baroness?"

"Um—"

"The baroness is lovely. And quite fond of our Imogen," Papa unhelpfully chimed in to the conversation.

"Oh, la! Well done, coz. You made no mention you had such lofty friends. We must call on her."

Imogen sighed. She supposed getting Winnie out of the house was the least she owed to Mrs. Garry, and the sooner she exhausted all the interesting aspects of Shropshire (interesting to Winnie), the sooner Winnie and Edgar would leave. Perhaps. She could only hope.

"Will you join us, Edgar?" Winnie turned to her husband to ask.

Imogen tensed, hoping the answer was no. She had managed to avoid any conversation with Edgar beyond superficial niceties. She was proud of herself for that. She did not relish squishing herself into the gig alongside him and Winnie for an afternoon social call.

"Depends, my dear. When do you plan to go? You know I've been quite enjoying my afternoon naps since arriving here. And Uncle Winston's cook makes the loveliest iced biscuits. Far better than anything our own cook ever bakes." Ah. All the naps and iced biscuits explained his thickening middle then.

Winnie looked expectantly at Imogen. "What time shall we depart tomorrow?"

She took a breath. It appeared they would be calling on the baroness tomorrow. Never mind that she had not even agreed. Winnie would have her way. She always did. Evidently she had wanted Edgar. Imogen had not realized it when she was in London all those years ago. Her cousin had shown him no partiality. Several young gentlemen had been courting her at the time and she had reveled in all their attentions.

In any case, Imogen was so very glad Winnie had snared him. Now she realized marrying Edgar would have been a grave mistake, leading to a future of unhappiness.

Even as uncertain as her life was these days

with Papa's questionable health, she preferred her life, *this* life, to the one she had so desperately longed for at ten and eight. Thankfully, her prayers had gone unanswered on that score.

She might be an aging spinster, but she felt happier and more fulfilled than she possibly could be in any alternate reality as Mrs. Edgar Fernsby. Just the thought made her shudder. Happy alone was better than miserable with someone. She heartily believed that, and she wondered why more women did not subscribe to that notion. She'd seen evidence of plenty of unhappily married women. She acknowledged that some women did not have the luxury of choice. She was fortunate in that regard because she did, and she never forgot it.

For some reason, Perry flashed across her mind. *Mr. Butler.* She needed to keep things in their proper place—starting with his name.

He had shown her what manner of husband he would be. At least in the marriage bed. He'd given her a taste of that passion. Just a taste . . . and now she longed for the full glorious meal.

Heat flushed through her, starting at her face and spreading through her body, pooling into the parts that he had paid particularly ardent attention. She did not think she would ever be able to touch herself there without thinking of him and remembering what he did to her on that rock.

She had fled from their conversation, letting Mrs. Merrit haul her away. Cowardly of her, she knew. As tempting as it was to see him again, nothing could come of it. It was just lust and to be avoided—*he* was to be avoided.

Desire was ephemeral in nature. It was not substantive. It did not last. Her experience with Edgar had taught her that.

She gave herself a mental shake, casting off all such thoughts of him. They were neither here nor there anymore.

She had fulfilled her promise. They were done. She had to remember that and focus on going back to the way she was before. *Before* he fixed his attention on her. *Before* he touched her. *Before* she started to like him.

Before she knew to long for anything else, for anything more.

"PEREGRINE? WHERE ARE you going?"

His mother's lofty tones stopped him cold. He turned with a respectful smile on his face, the familiar longing to have his own home, his own independence, seizing him. "Into town."

"At this hour?" She stood at the top of the stairs, wrapped in her elegant dressing gown.

The hour was not so very late. They'd had dinner and he had even sat with her for a while in the drawing room afterwards, pretending as though it felt normal to do so—as though it could be his life.

"I won't be gone very long."

"Where could you be going at this hour?" she pressed.

"For a ride."

"At night?"

"There's a full moon."

That was not true, but his mother did not know that. She was an abject *in*doorswoman. The only time she stepped outside was on the way to her carriage.

"Hm." She looked down her slim nose at him. He felt her disapproval keenly. It did not help that she loomed above him several steps. He swallowed back his aggravation at being questioned. He was a grown man. He had not apprised his mother of his activities since he was a lad.

"Do not be too late," she directed. "You'll be tired tomorrow and I wanted to go over our upcoming travel plans. We have several decisions to make. I'd like to visit Aunt Judith, but then there is your sister. She always expects me to be there for Thomas's birthday celebration."

This was his mother's life. These were his mother's plans. She was lumping him into them as though he were a child to be dragged along with her.

It was miserable.

He supposed he should be grateful for her unwavering support—even though she was the cause for the current circumstances of his life—but he longed for his freedom. Her actions might have determined his present situation, but it did not determine his future. That was up to Perry.

"Ah. I won't be about much tomorrow. I have some errands. Do not wait on me. Feel free to decide whatever you like." She did not know it yet, but he would not be accompanying her.

"Errands? Such as?" She crossed her arms over her chest.

"Just some business to attend to."

"Business? What manner of business do you have in Shropshire?" The level of derision in her voice was insulting. Then her expression suddenly transformed into one of hopefulness. She grasped the railing and descended the stairs. "Is it a marital prospect? Did you sort out that vile . . . matter?" She fluttered her fingers, clearly unable to put to words the rumor that he had the pox.

He nodded and waved a hand reassuringly. "The rumors have been put to rest." At least he assumed so. It had been two days since he bumped into Imogen leaving Mrs. Hathaway's house, when she had assured him everything was set to rights. He had not verified it one way or another.

Not that he was overly concerned anymore.

People could talk. People always talked. He was not worried as his mother was. His future did not depend on finding a rich heiress. At least not anymore. He'd let that particular ambition go, replacing it with actual ambition.

"Well, that is a relief." His mother stopped two steps above him. "Are you calling on the baroness tomorrow? Or perhaps Mr. Blankenship?"

"No. That is not my errand."

His mother's smile faltered. "No?"

"No," he confirmed, and before she could press for more information, he started away. "If you'll excuse me, Mother. I'll see you in the morning."

He left her staring after him, feeling her disappointment like a dagger in his back as he stepped out into the evening and closed the front door to the dower house firmly behind him.

He made quick work of fetching his mount from the stables and saddling the horse himself. He rode for town, his destination an amorphous thing in his mind. He rode without putting it into definitive words, but he knew.

He knew as well as he knew the shape of his own hand. It was instinctive. A burning impulse that he could not resist. He felt it in his bones, in the rush of blood through his veins, in the primal pump of his heart.

He was going to see her.

Chapter Nineteen ❧

$\mathcal{I}$mogen was still awake, the lamp beside her bed only just put out, and her head still settling into the pillow when a scrabbling sounded at her window that had her lurching upright with a gasp.

Her first thought was highwaymen, and then she called herself ten kinds of silly. That's what came of reading too many gothic romances before bed and taking to heart Mrs. Hathaway's tales of wild rogues holding up coaches on the road south to London.

She fumbled in the dark, groping for the lamp, just managing to illuminate the room in time to spot the man emerging halfway through her bedchamber window, one long leg slung over the sill and a hessian boot on her floor. Not a highwayman. She recognized the dark hair and profile of Perry at once and quickly swallowed back the scream in her throat.

Gulping down the sound, she pressed a hand over her galloping heart, watching as he unfolded himself into a standing position.

She *should* scream. In many ways he was as dangerous to her as a highwayman. Ever since their kiss she could not trust herself with him any more than she could trust him.

Kiss? Ha! What transpired between them at Mrs. Blankenship's garden had been child's play compared to what took place at the pond. The things they had done on that rock were scandalous. She did not know men did those things. She did not know that a woman could *feel* those things.

She flung back the coverlet and jumped to her feet. Snatching a pillow off her bed, she tossed it at him. It bounced off him like a feather.

A man had invaded her bedchamber. She should be terrified, but she could only summon outrage and reach for another pillow.

She *should* be screeching with all the quivering virtue of a maiden. It would be the ordinary and expected reaction. *If* she were ordinary. And yet she knew she was not. She was a spinster with more carnal knowledge than she ought to possess.

She took a measured breath. It would do no good to cause a commotion. She would spare Papa the ordeal and scandal of discovering Mr. Butler in her bedchamber. His health was fragile. She would handle this herself as she did most all things since Mama died and Papa was struck down with his first fit of apoplexy. She did not need anyone taking care of her or managing this situation for her. She was a capable person. She could send him on his way *back* at her window all by herself.

Hugging the pillow in front of her like a shield, she demanded, "How dare you! What are you doing climbing through my window? Are you mad?"

He dusted off his clothing. "Oh, I am a great many things right now, none of which I had ever imagined, so that is quite possible. I would not discount it."

She closed her mouth with a snap, absorbing that. She assessed him, taking in his broad chest lifting on several labored breaths. He was strong and fit. She did not think a simple climb up her trellis would wind him so greatly. So there was something more happening here. The way he stared back at her, intent and devouring, she had a suspicion that it was something to do with the crackling energy swelling between them.

She looked him up and down, noting that he had eschewed his customary dress again. It was just his boots, trousers and a fine lawn shirt. No vest. No jacket even in the chill evening air. She inhaled, wondering why her lungs felt so uncomfortably tight. It was as though she could not draw enough air. That V of bare skin at his throat and the top of his chest mesmerized her. She studied that patch of skin, marveling at how warm and inviting it looked. She moistened her lips and crossed her arms tightly, needing to pin her hands to keep them from reaching out to touch him.

Goodness. One illicit afternoon with him and she was insatiable. She did not even know herself anymore. Apparently she could not be in his company or within five feet of proximity without wanting to put hands on him, without wanting his hands and his mouth on her again. *More.* She wanted more. To fly out of her skin again.

She sniffed and glanced down at herself, suddenly conscious that she wore only her nightgown. A prim floor-to-the-neck nightgown, but a nightgown nonetheless—even if it was hidden behind a plump pillow.

No man had seen her in so little clothing before—well, in a manner. She had not fully disrobed with Perry at the pond, but he had seen plenty of her from the waist down. Her cheeks went scalding hot at the memory.

Mr. Butler followed her gaze, tracking her form, up and down. Something passed over his eyes. A dark storm slid over the icy gray and she shivered.

She fiddled with the high collar at her throat. "You cannot be here. We have houseguests. And my father is just down the hall."

He cocked his head and looked decidedly unmoved. "Reasons that don't seem to affect me." He shrugged. "I wanted to see you."

"You are not above the rules, Mr. Butler. You cannot simply barge into my chamber."

"I didn't barge. I was quite stealthy. *You* gave me the idea. I seem to recall you scaling the ivy escaping your house. It was easy enough to slip inside."

She advanced on him and stabbed him in the center of the chest with a finger. Recalling her vow not to touch him, she quickly withdrew her finger. "This is inexcusable."

"And what of *your* behavior? Are you so above reproach, Miss Bates? You who creates rumors with the same ease one sips tea."

"I've made amends for that and your name is restored," she hotly defended. Doing so was to have severed their connection. There should be no reason for him to be here now. She had done nothing more to anger him or foil his matrimonial plans. She had not *recently* invited his wrath to precipitate this intrusion. "This is highly improper."

"You are quite fetching in your outrage." A corner of his mouth kicked up mockingly and she knew he was recalling their tryst at the pond. And why not? She had been thinking of it in an unending loop since then.

She shook her head, her cheeks like fire now. "Stop that. I think that you—"

A gentle knock sounded at her door and they both fell instantly silent.

She blinked, staring at the door like it was something alive—a beast that might jump out and bite her if she made so much as a move.

Moments ticked past and she began to doubt, to hope, that she had misheard it. That there was no knock.

Until another came, vibrating on the air.

Imogen looked back at Perry in horror. Had they been too loud? Had they roused someone? Papa?

Perry looked at her with a mild expression that seemed to ask: *Expecting someone?*

Of course, he was not concerned. His reputation was not at stake here. Only hers.

Shaking her head, she stepped forward to the door. Flattening a palm against it, she swallowed thickly and cleared her throat, asking in what she hoped was a normal voice and not one that revealed that she had a man in her bedchamber. "Yes?"

A whispered voice floated back through the door. "Imogen, it's me."

Me happened to be Edgar.

Repelled by the sound of his voice, she stepped several paces back, putting herself side by side with Perry, as though they were allies in this instance and not . . . *whatever it was they were*. Adversaries seemed too strong a description, but they were certainly not friends and definitely not allies. They were . . . something else.

"Friend of yours?" he asked, an undercurrent of tension vibrating in his voice.

Imogen waved a hand wildly in front of her lips. "Shush," she whispered and then to the door, a fraction louder: "Go away, Edgar."

Too late, she realized her mistake. She should not have said his name. She winced.

Perry's eyes narrowed on her. "Edgar?" he asked, his dagger gaze shooting to the door. "Who is this Edgar?"

"My cousin's husband." She mouthed the words more than she spoke them, but from the look in his eyes he had no difficulty reading her lips.

"Please, Imogen." Edgar's hissed voice continued through the door. "Don't be like this."

She shook her head. Unbelievable. They had scarcely spoken since he and Winnie arrived here, and now he dared to come to her chamber in the middle of the night.

"Go away, Edgar. Leave me alone."

A flush of angry color crept up Perry's face. "Has he been harassing you?"

She expelled a breath. His mere presence in this house was a form of harassment.

"Um. Not precisely." She shifted her weight from foot to foot, glaring at the door, wishing Edgar gone—wishing he and Winnie had never come at all—wishing for an end to this untenable situation.

"Not precisely," he echoed, shaking his head in a way that felt actually restrained and that only spiked her temper. Blasted man! What did he have to be angry about?

She curled her hands at her sides to stop herself from striking Perry in the chest. That would be unnecessary contact, and it seemed very advisable that she *not* touch him. Even as cross as she felt, she was still under a heady haze of desire when it came to him.

She was not the one who had done something wrong here. She had one man scratching at her door in the middle of the night and another one standing in the center of her bedchamber through no doing of her own.

He continued, "How does a man *not precisely* harass you? He either does or does not. What's he doing at your door begging entrance into your bedchamber?"

Was that accusation in his voice? Did he think she had a lover in this house? That she would take a married man (her cousin's husband, no less!) into her bed.

Was he *jealous*?

The idea intrigued her more than it should. She did not want Perry's interest or his jealousy or his *anything*. Truly.

"You are one to talk," she shot back at him. "I did not invite him." She waved at him. "Just as I did not invite *you*!"

He angled his head sharply. "Oh, come now. You want me here."

She blinked, heat flashing through her. "Oh!" She puffed out an indignant breath. "The arrogance of you."

A familiar squeak scraped over the air. The noise was slight, but she knew it well. She had been meaning to oil the latch for weeks. She turned to stare at her bedchamber door once again, gawking in distress as the latch began to turn down.

Edgar was entering her chamber.

Chapter Twenty ⤙

$\mathcal{T}$here had never been a need for locks in the vicarage before, but now Imogen yearned for one on her bedchamber door. And locks on her window, for that matter, as this was, apparently, a night for intruders.

The door swung inward and Edgar slunk into her bedchamber in naught but his dressing gown. As though he was in the habit of strolling into her chamber all the time.

She felt the tension radiating from Perry beside her, but she could not take her horrified gaze off Edgar. The wood planks of her floor creaked beneath the weight of his bare feet. She could not believe he was here—that his long, bony feet were treading over her floor.

He wore a haughty grin that quickly faded away once his gaze swept over the room—once he realized she was not alone and there were three of them in the chamber.

She actually felt a flash of relief for Perry's presence beside her.

Edgar's gaze shot between her and Perry several times before settling on Perry. He squared his shoulders in his floral-patterned dressing robe as he looked Perry up and down. "What are you doing in here, sirrah?" he demanded.

"What are you doing in here?" Perry countered, taking a threatening step forward. Imogen's hand shot out to close around his arm, stalling him from doing anything rash.

Edgar opened and closed his mouth several times before turning his accusing gaze on Imogen. "Imogen? What is the meaning of this?"

"My exact question to you," she returned, lifting her chin up a defiant notch. "What is the meaning of you entering my room uninvited?"

"Indeed," Perry cut in. "As you can see. She already has company."

"Perry," she hissed, mortified. He made it seem as though they . . . as though they were in the midst of an assignation.

"Perry, is it?" Edgar asked tightly.

"And you're Edgar, Imogen's cousin's husband. I wonder what your wife would think of you here? Hm? Shall we call for her and ask for her thoughts on the matter?"

Edgar's lips pressed into a hard line.

"No?" Perry tilted his head.

Edgar answered with a hard shake of his head.

"Sound decision." Perry sent a long measuring look her way before facing Edgar again. "Permit me to suggest another sound decision for you."

Edgar visibly swallowed. "And what would that be?"

Yes. What would that be?

"Pack your things and leave here in the morning."

"I beg your pardon?" Edgar sputtered. "It is not your place to—"

"You heard him." Imogen found her voice, appreciating that at least she now had the ammunition to hasten Edgar's departure. "You're not welcome here, Edgar." He was demented to think he ever would be, especially after this latest offense. "Take Winnie and be on your way at first light."

Edgar attempted a smile. "Come now, Imogen. We cared for each other once."

"No. That is not how I remember it. *Caring* does not describe our past association." She knew that now. Pain and manipulation best described their history. "I don't know what you thought would happen here tonight, but you need to be gone from this place." Imogen would not feel safe in her bed until he was gone. She would not sleep a wink as long as he was under her roof. "Be gone in the morning or I will tell Winnie what you attempted here tonight."

His expression grew tight and pinched, his lips compressed as though he'd sucked on something sour. His gaze flicked back and forth between her and Perry. "Very well. I see that I made a mistake."

"Yes. You did."

"Well." He nodded once. "Good night." He left then, closing the door behind him with a smart click.

She faced Perry again, her shoulders sagging a bit. It was on the edge of her tongue to thank him, but she stopped herself. She would not thank him. He should not be here. She quickly put aside her relief for his presence in her chamber. Helping her did not absolve him from invading her room.

Sighing, she buried her face in her hands for a moment before lifting her head and settling her gaze back on Perry. "You should go."

"You want me to leave you?" He glanced to the door with a baleful look, as though he longed to go through it after Edgar. "There's no lock on that door and he's still in this house with you."

"Very well." Nodding, she moved to her desk and picked up the chair. Walking it across the chamber, she secured it beneath the latch. "There now. Satisfied?"

His lips curled. "That would not stop a toddler."

"Well, fortunate for me there is not a toddler in the house."

His lips twitched. "Only your cousin's randy husband."

"I think I'm safe from him tonight. And tomorrow, in fact." She gave a small wincing smile. "Thanks to you." Very well. That was a semblance of gratitude.

"You stood up for yourself quite admirably," he said.

Silence stretched between them. That crackling energy was back.

"I know I should not have barged in here. I hope I did not . . ." His voice faded. Clearing his throat, he finished, "I wanted to see you."

She motioned to the window. "Apparently."

"We were interrupted the other day—"

"We'd said everything that needed to be said." She shook her head. "*I* said everything I had to say." She wrapped her arms tighter around the pillow she still clutched, hugging it herself.

"You said a year from now you won't cross my thoughts, and I need you to know that's not true."

"You can't know that," she whispered.

"I can. I do. You're under my skin. A fire in my blood. I've never felt this . . . never wanted a woman the way I want you." He stepped forward, slowly closing the distance between them. "I'll never forget you."

She inhaled. Exhaled. She'd been fooled by seductive words before, but none like this. None she felt as tangibly as this.

Trust did not come easily for her, but she understood what he was offering. It was temptation. More of what happened at the pond. No promises beyond. That's it, and she'd take it.

Against her better judgment, her hand stretched out to rest on his chest, palm down against the cool fabric of his shirt, his skin warm through the linen, his heartbeat fast beneath her fingers. She smiled shakily. Her heart was beating just as fast. Faster even.

His hand followed, his bigger one covering hers. She sighed, reveling in the sensation. All that warm skin and strength over hers. Suddenly he bent down and swept her up in his arms. She swallowed back a small yelp.

It was a short walk to her bed, both terrifying and thrilling. She trembled in his arms and closed her eyes in a long, fortifying blink.

He lowered her down on the bed and proceeded to strip off his shirt, grabbing it from behind his neck and pulling it over his head in one smooth move, revealing the muscled perfection of his chest. She watched, still hugging her pillow as though it were protective armor.

The candlelight danced over his body, and her gaze followed it, licking over every inch of his smooth skin, every hollow and curving muscle.

Her palms tingled, imagining the texture, the sensation of him. Her fingers flexed in the softness of the pillow. Her breath fell harshly, eyes burning for lack of blinking. She shook her head once, hard and swift. It did no good. She couldn't manage to gawk less.

Accept this. Take what he's offering—take what you want.

The dark whisper didn't have to work very hard to convince her.

He bent and removed both boots, not tossing them, but setting them carefully beside the bed as though not to make a sound. Straightening, he fastened those slate-gray eyes on her.

His hands moved to his trousers and then stopped, lingering for a long moment. Her gaze locked with his. He arched a dark eyebrow in question. This was it. He was giving her a choice.

She nodded.

He removed the last of his attire, shamelessly and unabashedly exposing himself—gloriously, beautifully naked. More beautiful than any statue she'd giggled and gawked at alongside

Winnie at the museum in Town . . . and certainly more abundantly proportioned. Heat swamped her face as that specific part of his anatomy grew before her eyes.

She tossed her pillow aside and propped up on her elbows, trying to peer around him to see more, to see all of him.

"You want to see me?" Still arching that dark eyebrow of his at her, he turned, rotating slowly. Her stomach dipped and twisted at the sight of his derriere. Tight and round, with an indent along the side of each curved and flexing buttock. Who knew the sight could be so arousing? It was . . . mouthwatering. Saliva rushed over her tongue.

She held out her hand, extending it to him.

He may have barged into her bedchamber, but she was inviting him into her bed.

Stepping forward, he lowered one knee onto the bed. His hand seized the hem of her nightgown.

Her hands shot to the little buttons at her throat, feverishly liberating them of their constraints. When she'd freed enough of them, he tugged the nightgown the rest of the way, dragging it up and over her head and tossing it to the floor.

He looked her over, staring at her face. It seemed just as important to him as the rest of her. He stroked her skin, sliding the rough pads of his fingers along the curve of her cheek. His entire hand spanned half her face and it made her feel almost delicate—a wholly new sensation. She had never been considered a small female, after all, but she felt like he could wreck her in the best, most glorious sense.

His hand continued its exploration, moving down her throat, tracing her collarbone. As each moment of prolonged contact passed, her breathing grew raspy and shallower. Her blood pounded, hot and heavy in her veins.

Her eyes dipped, straying to his swollen manhood jutting forward, so close now that she could reach out and touch it. *And why not?*

He was here for the offering. She wanted to touch it. *Him.*

She yearned for him with a fierceness that should have shamed her, but it did not. Perhaps a modicum of this had always been there. This longing. This craving. For no other reason had his unkind words hurt her so much when she was a girl at his birthday party—or all those times she had visited his house as a child and been largely ignored by him. He'd enamored her. She'd thought him as beautiful and glittering as some distant star. And that was the truth she had never permitted herself to acknowledge before.

Now that star was before her. Bright and burning, but hers to touch and hold.

Perhaps this was it. *He* was it. Her one chance, her one taste of passion until she returned to a life of spinsterhood.

Holding his gaze, she scooted back on her elbows, her arms trembling with tension as she made more room for him on her bed.

He watched her for a long moment, his gaze scouring her in a hot sweep that she felt deep in her bones.

"You are certain you want this?" he rasped, his voice a husky growl—the words like a gauntlet thrown down, waiting for her to pick it up and accept. And of course, she would.

She nodded her assent and he lowered his second knee to the bed. The mattress dipped from his weight. He moved in, walking on his knees like a great seductive beast intent on devouring her, his muscles undulating beneath his smooth taut skin. Her thighs instinctively parted for him, welcoming him in, even as she was both thrilled and petrified.

The intensity of his gaze as he looked down at her was like a physical touch. She forgot to breathe under that stare. Her hands fluttered to rest on his shoulders—so delightfully, shockingly naked.

"So lovely," he murmured, brushing the hair back off her forehead.

She laughed nervously. That was the first time

someone said that . . . someone who actually meant it. And he meant it. He was not a pretender. Not a man to say things he did not mean. She knew that much about him.

He smiled wickedly, knowingly, as he settled deeper between her knees, the warmth of his body, his skin, singeing the insides of her thighs. His chest pressed against hers, grazing her sensitive nipples into stiff points. She arched her spine, enjoying the sensation, craving more, to which he delivered.

Dipping his head, he sucked the tip of her breast deep into his warm mouth. His teeth scraped the hard point, spiking her need.

She cried out at the intense pleasure and he quickly covered her mouth, gently admonishing her with a "*Ssh*" against her ear. "You don't want to wake the house, do you?" She felt his smile against the whorls of her ear.

She nodded and he slid his hand away, dragging it back down to her breast, fondling the mound until her entire body was an inferno, boiling from the inside and ready to burst.

His manhood nudged at her core, the hard heaviness of him rubbing against her. The intimacy of him over her, splayed between her thighs, prodding her, left her gasping, desperate to be filled. Her inner muscles clenched, aching with need.

Perry seized her lips in a consuming kiss. There was no sliding into it. No gentle easing. Nothing soft or mild. His tongue delved into her mouth, stroking her own tongue until she moaned, a writhing wreck beneath him. She pushed up toward the hard length of him.

He seized her head with both hands as their kiss grew wild and hungry. His hand descended on her breast in a fiery trail. He tweaked her nipple, rolling and pinching it, coiling her passion higher, tighter. She felt that familiar swell building and coming over her again. Just like at the pond with the warm rock bed under her. This time she had a soft bed and it was an improvement.

The head of him prodded her opening. Moisture rushed between her legs. She wiggled her hips eagerly until his manhood began pushing inside her.

She inhaled sharply at the tip of him entering her.

He paused. "Is this . . . do you want me to stop?"

She shook her head. "No!" The very idea of him stopping filled her with panic.

He smiled slightly, knowingly, and then gave the faintest teasing nudge, deepening his penetration. The motion had her puffing and wiggling. "Say it. Say what you want," he encouraged.

"What I want?" She was confused . . . and in torment and could scarcely form a thought.

"My cock," he supplied. "You want my cock, Imogen? Ask for it."

At his profane speech, she grew wetter. The ache between her legs was almost painful now.

Anxious for all of him, she pushed up against his hardness, seeking relief.

"Say it," he instructed. "Cock."

"Cock," she snapped. Then softer, pleading, need thick in her throat: "I want your cock. Please."

He gave her what she wanted and met her hunger, lodging himself deeply, seating himself all the way with a rumbling groan.

There was no resistance. Just a general stretching and burning that wasn't completely comfortable, but any discomfort diminished alongside the delicious friction of him as he set a pace, moving inside her.

His lips brushed her head. "Your quim feels so good . . . perfect."

Nodding wildly, she panted, her fingers clenching on his shoulders, hanging on as he withdrew and drove inside her.

Her nails scored his shoulders. Moaning, she wrapped her legs around his waist.

His fingers clasped the generous flesh of her thighs and she felt the imprint of each one like a fiery mark. He growled deeply and thrust again. And again. And again.

He reached between them, finding her slick warmth, that tiny nub of pleasure he had lavished such attention on at the pond, and put his fingers to it, pushing and rolling and rubbing until she began to tremble.

The pressure gave way inside her. Snapped like a band. Shudders racked her, starting at her core and eddying out through her body as she burst.

She collapsed back on the bed, her body a limp, boneless heap. Gasping and winded, her chest heaved as though she'd run a great distance. He thrust a few more times and followed fast on her heels with his own release. He quickly withdrew from her body at the last moment and spent himself in her bedding.

He dropped down on the bed beside her with his arm wrapped around her, tucking her into his side. His breath fell hard beside her, ruffling her hair. "That was . . ."

"Lovely," she supplied.

"Lovely," he agreed with a chuckle.

"Marvelous," she added.

"Yes. That, too." His hand stroked her arm in gentle, rhythmic movements, up and down, from her elbow to her shoulder.

"That's nice." She sighed and nestled closer into his side. Just for a little while.

It couldn't last. She knew that, but for just a moment she would enjoy it. She'd enjoy him. She would revel in his closeness, in his touch, in the warmth of his body and not think about how he would eventually have to leave her.

She settled her hand on his chest, enjoying the sensation of his heart beneath her palm, wondering if it matched the beat of her own.

Chapter Twenty-One ❧

$\mathcal{I}$mogen woke with a long luxurious stretch. She let her hands drop above her head and remain there. She had no difficulty recollecting what had transpired last night. Even as the early morning light streamed through the window, she recalled every moment of what happened in her bed. And if her memory was somehow faulty, she had only her body to remind her with all its new and unfamiliar aches. The delicious soreness asserted itself any time she made the slightest move.

She had not meant to fall asleep, but she lost that battle. She'd fought to stay awake, unwilling to miss a moment of their time together, but her tiredness had won out. Perry made for a most comfortable pillow.

She'd slept hard, not even stirring when he left her bed. She had been dimly aware of him leaving, recalling his weight lifting from the mattress, his form dressing beside the bed in the purpling air that hinted at the coming dawn.

Of course, he had left her. He couldn't stay through the morning. They weren't anything more than a fleeting affair. One night. That's all she had wanted—all she could have.

She poked and prodded around inside her head. There was a whirl of emotions in there, but not regret. She didn't regret what she had done. It might be all she ever had. One night with someone holding her and loving her. Her only intimacy with another human. No. She would not regret that.

She stretched again and her hand brushed something on the pillow. A faint crinkling sounded and she turned her head, glimpsing the parchment. She couldn't help smiling. So she had not been left completely alone, after all. Reaching for it, she held the note up over her face, her eyes scanning the neat masculine scrawl in the light of dawn.

I'll see you at church. I'll be the man staring at you the entire time.

Her smile deepened slowly. She could not help it. As unaffected as she wanted to be, as calmly and levelheadedly as she wanted to approach this thing that had happened between them, she could not help it.

One hand clutched the letter, bringing it to her chest whilst the fingers of her other hand covered her lips, as though she could somehow suppress that smile and the twinge of hope stirring inside her.

Hope that perhaps this was more than a single foray into passion.

Hope that it could be something more—that it could last.

PERRY COULD NOT look away from her.

He was aware that it was not the most inconspicuous behavior, but there was no preventing his gaze from going to Imogen, the proverbial moth to flame.

She, much to his chagrin, did not seem to be afflicted with the same compulsion. She sat straight in her pew, facing forward, listening to her father haltingly deliver his sermon with a serene expression on her face.

The baroness and her daughter occupied the space beside Imogen, so he could only assume that the Bates's houseguests had departed. There was no sight of that scoundrel, Edgar, and he was relieved to know that he and his wife had indeed left. He couldn't have stayed away if the man still resided with Imogen under her roof.

Imogen looked fetching in a pale cream gown with thin lavender stripes. So modest. A customary costume for demure young ladies. Only he knew what she looked like beneath it. Only he knew what it felt like to have her claw his back and the memory made him instantly hard. He brought his prayer book over his lap, hiding his erection.

He had full carnal knowledge of Imogen Bates, and he didn't know how he would ever pretend otherwise.

The service ended, and they all filed outside. His mother lingered to talk with Imogen's father. She'd always had a fondness for the man. He supposed that was because of the hours his father had spent with the Reverend Bates.

She then moved on to chat with the baroness, the only other person she deemed worthy of her company.

He found his own spot to stand nearby. Out of the way. Against a tree. A safe distance to watch Imogen. She played the gracious hostess, listening to every blue-haired lady with what appeared to be keen interest. Not simply because it was her role to do so, but because she *did* care. Because there was not a fiber of her being that did not care about others.

Had he really compared her to a rotten lemon? He shook his head. What a fool he had been. Everything about her delighted him. He could listen to her talk about wheat mites or anything else and be quite content.

She slipped back inside the church. Most of the congregation had thinned out by now. The vicar was once again in conversation with Perry's mother.

Perry glanced around and then slipped inside the church after Imogen.

He entered stealthily and she didn't look up from where she was gathering hymnals and stacking them.

He crept up behind her and circled her waist, hauling her flush against him.

She gasped, her hand flying to his arm wrapped around her waist.

He nuzzled the side of her hair and spoke into her ear, "I've missed you, Imogen Bates."

"Perry! It's just been a few hours since you last saw me." She laughed softly and then gasped again as he bit down softly on the lobe of her ear.

"Let's return to that warm bed of yours."

She slapped his arm lightly. "You should not be doing this here. What if we're seen?"

"Then where should we do this?" He unwrapped his arm from her waist and she turned to face him.

She stared at him in a scolding manner. "We shouldn't be doing it anywhere."

He frowned, not liking the notion of that at all. He brushed his thumb down the curve of her cheek. "You mean no more of this?"

She released a shuddery breath. "That was my understanding," she whispered.

He bent his head and kissed her long and deep. True. He might be hoping to seduce her and make her forget her reticence.

Lifting his head, he stared down at her, watching her as she slowly opened her eyes, looking up at him dreamily.

"You're incorrigible," she breathed.

"And you love it," he countered.

Her dreamlike haze dissipated and she stepped back, her expression admonishing. "Behave yourself," she lightly scolded.

His timing and choice of place could have been better, he supposed, because additional sunlight flooded into the church just then as the double doors opened.

"There you are, Mr. Butler," a voice intruded.

He turned to watch as Mrs. Berrycloth advanced down the center aisle in a dashing plum gown. No demure maidenly colors for her. He longed to see Imogen in such colors. Rich hues that brought out the amber in her brown eyes.

"Mrs. Berrycloth," he greeted.

The widow flashed a smile for Imogen. "Miss Bates." She then turned her full attention back to Perry. "I thought I might take you up on that offer for an afternoon walk."

He stared at her for a long moment, blinking and not recalling what she was talking about.

"Remember?" she prompted. "You suggested

we take a stroll together." She reached out and stroked his arm. "It wasn't that long ago. Have you forgotten it?"

Yes, indeed he had. An unfamiliar heat crept up his neck. He could feel Imogen's eyes on him.

He was no longer interested in pursuing any of the town's heiresses. He had been clear on that matter—to himself and Imogen. He would not use an heiress to secure his fate. Apparently, however, he had a few loose ends to tie up.

Mrs. Berrycloth was every bit an heiress even if she was not in the first flush of youth any longer. She had been married multiple times and had accrued quite a tidy sum that would last her lifelong, which was why he had ever thought to consider her as a potential wife in the first place.

The lack of a papa managing her purse strings could be seen as a benefit to many gentlemen. Additionally, she was an attractive woman. There was much appeal to her . . . and yet he did not find her appealing.

She was precisely what he had thought he wanted. The operative word being "had." Things had changed.

He had changed.

He did not want her, and yet he found himself presently in this awkward situation.

"Ah . . ." Again, his gaze went to Imogen. "When were you thinking—"

"Is right now an acceptable time for you? I walked to church this morning. You could escort me home." She stared at him in patient expectation.

"Ah . . ."

"On a lovely day like this?" Imogen suddenly spoke. "You both should go around the village and cut through the Pritchards' orchard."

His gaze whipped to Imogen at the cheerful suggestion. What was she doing? Was she actually throwing him at Mrs. Berrycloth? He narrowed his gaze on her. He was not a toy to be cast aside. Did she think herself done playing with him and ready to be discarded now?

"Ah! Delightful suggestion!" Mrs. Berrycloth's eyes danced and she looked at him in bright anticipation.

"I, ah. Yes." He nodded. "Of course." He motioned to the church doors, inviting her to precede him. There was no choice but to accept her request. He'd been asked directly by the lady, after all. It was the gentlemanly thing to do. He had no ready excuse and Imogen had just sanctioned the event. *Bloody hell.*

Mrs. Berrycloth passed him and proceeded down the center aisle, moving for the doors.

"What are you doing?" he growled for Imogen's ears alone.

She looked up at him with mock innocence. "You asked the lady to step out for a walk."

"That was a while ago. Before us."

She blinked at his plain language, and then slowly shook her head.

He pressed, "Is that what you want then? For me to spend my time with other women?" His gaze scoured her face, needing to hear her deny this.

She averted her gaze, turning her face away.

He glared at her furiously, whispering, "You know we have something here, Imogen. Do not run from this. Do not push me away."

She turned her gaze back on him, her eyes bright with an emotion that looked akin to pain. "What is the point? This cannot be."

"Says who? No. I do not accept that. And I don't believe you do either." With a disgusted shake of his head, he started down the aisle after Mrs. Berrycloth, only to stop at the sound of Imogen's harsh whisper.

"Do not be a fool, Perry. You know as well as I do that we cannot have anything lasting. And I'm not the manner of female to be any man's mistress."

He opened his mouth, but had no chance to speak before she was striding past with a resolute look on her face, leaving him standing in the aisle of the church, her footsteps a soft fading tread on the runner.

Chapter Twenty-Two ⤜

$\mathcal{I}$mogen turned down her bedding, longing for a night's sleep. There had been little slumber the night before and her brain needed a solid rest so that she could return to thinking properly.

She had stripped her bed and put fresh sheets on before they left for church this morning. Fortunately for her, she often did such household chores herself, so the act didn't raise any eyebrows. She didn't need Mrs. Garry handling her sheets after last night and seeing the evidence of her tryst.

The scrabbling at her window was familiar at this point, but still unexpected. Crossing her arms, she turned and watched warily as Perry pushed himself inside her bedchamber.

"I really need a lock on that window," she declared, uncrossing her arms over her chest.

He straightened, brushing at his clothing. "Then I would simply have to come through the front door and that wouldn't be very discreet. I'm happy to do that, of course, if you prefer."

She did *not* prefer that. She needn't have members of her household getting their hopes up that she was entertaining Mr. Butler's suit. And hopes would rise. They would be excited. Papa liked him very much, and Mrs. Garry had voiced her opinion more than once that Imogen should be happily married with children by now. Despite Imogen's reassurances, the housekeeper worried what would happen to Imogen when Papa was gone. She didn't want her left alone in the world.

"You're unconscionable," she accused.

"I'm unconscionable?" He pointed to himself. "You're the one pushing me at other women."

"You asked her to step out and walk with you."

His gray eyes fastened on her, brighter than she remembered. "That was before."

"Before what?" she snapped.

He shook his head and reached for her, both his hands seizing her by the arms and hauling her against him. His mouth covered hers and she didn't even hesitate. She melted against him, opening her mouth to him and kissing him feverishly in turn, meeting every thrust of his tongue with her own.

Her heart took flight inside her chest, wild as a bird set free.

They moved in unison, backing up toward the bed with shuffling steps, their mouths fused.

Everything sped to frenzied motion. The blood

rushed, a dull roar in her ears, and she thought she could hear the muffled beat of her heart through the roar.

Their lips broke just long enough for them to tear off their clothing. Garments flew on the air in a blur. They collided together again. This time gloriously naked, bare skin rubbing sinuously against bare skin.

Everything was fierce. Desperate. Violent in its intensity as they fell together on the bed.

Roaming, fondling hands. Kissing, biting lips. Panting, groaning breaths.

"You still think I want to court other women?" he growled, his hand skimming her face. Hard fingers delved into her hair, unraveling her plait as he gripped her scalp. His hot mouth crashed over hers before she could answer.

He settled atop her, finding his home between her thighs. It felt so right, so natural, to have him there, his hot cock aligned with the weeping seam of her.

His head dipped to kiss her breasts, and she moaned, arching her spine, wanting more.

His mouth closed around one nipple. Her fingers clenched on his flexing biceps. He shifted and his cock drove into her, sliding into her slick heat.

She panted, clinging, straining against him,

urging him closer as she tilted her hips, taking him in deeper, needing him as one needed water, air, sustenance.

"Yes, yes, yes."

His thrusts were relentless, the friction unbearable.

His eyes gleamed hotly down at her. He wrapped an arm around her waist and flipped them both, settling her on top of him.

"Perry!"

"Ride me, Imogen. Take me as you please."

His eyes locked with hers as she started to move, uncertain at first and then gradually building a rhythm, gaining speed as she rode him, pushing her palms down on his chest for leverage as her hips worked over him.

Gaspy little cries escaped her that might later embarrass her, when she reflected. But not now. Now there was only this. Now only raw hunger.

His low groans encouraged her, fed her passion. An aching pressure built inside her as she moved, increasing the delicious friction and tightening the coil in her belly. Her eyes widened as she felt the familiar swell coming. The pressure built and built and she increased her movements, becoming wild and completely lacking rhythm as she raced toward it, searching for her release.

"I'm close. Come with me," he choked, his chest tensing, muscles bunching tightly beneath her fingers. Her nails scored his skin as she worked desperately over him. "Get there, Imogen."

"I'm almost . . ." She rocked and felt him deeper. He hit an angle that made her fly apart. She cried out, every nerve bursting. A full body tremor started at her toes and worked its way through her. "Ohhh."

His arm came around her waist again and he flipped her on her back. He drove into her, still going, still pumping hard. Sharp gasps spilled from her lips as her climax came hard and fast. He raced toward his own release, pounding into her, launching her into another climax.

He groaned and stilled inside her, his weight a delicious thing on top of her.

She went limp, folding both her arms around his smooth shoulders.

His arms slid around her, coming around her back, hugging her closer, his lips nuzzling in her neck. As solid and heavy as he was, she didn't want him to ever move. She wished they could stay like this forever. Never leave each other or this bed.

It was a lovely wish.

"Imogen," he whispered.

"Hm?"

"I don't want walks with anyone else."

She exhaled. Perhaps it didn't have to be just a wish.

PERRY WATCHED IMOGEN for several long moments, studying her as she slept and imagining waking to this—to her—every morning. He could not envision a better life. Not even when he had been the duke.

Certainly he had to figure some things out. He wasn't going to bring a wife to his mother's house.

Wife. Yes. He was thinking of that. What else could he be thinking at this point?

He wanted to marry her. It felt right. The notion of building a life with her thrilled him more than anything he'd ever had—anything he had done or ever wanted to do. And build they would. Nothing would be given to them. No royal dukedom with all its contingent wealth would be handed down to him for the simple matter of his existence.

They would start a life together. Build a life together.

But until then, he should remove himself from her bedchamber. Morning light already spilled through the window. He needed to make haste and go before her father or housekeeper roused themselves. He did not want to scandalize the household with his presence in Imogen's bed-chamber.

He eased from bed and quickly dressed himself. Moving to her desk, he searched for a piece of paper to leave her another note. He smiled as he contemplated what kind of clever message he would leave her this time.

Not finding anything on the top of her desk, he opened a drawer and ruffled through for some stationery.

His gaze arrested on one piece of paper, his name leaping out at him. Well, rather his old name: the Duke of Penning. He lifted it from the drawer, scanning the words.

His hand started to shake.

The paper dropped, fluttering through the air and landing on her writing desk with a whisper. Strange. That slight whisper sounded as loud as a horn in his ears.

His own letter-writing task forever forgotten, he turned, staring at her where she slept, her brown hair soft all around her on the pillow.

He could still feel her. Her hair wasn't the only soft thing about her. Her skin. Her breasts. The pillow of her lips.

Perry blinked once hard, as though attempting to shake the very real memory of those sweet things from his mind. A moment ago he had thought to never lose those things. He had thought to keep them forever. Now he felt the desperate need to forget. To put those things so far from his mind that he never wanted them again. Never wanted *her* again.

He'd lost everything. *Because of her.*

And then he'd decided to give everything up—*for her.*

The irony was bitter and terrible and he felt a little like he was dying inside.

He'd cast out any hope or desire for an heiress. He'd given up the notion of reclaiming a semblance of his old life. A life of comfort and affluence. He'd decided to happily settle for whatever life he fashioned for himself as long as he could spend it with Imogen Bates.

All this time he could have been playing the doting suitor on any number of prospective ladies, but he had forgone that, immersing himself in Imogen Bates.

Clearly a waste of time and energy.

What a daft fool he'd been.

He released a soft bark of laughter. She must have enjoyed tying him up in knots—seeing him brought so low and then watching him pant after her all the while knowing she was the reason for his downfall.

She stirred in the bed. "Perry?" She moved beneath the coverlet, her legs kicking it free.

He crossed his arms over his chest as though

to trap them, as though he needed to be certain he would not reach for her.

She lifted her head, pushing that honey-brown hair back from her face as she scanned the chamber, her gaze searching and landing on him. "Ah. There you are." She patted the bed beside her. "Come back to me."

He didn't move. He could not even summon the will to speak.

She glanced to the window as though assessing the time and pouted prettily. "I suppose you must go." She sat up, holding the coverlet over her chest. Still modest. Even after everything. She looked shy for a moment, tucking her hair behind her ear as she murmured, "I will miss you."

He didn't have to harden his heart to resist her sweet charms. It was already hard. It felt like a stone in his chest. A dead thing. Cold and bloodless as a rock.

She must have finally sensed something was not right with him.

"Perry?" The pretty pout disappeared. "What is it? Is something amiss?"

He turned back to her desk and lifted the letter he had dropped as though it scalded him. He carried it over to her, not getting too close. He couldn't get close to her. He dropped it in her lap and took several steps back. Distance was good. Necessary even.

She glanced from the paper to him curiously. Settling her gaze back on the paper, she picked it up, canting her head as she examined it.

It didn't take long.

Recognition lit her eyes. The color drained from her face.

She lifted that big brown gaze of hers to his and slowly shook her head. "Please, Perry. I can explain—"

"Can you? That would be a neat trick." He stabbed a finger at the damning parchment. "Can you explain that letter from some curate, confirming my birth date was in fact in January and not the month of May."

"Perry . . ."

"You were the one. You! You outed me. You snooped and discovered the truth of my birth."

"Not on purpose. When I took over my father's book and ledger keeping, I uncovered a few inconsistencies and merely sought to update and organize his records. The previous vicar had handled all the records abysmally. I knew your birth date. I was at most of those celebrations." She began stammering. "I—I simply wrote to the curate so that he could correct his records since he had the wrong birth date recorded. You must believe me."

"Must I? Because you've been so honest up to now?"

"I did not know it would spur an investigation—"

"So you discovered the truth *accidentally*? You realize the distinction is not important." He shrugged. "You made certain to alert the world of your discovery and ruin me."

"No." She pressed her fingers to the center of her forehead as if fighting off an aching head. "I did not! It was not like that."

He shook his head. "You cannot even accept responsibility? You cannot admit the harm you've done me."

She sat up straighter. "I did not mean to!"

"And yet you did," he snapped. "You did. You took my life away."

Her voice fell small, almost whisper-like. "I'm sorry, Perry. I can admit that. I am so sorry. God, you have no idea how sorry I am. I didn't mean to, but it happened. And . . . isn't a part of you glad to know? To have the truth out?"

He went hard as stone, seeing her then, seeing how little she truly cared for him—still.

"*Glad?* How could I ever be glad about any of this? You stole my birthright," he said softly, perhaps unfairly, but the poison of her betrayal ran swiftly through his veins, the sting so hot that he could scarcely even think about what he was saying. "You must have hated me." He shook his head. "Really truly hated me to do such a thing."

She shook her head, too. "That had nothing to do with this. I didn't like you. That is true, but then you didn't like me either."

"You're correct. I didn't." There was a long pause, and then he added, lashing out, "And now I don't again."

She flinched. It was the barest flicker of emotion. The reaction passed over her face and vanished quickly. He didn't miss it though, and he felt a stab of guilt and pain that he quickly shoved aside.

She had wronged him. She had destroyed his world.

He should feel no compunction over hurting her feelings.

"You should go." She nodded toward her window. Her voice was thick, as though her mouth was stuffed full of cotton and he suspected she was holding back tears. "And never come back. Rest assured, I will be getting a lock."

He nodded once in agreement. "Fear not. You don't need one. I'll never climb up your trellis again. There is nothing for me here."

She watched him with bright wide eyes as he gathered up his jacket, slipping it on before he tugged on his boots. He moved to the window and opened it, peering out to make certain there was no one out and about in the morning. It would not do at all to be spotted climbing down from her window. He didn't wish to be caught in a compromising position with a woman he wanted to be rid from his life. The last thing he wanted was to be coerced into matrimony with her—especially after they had just asserted their eternal acrimony for each other. That would be a nightmarish union.

He swung one leg over the sill, freezing when her voice cracked over the chamber.

"Oh, and Perry?"

He looked over his shoulder at her, arching an eyebrow in question.

"Good luck finding your heiress. You will need it."

He narrowed his gaze on her. "Is that a threat? Do you intend to thwart me again? Is that what you are thinking?"

Her shoulders squared. "Don't be ridiculous. Contrary to what you believe, I am not the reason for everything that is wrong in your life." She cut a hand almost wildly through the air. "I thought you had changed, but you haven't. You're still that hard-hearted spoiled boy who laughed at me and said terrible things, who thought himself above everyone else in the world."

He released a hot breath. "Perhaps I was that lad once, but you've seen to it that I'm not. I'm quite aware of my life's limitations. If I marry someone, it will be someone who doesn't live to torment me. Someone who won't lie. Someone with integrity."

"Ha!" She hopped from bed, whipping the coverlet around her body—her shapely body that he could still recall perfectly in his mind's eye. "Oh, let us be honest. Whomever you find, you shall torment her, too. You will be miserable and so will she. Whatever woman you marry shall be attached to a man"—she gestured wildly at him—"who will spend his life mourning for what he lost. *You* will never be happy."

A long spell of silence followed this declaration. Her chest rose and fell on heavy breaths.

"Perhaps," he allowed, his gaze locked on her lovely face—the sight of which only made him ache, for multiple reasons he could not examine closely right now when he was already in such turmoil. "And I have you to thank for that. Do I not?"

She'd ripped his heart out and didn't even realize it.

Without waiting for her to answer, he turned from her and took his exit the same way he had entered, through the window.

Climbing down the trellis, he thought he heard the sound of her choked sob floating above him.

Chapter Twenty-Three ❧

$\mathcal{P}$erry did not return home—or rather, to his mother's home.

He knew it would be impossible to go there without talking to someone, either to his mother or Thurman. Any time he was in the house, they seemed to find him. He could be hiding in a mouse's den, and they would find him.

They had interrogation down to an art form, and that was the very last thing he was in the mood for.

So he walked.

He walked the countryside as the sun lit up the morning sky. He crossed through pastures and fields, jumping fences. He walked through woods as morning faded to afternoon and the sun grew warmer on his skin.

He walked aimlessly, thinking over the letter he had discovered, thinking over the words he had said to her. The words she had said to him. He thought of her attempt to apologize and her insistence that she had accidentally outed him.

He thought about all the things.

Gradually he realized it could have been as she said. She could have made an innocent inquiry that led to the revelation of his birth.

Did it really matter?

Whatever the case, it was the truth.

How could he blame her for the truth, for the reality of his life?

He only knew that moments before he read that letter he had been blissfully happy, in love with the woman beside him and planning a future with her.

And then he had wrecked that.

He wanted to feel blissful again. He wanted love.

Sighing, he dragged a hand through his hair, realizing it could be too late for that now. He'd been an arse and had quite perhaps pushed her away forever.

A terrible hollowness spread through his chest.

Perry glanced around, taking measure of his location with sudden awareness. He'd walked far, his feet following a familiar path, for he stood on a familiar hill overlooking the familiar sight of Penning Hall.

His feet had carried him here involuntarily. He looked down at the grand mausoleum with its stone face and countless windows. The vast green grounds. The burbling fountain with its swans. And he felt nothing.

No ache. No loss or sense of longing.

"Mr. Butler," a voice called. "Good day."

Turning, he spotted his former housekeeper walking toward him. "Miss Lockhart," he greeted. "Good day."

She stopped beside him and looked from him to the panorama of the grand house she so diligently maintained. "Lovely view," she remarked.

"Indeed, it is."

Miss Lockhart was relatively young. Not much older than himself. She was certainly young for her position, but she had seemed a natural fit for the role. She grew up at Penning Hall, at the skirts of her aunt, the former housekeeper. When her aunt had expired ten years ago, she had temporarily stepped into the position, but she quickly proved herself in his father's eyes. What started out as a temporary arrangement became permanent.

He felt her thoughtful stare on the side of his face. "We all miss you," she declared.

He smiled slightly. "That is kind of you to say."

"Do you?" she asked abruptly. "Miss it very much?"

He studied the house. It was just stones. Brick and mortar. "I find that . . . I don't actually." He faced her. "Not anymore."

She arched an eyebrow. "Oh. I'm . . . that is

good, Your Grace." Her cheeks pinkened. "Forgive me. Mr. Butler."

"Old habits." He shrugged. "When the new duke arrives, that will cease."

She sighed and crossed her arms, looking back down at the hall. "That should be at the week's end. He and his retinue are coming."

"Oh?" The man to take Perry's place would finally be here. He let that information roll around in his head for a bit, and felt . . . nothing. No reaction. No sadness. No resentment. It did not affect him. "Good. That's for the best. It's time for all of us to move on." As he had. As he would. Nodding, he stepped back. "It was a pleasure seeing you again, Miss Lockhart."

"Oh. Am I keeping you from something?"

He shook his head, his slight smile deepening. "No. Not at all."

There wasn't anyone or anything keeping him back anymore.

Least of all himself.

IMOGEN WAS TENDING the garden with Mrs. Garry, gathering peas and dropping them in a bowl with satisfying clinks and trying not to think of Perry's departure as the most devastating thing to happen to her. Even if it was. Not even Edgar's betrayal compared to Perry walking out of her life.

It was simple to understand why she felt this way. She never loved Edgar.

She loved Peregrine Butler.

She loved him and wanted only the best for him. He deserved only the best of everything in life, and it crushed her to know that she was the reason he would not have everything. She'd seen to it that he didn't have anything.

He thought she had betrayed him, and she supposed she had. She had not meant to, but she had outed the circumstances of his birth to the world.

She had not realized what would happen when she wrote to the cleric of the shire of his birth. She had no suspicions. She thought she was correcting a simple error in the mess of her father's bookkeeping. Not destroying a man's life. The mistake had been hers, but he had paid the price.

She blinked burning eyes, and picked peas faster, appreciating having something to occupy her fingers if not her mind. Her thoughts could not help straying to Perry. It was best he knew the truth now, of course. She could not have kept it from him forever. He had to know she was the one who had instigated the events that led to his disinheritance.

Inadvertent or not, she had ruined his life.

She closed her eyes in an awful, squeezing

blink. *Goodness.* That thought rang terribly in her mind.

Opening them, she got back to the task of picking peas.

She had it in her mind to prepare a few vegetable tarts, some of which she would deliver piping hot to the Blankenships to thank them for their annual hosting of the ball. She should have already done so. It was the kind of thing her mother had done and she tried her best to live up to her mother's example—the spreading of salacious rumors notwithstanding.

"My bowl's full," Mrs. Garry announced, straightening and stretching the kinks out of her back.

Imogen opened her mouth to respond when she heard the distant shout of her name. She stopped and glanced around.

Young Teddy from the Henry farm to the east of them was running with a vengeance through the field, his skinny legs lifting and cutting through the tall grass.

He called out wildly, his voice cracking on the air. "Miss Bates! Miss Bates!"

She lifted a hand to shield her eyes, peering into the direction of the afternoon sun. "Teddy? What's wrong?"

Mrs. Garry stepped beside her, muttering, "I can wager what's wrong."

Imogen nodded grimly, dread settling in the pit of her stomach. Indeed. She could, too.

"It's Ma! He's killing her! He's really killing her this time."

At this panicked confirmation of her fears, she dropped the bowl of peas and grabbed her skirts.

"Miss Imogen!" Mrs. Garry squawked.

She clambered over the fence of her property— something she had done countless times as a girl, but older now and weighed down in her skirts, she executed it with far less grace.

"Come, Miss Bates! Hurry. He's really going to kill her this time!"

"Fetch the constable!" she shouted back to her housekeeper.

"Miss Imogen! No! Come back! You can't go alone!"

She didn't obey. She didn't stop. The Henry family lived under a perpetual dark cloud. If Teddy was running to her for help, then things were past dire. Help was needed.

She made good time, speeding across the field, trailing after Teddy who had quite a good lead on her. She was quick, but not as quick as a fourteen-year-old lad.

She clambered over another fence, this time falling inelegantly on the other side and scraping her elbow before hopping back up to her feet.

Her arms pumped at her sides as she raced the

rest of the way to the Henry farm. By the time the house came into view, Teddy was already there.

She spotted the lad as he latched onto his burly father. He'd plastered himself like a little monkey to the bigger man, his spindly legs latched around his thick torso.

It was chaos.

Mr. Henry jerked around wildly in the small yard in front of the house, trying to toss his son from his back to no avail. The smallest children sat in the dirt crying amid darting chickens and a barking dog and a few grunting hogs that had escaped their pen.

Mr. Henry was dragging his wife by the hair, his fingers buried deep in the strands, locked at the roots. She resembled a limp rag doll, scarcely struggling. Blood marked her face, dribbling from her nose. One eye was swollen shut. Her arms curled around her swollen belly protectively.

"Mr. Henry! Stop!" Imogen charged into the fray.

He lifted bleary, bloodshot eyes to Imogen. "Mind yer business, lass! This is a family matter."

Imogen clamped down on his arm, shaking it in an attempt to free his grip. "Unhand her!"

"Stop it, Pa!" Teddy bellowed.

Mr. Henry whirled around with a roar, effectively dislodging both Teddy and Imogen.

Imogen dropped down to the ground beside the boy.

It was madness. Mrs. Henry was sobbing, pleading with her husband. "Please, please, Archie."

He gave her another shake by her hair, snarling at her. "Wot did I tell ye about disrespecting me?"

Valiant Teddy was not even close to giving up his defense of his mother. He started lashing out with his legs, kicking at his father. He landed one solid kick to the older man's knee.

Mr. Henry howled and released his wife, clutching his leg. "Ye little bastard!" He raised a thick arm to strike his son, but Imogen dove in the way, covering the boy, shielding him with her body.

Pain exploded in her back, just below her shoulder. She cried out, arching against the impact.

"Pa!" Teddy looked over her shoulder with a stricken expression. "No! Don't hurt her, Pa!"

Imogen clutched the boy tighter and braced herself for another blow.

It never came.

There was a loud grunt and scuffling behind her.

She cracked open one eye and then the next.

There was no pain radiating through her body. She was . . . fine. Unharmed.

Loosening her arms from Teddy, she peered around her—just in time to see Perry lowering his fists and standing over Mr. Henry who was writhing in agony on the ground. Clearly Perry had used those fists to knock the man down.

"Perry?" she whispered.

He looked like an avenging angel, his dark hair windblown, his gray eyes like a storm as his chest lifted high and deep on serrated breaths. His fists uncurled, relaxing at his sides as the threat subsided.

He moved from where he stood over the wretched man and crouched down beside her. "Imogen?" He brushed a hand down her face, his gaze assessing her, roaming over her body, searching for evidence of injury. "Are you hurt?"

"I'm fine," she assured him, motioning to Mrs. Henry. "She is the one who needs attention."

Teddy and the other children surrounded Mrs. Henry. The constable and Mrs. Garry arrived in a wagon and joined the children to fuss over Mrs. Henry.

Perry didn't leave Imogen's side. Several minutes passed and he said, "She is well cared for now and you look quite pale." He pressed the back of his hand to her forehead. "Allow me to escort you home."

"What are you doing here?" she demanded shakily.

"I came for you and spotted your frantic house-keeper. She told me where you had gone."

Imogen watched as the constable shackled a foul-tempered Mr. Henry and secured him in the back of the wagon.

Mrs. Garry harangued them through it all, insisting they lock Mr. Henry away forever. "He's a menace! Not just to his family, but the entire community. What would he have done to my Miss Bates if Mr. Butler had not arrived in time?"

"We will handle him, Mrs. Garry," the constable gruffly assured her. "This is one time too many for his shenanigans."

"Shenanigans," Imogen murmured under her breath. It seemed a very insignificant word to describe the horribleness she had just witnessed. What would have happened if Teddy had not gone for help? If she had not arrived? If Perry had not?

Mrs. Garry helped Mrs. Henry and her children into the house. She looked back over her shoulder and called, "I will tend to Mrs. Henry here. Can you manage, Miss Imogen?"

Imogen opened her mouth, but before she could speak Perry called out, "I have her, Mrs. Garry. Fret not."

Imogen looked at him sharply. "You *have* me?"

He stared back down at her. "Yes. I'll escort you home."

With a sniff, she started walking, trying not to wince at the tenderness in her back. "I can get home on my own."

He fell in beside her. "But I'd rather walk you."

She released a snort of laughter. "I thought you were angry at me, Mr. Butler."

"It's Perry. Or did you forget?"

How could she forget that? She fell silent as they continued through the tall grass. When they reached the fence, she stopped and gathered her skirts, ready to climb over. Before she realized his intent, he scooped her up in his arms and set her down on the other side of the fence.

"I'm capable of climbing a fence. I do it all the time."

"But now you have me. I know you can do things, but you'll have to forgive me for wanting to be there for you."

She whirled around to face him, watching him as he vaulted the fence. "I do not *have* you. You *despise* me."

"You do have me," he immediately countered. "If you want me. And I don't despise you. How could I? I'm in love with you."

She stared at him in astonishment, searching for her voice. It took some time. "No," she whispered hoarsely. She shook her head, reprimanding her heart to slow its sudden wild beating.

"I destroyed your life, remember? I think that's what you said."

"That was badly done of me. I said many things I regret. Many things I didn't mean. I was surprised, and I acted like an arse. Forgive me."

She blinked in disbelief.

He went on, "It does not matter. Accident or not, I don't even care. I'm not the duke, and I don't care."

Mystified, she shook her head. "Who even are you?"

"I'm the man in love with you."

She staggered back a step. It was just as astonishing to hear that a second time. *In love with me?*

"Forgive me," he said again. "Forgive me, Imogen."

"Forgive *you*?" She blinked burning, tear-blurred eyes. "Can you forgive *me*?"

"Of course I do. You didn't do anything wrong. Now say you forgive me, and let me love you."

She ignored the treacherous little thrill wiggling through her, still frightened. None of this could be real. It could not be her reality.

"I can't make you happy. I'm not what you want. I'm a poor vicar's daughter. I don't have anything to help restore you to your old life."

He closed the distance between them then, his hands closing on her arms in a demonstration of sudden earnestness. "Don't you understand? I didn't even know who I was until I lost everything. It took losing everything to find me. To find *you* . . . and I could not be more grateful for that."

She blinked several times, marveling at the tears springing from her eyes.

"I . . . I'm frightened," she admitted.

Frightened of believing in them and trusting this.

Trusting what her heart was telling her to do.

His hands flexed on her arms. "Do you love me, Imogen Bates? Even a little?" His gray eyes scanned her face, devouring her, missing nothing.

She nodded slowly, choking back a sob. "I do. Of course. More than a little," she sobbed.

He kissed her then. Swept her up in his arms and lifted her off her feet, kissing her and spinning her in a small circle.

She laughed joyously against his lips.

Even when he stopped spinning her, she still felt like she was flying.

They ended their kiss, and he rested his forehead against hers, his warm breath colliding on her lips. "Shall we go together to tell your father and ask for his blessing?"

"Of course. Then you won't need to climb in and out of my window anymore." She grinned. "As delightful as that was."

"Perhaps I'll surprise you every once in a while and do just that."

"As long as you don't have to sneak out before I wake up."

"Oh, Imogen. I promise to be there beside you every morning for the rest of our lives."

Epilogue ✦

One year later . . .

*T*he Hare and The Basket was bustling. As it was most nights.

Ever since Perry had purchased the place from Mr. Compton and renovated the main room, it had become quite the attraction for locals and those passing north and south, en route to either Scotland or London.

The place was a smashing success and Perry was already looking for ways in which to expand. His next goal was to add a full-fledged restaurant next door, a fine dining establishment, connecting to the tavern. Given the profits he'd made from the tavern, he would not even require investors this time to help with the addition of a restaurant.

His ideas were endless and they filled him with continual excitement. Every morning he woke up early, thrilled to be alive.

Astonishing how many times a life could change.

He went from being an overprivileged duke to a man without station or wealth.

Now he was a successful entrepreneur. In love. Married. Eager to start every day.

Thurman was deep in conversation with a table of gentlemen by the fire. He opened a box, bowing forward to offer each of them a fine cigar.

Thurman had been another surprise in all of this.

While Perry's mother had been shocked and decidedly *not* thrilled at his decision to buy the tavern from Mr. Compton and take it over, Thurman had merely listened, saying nothing. Until later.

A smile twitched Perry's lips as he recalled his mother's reaction. In truth, Perry could not guess which had shocked her more—her son becoming the proprietor of a tavern or his marrying Imogen Bates.

Thurman was not so scandalized.

A full day passed following Perry's announcement that he was acquiring investors to help him take over The Hare and The Basket *and* he was giving up his quest for a wealthy heiress before Thurman cornered him.

After pressing Perry for more information on his plans for the tavern, his mother's butler had requested the opportunity to go into business with Perry. It seemed he had a bit of a nest egg set aside, and he had always dreamed of having something for himself. He did not want to spend all of his life in service. He wanted to be his own man apparently. Just as Perry did.

Thurman had simply lacked an inspiring idea, but it did not take long for Perry's budding inspiration to become his own, and Thurman brought his own value to their enterprise. His financial contribution was not the only benefit. His years in service gave him a unique perspective that Perry lacked. They made the perfect team.

Together, they dove into the renovation of the tavern. After a brief closure, The Hare and The Basket reopened under their ownership, grander than ever.

Perry ducked into the back office and slipped on his coat.

Thurman entered the room after him, cigar box tucked under his arm. "Off for the night?"

He nodded. "Dinner awaits." At the mention of that, he asked, "You're still dining with us on Thursday?"

"I would not miss it."

Nodding, Perry bade him good-night and slipped out the back door of the building.

He rounded the side alley and came out the front, spotting his former valet, Carter, as he was about to enter the building.

"Mr. Butler," the young man greeted, stepping forward to warmly shake his hand. "Good to see you."

"Carter," he returned. "Evening off?"

"Indeed, His Grace retired early for the night."

"Ah, good for you. I hope the new duke is treating you well."

"Oh, yes, of course." Carter nodded agreeably, but Perry knew if the new duke was not treating him well, Carter would not be the one to say it. He took his position as valet very seriously and never carried tales. Just one reason he was excellent at his job.

Carter's gaze flicked to the front of the building. "I cannot tell you how nice it is to have such a fine establishment to come to when I've the free time. You've done wonders here."

"Well, thank you. That was the goal. We wanted the tavern to serve as a comfortable refuge. I'm glad you're enjoying the place."

"Indeed." Carter continued to nod agreeably. "I am so very glad you've found your footing and met with success."

Perry grimaced slightly, well aware that when they had last parted his valet likely thought he would end up dead in a ditch. He had not been in a good place at the time.

"Well, I am late for dinner. It was good to see you, Carter."

"Ah, yes, of course. Please send my regards to your kind wife."

"Indeed, I will."

Carter's gaze turned very thoughtful. "I was so very glad to hear of your marriage to the vicar's daughter. Whoever would have thought that when . . ." His former valet's voice faded. Clearly he did not know how to speak of Perry's less than blissful past.

"When I lost everything?" Perry finished for him.

It was the simplest way to characterize the events that had transpired nearly two years ago. That time had been abysmal.

Carter ducked his head and nodded rather sheepishly.

Perry clapped him on the shoulder. "In truth, it was the best thing that ever happened to me." He gestured around him, letting the vague motion encompass all the riches he had in life, both the physical and intangible.

Carter beamed. "I'm so very happy for you . . ." His voice faded yet again and Perry knew he still struggled with how to address him.

"Call me Perry," he provided.

"Perry." Carter nodded, looking much relieved.

Perry gave a final nod and motioned for him to continue inside the building. "Have a good evening."

That said, Perry stepped forward and continued on, humming lightly under his breath as he
strolled through the village amid the settling
dusk.

The vicarage soon came into view ahead of
him, the setting sun above the treetops gilding
the ivy covering the front of the house and setting it gloriously afire.

Home.

He was aware that it would not be home forever, and he and Imogen had not so distant plans
to build a house. His father-in-law was beginning to entertain the notion of retiring from his
post, so plans were in development. He and Imogen were already eyeing a certain property, and
had made an appointment with a London archi-
tect so that they could begin on the designs for
the house.

For now though, the vicarage was home.

Any place with Imogen was home. They had
each other, and that was enough. More than
enough. It was everything.

Together, they had everything.

He stopped on the walk leading up to the front
door. The parlor drapes were pulled open and
for a moment he stopped there to study the happily domestic scene through the parlor window.

His father-in-law sat in his wingback chair
and Imogen fluttered about the room with her

usual energy. She draped a blanket over her father's lap and then poured him his claret from a nearby tray.

As she straightened he was granted the view of her slightly swelling belly. Her hand went there. Her fingers curled around the gentle mound protectively, as though assuring herself that their babe was indeed tucked safely below her heart.

Their family was growing and Perry was beside himself with joy.

They had each other and that *was* more than enough, but now they would soon be blessed with even more. There seemed to be no end to the riches in his life.

Imogen's gaze alighted on him through the window and a wide smile curved her lips in happy greeting.

He smiled in turn. Lifting his fingers to his lips, he pressed a light kiss there and then carried it to her on the air with a float of his fingers.

Her smile beamed brighter and she waved him in with an eager hand.

Grinning, he hurried forward and entered the house.

❧•❧

Don't miss

The Rake Gets Ravished

The next book in *New York Times* bestselling
author Sophie Jordan's Duke Hunt series.

Available from Avon Books
March 2022

*G*ive in to your Impulses!

These unforgettable stories only take a second to buy and give you hours of reading pleasure!

Go to *www.AvonImpulse.com* and see what we have to offer.

Available wherever e-books are sold.

AVONIMPULSE